SHORTCUTS
TRACK 1

EDITED BY MARIE HODGKINSON

SHORT CUTS

TRACK 1

Paper Road Press
paperroadpress.co.nz

Landfall © Tim Jones 2015
Bree's Dinosaur © AC Buchanan 2015
The Last © Grant Stone 2015
Mika © Lee Murray & Piper Mejia 2015
Pocket Wife © IK Paterson-Harkness 2015
The Ghost of Matter © Octavia Cade 2015

This collection first published 2015. All authors have asserted their moral rights.

Thanks as always to Elizabeth Heritage, for her excellent publicity work for Paper Road Press.

Paperback: 978-0-473336-48-6
Epub: 978-0-473336-49-3
Mobi: 978-0-473336-50-9

Cover art by and © KC Bailey
Design © Marie Hodgkinson, Paper Road Press Ltd.

CONTENTS

FOREWORD

S A LITERARY FORM, THE NOVELLA HAS SEVERAL DISTINCT advantages: in being longer than a short story, it can spin its yarn with greater complexity; but, being shorter than a novel, it can readily occupy those quieter times when we are waiting for a bus, or a friend for coffee, or simply enjoying the peaceful hour before sleep.

So, lucky reader, you are in for a treat. The six novellas in this volume are all very different. Here you will visit an enchanted forest, be shocked by living dolls, and caught up in the bleak world of asylum-seekers. You will also be introduced to the triumph and sadness of Ernest Rutherford's life, captivated by the dinosaur being constructed next door, and follow the intricate, tattooed path of medical discovery.

Enjoy it, as Paper Road Press gives you 'six of the best'.

PHILLIP MANN

Introduction: Why Shortcuts?

WELL, SINCE YOU ASKED ...
Basically it's all about puns. Terrible, terrible puns.
Get it? Paper **Road** Press? Shortcuts? **Track** 1?
Aha, ha, ha.

Anyway.

I founded Paper Road Press in 2013 and named it after one of my favourite cartographic phenomena. A 'paper road' is a road that exists only on paper, not in real life. Maybe they were meant to be built but somehow the idea died out between crisp papery plans and the muddy reality; maybe they really did exist, once, not that you would know it if you tried to walk down one. In Dunedin, where I grew up, and Wellington, where I live now, there are many roads that surreptitiously fade out or dwindle into cliff-side steps, much to the chagrin of anyone trying to use a maps app to drive around. Paper roads – intriguing, occasionally frustrating, uncompromisingly dubiously real – seemed the perfect metaphor for the speculative fiction I planned to publish.

So when I started bandying around the idea of publishing a series of shorter works, calling them 'shortcuts' seemed the obvious choice. Shorter than novels, longer than short stories, these texts would be the sort of story you could read on your commute, your lunch-break, or any other odd time when you just want to slip away for a bit. The seven authors whose work is featured in this collection took the series' theme – to 'be inspired by the extra-ordinary possibilities of our land, history and cultures' – and ran with it in a glorious confusion of directions:

One night. One life. One decision. Tim Jones' *Landfall* explores the desperation of climate refugees in a not-too-distant New Zealand.

Bree's Dinosaur, by AC Buchanan, is a story of displacement – of place, family, and self, and trying to make sense not only of the world's mysteries, but the solutions it offers.

Grant Stone takes an outsider's perspective in *The Last*, as music journalist Rachel flies in to Auckland to interview musician Katherine St John, a fellow English expat who disappeared from the limelight after her last record. She's brought her music to the other side of the world – but what else did she bring with her?

In *Mika*, Lee Murray and Piper Mejia introduce us to a woman on an odyssey to find a cure for the disease that ravages her people. As she ventures into America, cultures clash, but it's only through connecting with others in this strange land that she will find what it is she seeks.

'Tech horror' is a well established trope, but it's not necessarily the machines you should be worrying about. IK Paterson-Harkness' *Pocket Wife* shows us what can happen when long-distance relationships get too close for comfort.

Lives, families and the atom are broken down in the final

story in this collection: Octavia Cade's *The Ghost of Matter* takes a new look at Ernest Rutherford's life and career.

I couldn't be happier with these stories. I hope that you enjoy them, too – and that they lead you down new paths, following bibliographies and tables of contents into other new worlds. Try not to get too lost.

As for 'Track 1'? Well, it suggests a certain continuity, doesn't it – a whisper, if not a promise, of numbers yet to come.

We'll see.

MARIE HODGKINSON
EDITOR & PUBLISHER
PAPER ROAD PRESS

LANDFALL
TIM JONES

THE TWIN TORPEDOES THAT ENDED THE LONG JOURNEY OF the *Jamalpur-2* from Bangladesh to the Tasman Sea were scarcely necessary. The old river ferry had been held together by little more than wire and faith ever since they were chased out of Australian territorial waters. Strong winds and heavy waves had put paid to their backup plan of landing the vessel in some isolated cove in southern New Zealand; looking at those forbidding mountains half-choked by clouds, Nasimul Rahman had been relieved.

So they had run north, north before the wind, the ship juddering and groaning with every new onslaught from the sea. Each day there were a few more deaths – not many, for those most vulnerable had died long before. Fewer than half of those who had been aboard the vessel when it made the imperceptible transition from the Mouths of the Ganges into the Bay of Bengal were alive to greet the Fiordland coast, but that had still left over 150 souls aboard.

Nasimul's wife Hasina was no longer among them. She had lasted through the tropics, kept alive by her hope that she would see land again, even if it was the unmitigated harshness of the Australian continent, where it was said whole groups of people could disappear into the interior without ever being noticed or pursued, if only they could find a way ashore through the frigates and the proximity mines and the thickets of razor wire. When Nasimul had slipped into desperation within a fortnight of the journey beginning, it had been Hasina's belief that kept him going. But, already weakened by dysentery, the plunge into colder climates had been too much for her. She had died somewhere in the long, hopeless reaches of the southern Indian Ocean.

Wife gone, son lost to cholera back in the camps before he had lived out his first year, Nasimul shivered and heaved up his food and crawled into a nest of damp clothing night after night, and somehow survived. The ship drove forward. The temperature warmed fractionally. The sky flamed red at dawn and dusk: ash and smoke from Australia, someone said. Perhaps the whole continent was burning.

And then, on another night of storm and cloud, the New Zealand Navy came, destroyers surging over the eastern horizon. There was no point in running, and nowhere to run. The *Jamalpur-2* wallowed in the waves and waited for the end, while the people aboard made for the last slender hope, the lifeboats.

No self-respecting Bangladeshi river ferry sailed without at least twice the number of passengers it was rated for. But death, nipping at their heels the whole way, had achieved what no government functionary had ever been able to and reduced the number of passengers on the ferry to almost exactly the number it was allowed to carry. So there were almost enough lifeboat places for them all: if they had been fit, if they had been healthy, if the ferry had run into trouble on the flat reaches of the Lakhya or the Meghna or the Ganges. Now, it was the sick carrying the sicker, the injured carrying the half-dead, and the grey wolves of the sea bearing down on their prey.

The davits won't work, thought Nasimul, eyeing up the rusted metal winches and the rusted chains that held the lifeboats high above the water. Yet all but one worked, each casting its freight of lives upon the waters. It was Nasimul's good fortune that he was in the lifeboat that failed to deploy. He was working to free it, precariously perched on the lifeboat davit itself, when he glanced downwards and saw the straight track through the curving waters. Before he could nerve himself to jump, the *Jamalpur-2* took matters out of his hands, throwing him into the water as it shuddered and began to break up from the force of the first and then the second explosion as the New Zealand Navy's torpedoes did their deadly work.

Nasimul was a strong swimmer. He was born over water in his family's tiny hut, perched on stilts above the banks of the mighty Lakhya, and he had been around and in water all his life. But this was like nothing he had ever experienced, and the first shock of cold and salt as he went under was almost too much for him. He struggled his way back to the surface and found himself clutching at something: a body. It was missing a leg. Floating beside the body was a curving length of wood from a lifeboat – perhaps the lifeboat he had been trying to launch. It was about two metres long and a little less than half as wide.

Nasimul managed to turn it over so that the concave side was upwards. It floated like the world's smallest and least safe canoe. He clambered aboard his impromptu vessel and, despite how cold and damp he was, despite his left hand and right leg trailing in the water, despite the cries that drifted across the water from the boats and the machine-gun fire that silenced them, boat after boat after boat, he fell asleep.

The cries grew fewer and the bursts of machine-gun fire less frequent, until both stopped altogether. The Navy returned to base. Night fell. Wind and tide and current took Nasimul Rahman and swept him towards shore.

×

Kimmy Potiki was a lazy bitch, thought Donna, chewing her gum and looking at the mess the lazy bitch had made of the stockroom. Kimmy was supposed to clean up before she knocked off at four, but when Donna went back there just before six, there were boxes and shit scattered around all over the place. Some of them had been pulled open and the clothes taken out. It wasn't good stuff, but it was warm stuff, and Donna thought maybe Kimmy and that dipshit boyfriend of hers were stealing stuff and selling it cheap at the market on Saturdays. Or maybe she had just pulled it out to make a nest: at the far end of the room, under a rack of coats, was what would pass pretty well for a bed if you'd been cold and wet and running from the cops and sleeping rough. Kimmy hadn't, but her boyfriend had. There were tinnies and knives and empty bottles, too.

Well, fuck Kimmy Potiki. There was no way Donna was going to make herself late by cleaning up after Kimmy, who'd have to take her chances that Mrs Alberts didn't come into the stockroom before Monday. Though it was Kimmy who had got her this job in the first place …

Fuck Kimmy Potiki. Donna worked as fast as she could, shoving clothes back into boxes without paying attention to what went where, kicking tinnies and bottles back under cover, straightening the place up to the point that anyone who just popped into the room for a moment might think nothing was wrong.

'You took your time,' said Mrs Alberts when Donna

returned to the shop. Donna just shrugged. It looked like Mrs Alberts was going to go off on her, but then she said, 'You'd better get going. You don't want to be late for your first patrol.'

'Okay,' said Donna, and added, 'thanks'. Mrs Alberts could be an old cow sometimes, but she was okay mostly. The shop would do for Donna till she found something better.

Mere was supposed to be waiting for her outside so they could go for smokes before Shore Patrol started, but Mere wasn't there. Maybe she had got bored of waiting. Maybe she forgot. Donna wished she still had her phone. She thought all that cancer stuff was bullshit.

Still, that was one of the cool things about Shore Patrol: they got radios, these little walkie-talkie things that were pretty much like phones except you couldn't text. The KFC on the corner was still open. She went there and ate and sat by herself until it was time to catch the bus. The bus driver was that one who had kicked them all off that time Kane chundered on the back seat. Donna kept her head down.

It was a dark walk down deserted streets from the last bus stop to the Shore Patrol building and its reassuring blaze of lights. Where the hell was Mere? Safety in numbers, that's what they were always told, safety in numbers. Why couldn't they at least light this part of the bloody street? Why couldn't the moon be shining?

But she got there OK. To be honest, she was early: she should have stayed later at KFC. She hung around until Mere arrived, then gave her a hard time about not waiting. Mere said she forgot. Donna said yeah right, it was a girl, wasn't it, Mere? It was always some girl with Mere. Donna had quite liked a couple of them, but most of them were stuck up bitches from the North Shore.

Mere wasn't telling. So they presented their passes, got

their pistols from the Serjeant at Arms (and why the fuck was it spelled like that?) and headed down to the firing range for fifteen minutes' practice. Donna was better at the static targets, and Mere was better at the moving ones. Two along from Mere there was this boy, David. He was really cute. Donna had given him the eye a couple of times, but whenever he looked at anyone straight on, it was Mere. And Mere was cute too, with her button nose and her big dark eyes, but she had never given a boy the come-on in her life. David was an idiot.

Donna took a critical look at David's shot pattern. It wasn't bad, but not as good as hers. Provided her targets stayed stock still, she was deadly. When they moved, she had trouble figuring out which way they were going.

Big Bob called them all together. His name was Robert Wilson, or Sergeant Wilson to his face. He had a fancy uniform he was always threatening to burst out of. In real life he was a clerk at the ration house. It wasn't hard to see how he disposed of the rations that went uncollected.

'We're a military auxiliary, but we're also a team. We help to defend our country, but we also take in young people and give them a sense of purpose. We train them in weapons and tactics, but we also train them in life. And when training is done, it's time to take the step up into active service, knowing that everything you give will be returned to you by a grateful nation.'

I bloody well hope so, thought Donna.

The Sergeant made his face adopt its most serious expression. 'We must never forget that the threat we face is very real: millions upon millions of poor and desperate people, displaced from their teeming homelands by the rising seas, who look south hungrily at our green and fertile lands. They'd overrun us in months if we let them, and the Shore

Patrol is a vital second line of defence that frees our nation's Navy and Army to do what they each do best.

'So tonight I'd like to call forward six of our new recruits who have shown they have the right stuff to answer their nation's call. Step forward, David McDonald …'

Donna waited for her name to be called with a mixture of excitement and dread. It was pretty crisp to be presented with the cap, the jacket and the badge, though she was glad the ceremony was happening in public: she'd felt Robert Wilson's fingers curl around her left buttock when he though no one was looking. Still, she stepped forward, and shook the wanker's hand, and took the cap (too small), the jacket (too big) and the badge (just right). Robert Wilson she could handle, or at least avoid. It was the patrolling she was scared about. It was all becoming real now.

But at least she'd have Mere with her, and for that matter David. Somebody had obviously noticed that they hung together at training, because the three of them had been put in the same patrol. The woman who ran this one was new to her – Staff Sergeant Anderson, a thin-faced, serious woman who looked them and the rest of the patrol up and down for a bit before giving them their orders for the night. After the induction ceremony, Robert Wilson had droned on for another five minutes about family and country and duty, but there was no bullshit from this lady.

'Tonight you will patrol the foreshore between Gloucester Park Island and the intersection of Beachcroft Ave and Arthur St. We're informed that the Navy sank a ship full of infiltrators yesterday, and that some of them may have escaped on small boats, so you are advised to be especially vigilant. We've also heard that the so-called Shepherds may be attempting to aid the survivors from the sunken ship. As I'm sure you know, this is illegal and punishable by a lengthy spell of mandatory detention. Anyone found aiding an infiltrator is to be apprehended and arrested.

'Apart from that, you're to perform your usual role of stopping and questioning anyone who isn't where they should be. Don't shoot unless you have to, and don't shoot any citizens. Questions?'

'What about a citizen who is helping or hiding an infiltrator?' asked David.

'Good question. The first rule is, don't shoot a citizen. The second rule is, don't allow an infiltrator to escape. Sometimes those two rules conflict, and you have to use your judgement. Do your best, and follow Corporal Reweti's lead.'

The Corporal inclined his narrow head.

'That's not very helpful,' whispered Mere.

What the fuck have I got myself into, Donna wanted to whisper back, but now the thin-faced woman was speaking again, asking 'Does anyone here have experience with dogs?'

'I do,' said Donna, thinking of the Staffie cross that protected her fearful mother from the world outside.

'Good,' said the woman. She left the room and returned a few moments later with a shaggy, red-brown dog that whined and panted on its lead.

'Meet Rufus,' said the woman. 'He's coming on patrol with you. He's not the brightest, but he'll hear and smell people you'd walk right past.' And she handed the lead to Donna.

Donna soon wished she hadn't. Rufus was a big red bundle of enthusiasm who appeared utterly incapable of doing anything on command. 'Nose like a bloodhound,' said Corporal Reweti encouragingly, as Donna wrestled Rufus into the electric runabout assigned to the patrol. By then, Donna was wishing her mother had never gone beyond having a budgie.

✖

The mud stank of brine, of fish, of chemicals. Nasimul lay in the mud and stank along with it.

He had been woken by something brushing against his trailing leg. Panicked, he tried to pull his leg out of the water and onto his de facto raft, and pain flashed along his nerves. But it was nothing more serious than cramp. Though it burned in his limbs, he tried again and managed to get the whole of his slender frame inside his impromptu boat. He drifted, wet, cold. I'm going to die like this, he thought. But death, although he sensed it hovering, refused to come into focus.

The tide carried him – he could not say where, but it carried him. The strong winds from the south had died away and a breeze blew from land that could not be far away, carrying familiar smells of wet vegetation, and other smells he did not recognise.

Sometimes he saw shapes off in the dark, but nothing came near until he heard a small boat approaching, the sound of its engine borne towards him on the wind. The boat was running without lights: he did not see it until it was within fifty metres of him. For a moment, he feared he might be run down, but then he realised the boat would pass a few metres to his left. He lay as flat as possible, hoping that no one on the boat would spot a dark man in dark clothes lying on a damp and waterlogged hunk of wood. No one did, and the boat passed him by. Where were they going in such secrecy? Why were they trying to hide? He did not know.

An hour later and an unknown distance closer to shore, twin beams of light swept across the water, approaching him from either side. Again he pressed himself flat, praying that they would pass him by. The edge of one light cone did sweep over him, but to the operator, he must have seemed just another piece of flotsam on the tide. The lights swept away, and nothing changed for an hour – for two hours – he could not tell how long. He went where the sea dictated.

He felt the curved plank on which he was floating brush against something. It broke free, drifted twenty or more sluggish metres, and then ran aground, if ground it could be called, on a mud bank.

Nasimul lay there, too weak and tired to do anything, until the barking of a dog – distant, but not too distant – spurred him to action. Plainly, he was not far from land. That meant opportunity – the chance of escape – but also danger. He did not know how long this moonless night would last, but when it ended, he would be as visible as if he had lit flares to announce his presence.

And he was hungry, and cold: this whole land seemed made from cold and mud. How could anyone live here, how could anyone even make it ashore?

Perhaps they could simply walk. That thought lasted him as long as it took to straighten one leg, bend his knee with aching slowness, and put part of his weight on the mudflat. His foot sank, smoothly and deeply, and the more weight he put on it, the deeper it sank. He pulled his oozing foot and calf out with an effort.

Would the tide rise and refloat him? He waited a few minutes, then a few more, but got no sense of whether this harbour was on the waxing or the waning tide.

He could not afford to wait any longer. He abandoned his faithful vessel, slid into the shallow water, and began to swim towards the tantalising smell of the shore.

✖

It had been a shit of a night. With each tired footstep, with each half-heard noise in the darkness that set Rufus, the stupid bloody untrained bloody mutt, barking and straining at his leash, Donna wondered what the flying fuck she was doing here with this bloody dog, with the bunch of grinning morons who were no help whatsoever – and Mere worst of all.

Think happy thoughts, think happy thoughts. She looked at David's arse rounding out his camo trousers. It didn't help.

She tried to think positive. Good things came if you joined the Shore Patrol. First there was the extra pay, which looked better and better the more Mrs Alberts cut back Donna's hours at the shop, because south of the Harbour Bridge no one could afford to buy clothes anymore. Then, if you stuck with it for long enough, there were the free fees to AUT and Unitech, and god knows Donna wanted to get trained and get out of working in a shop that never sold anything and into a job where she could actually get shit done and get paid for it, maybe a mechanic or something.

Or maybe the regular Army. Donna was short and not that muscly, but from what she heard, the Army would take pretty much anyone it could get who could stay off the pills and shoot straight. Donna knew she could shoot straight.

But for now she was stuck with Rufus.

In the right hands – say, the hands of a loving owner with a big house and big grounds and a lot of time on their hands – Rufus the red setter would have been a lovable scamp. But in a paramilitary setting in which stealth, concealment and surprise were meant to be the modus operandi, Rufus was about as useful as tits on a bull. He had proved at their last break – five minutes for hot, bitter coffee from a flask – that he could hump an enemy's leg to death; at least, he could hump David's leg to death, and that was pretty much the same thing. To be fair, though, he had settled down a bit since the humping incident, seeming to accept that this night was just a very long bout of walkies.

So here they were, swinging down Arthur St one more time. In these years of the relentlessly rising sea, wealth bought elevation: the only people who lived close to the ever-advancing shore line were those who could not afford to live further away. The top end of Arthur St was still well lit, houses diligently repaired after each ravage of the wind and rain, but as they neared the sea, the streetlights disappeared, the footpath devolved to gravel and mud, the houses slumped and shrank back from view. If anyone still lived here, they had no wish to be discovered.

Beachcroft Ave, and beyond it, the old waterfront motorway, deserted, half-awash. There were no lights above or below. The country was up to its eyeballs in debt trying to pay the massive cost of managing its retreat from the sea: no one was going to waste a cent down here, where the battle was already lost.

Donna mooched down the street, and the patrol mooched with her: Mere, David, and the old lags, Norman the former car detailer (and boy, did he know a lot of details about cars), and Corporal Reweti, officially in command but seemingly possessed only of the desire to smoke one after another of his thin, poisonous rollies.

'How long to go, Sarge?' asked Donna.

'Corporal,' corrected Corporal Reweti. And, 'ten minutes less than when you asked last time.'

Still the best part of two hours, then. Bloody hell.

Along Beachcroft Ave they marched, and it seemed to Donna that the night might never end, that already, on this her first night of duty, she had passed out of time's regular cycle and into a parallel kind of time, military time, where everything was repetition. Put one foot in front of another for long enough and you would find yourself back where you started, on and on, while the clouds refused to lift and the sun refused to rise.

So maybe mechanic was the go, not Army. She could—

Rufus pulled the lead out of her hand with a jerk so strong that it wrenched her wrist. He had seen what no one else had seen, heard what no one else has heard, and without waiting for orders to be passed down the proper chain of command, he was off in hot pursuit.

'Shit!' said Donna. 'Fucking dog!' Wrist still smarting, she chased after the rapidly disappearing beast.

Corporal Reweti was lost deep in a dream of nicotine when Rufus and Donna took off. The Corporal wasn't clear what had spooked either of them, but it seemed reasonable to assume that it had military significance. 'Well, don't just stand there!' he ordered the rest of the platoon. 'After them!'

So they ran after the wildly barking Rufus. One thing's for sure, thought Donna as she panted after the dog, any infiltrators will have made a run for it by now. They'll be miles away, doing … her imagination failed to come up with a picture of what they would be doing, seeing as she had never seen an infiltrator herself and had no idea where these particular infiltrators were from. Infiltrating, anyway, and trying to blend in, trying to look like regular New Zealanders – whatever they looked like.

Rufus led them to the doorway of a long-abandoned, half-decayed house that would soon have high tides washing beneath its warped and peeling door. And there he stopped, quivering.

'You stupid mutt,' said Donna, but then Corporal Reweti arrived and told them to be quiet, they didn't know who or what was on the other side of that door, or what they might be armed with. 'You two,' he said to David and Norman, 'check round the back. If you find a back door, stand outside it and wait for my call. And have your guns drawn. If any-one tries to come out, apprehend them. Otherwise, await my command.'

David, inflated by his new responsibility, disappeared around the back of the property with his shoulders high. Norman strolled after him, dreaming of classic cars: Daihatsu, SsangYong.

Donna and Mere stood beside Corporal Reweti, their guns also drawn, waiting for orders. Rufus, finding nothing better to do, lolled with his tongue out, giving Donna the chance to recapture his lead.

They waited long enough that Donna got bored. God, she thought, if every night is going to be like this I am going to go crazy in a week. I am going to be begging Mrs Alberts to give me more hours, even if I have to spend all of them cleaning the toilets and looking after her snotty grandkids. I am going to—

'Now!' And Corporal Reweti kicked the door in – first time, too. They pounded up the stairs, Rufus going crazy, Donna trying her best to hold him back. At the back of the house, more noise, and the sound of splintering wood. Just ahead of her, Corporal Reweti kicked another door open, gun drawn. 'Put—' he said, and a shot winged past him, splintering the doorframe. Donna froze, and Mere dived past her just as Corporal Reweti fired. A scream from in-side the room, and then, as Donna peered around the door-frame, she saw Mere tackling a man and knocking the gun from his hand while next to him a woman cried out in pain and clutched her left shoulder.

While Mere and Corporal Reweti subdued the strug-gling man, Donna tied Rufus to the leg of a sagging bed and bound up the woman's wound. The bullet had passed through the fleshy part of her shoulder, leaving a messy exit wound. A few centimetres to the right, and she would have been in a lot of trouble. But if Corporal Reweti had been trying to hit the man with the gun, he sure wasn't much of a shot.

There was a lot of blood, but Donna had seen blood before. By the time she had torn up bed sheets to bandage the wound, her racing heart had quieted, though that only brought the memory of her cowardice in the hallway into sharper relief. Mere had been so brave …

The woman was short, brown-skinned and very frightened. As she should be – from what Donna had heard, detention centres were not good places to be. And as for the man – tall, Pākehā, struggling less now after a couple of good socks to the jaw – he was facing a long, long time inside, or worse. She didn't know which of them she envied less.

It ended up with four of them manhandling the guy out of the house, and Donna being left with the woman. She didn't seem like much of a threat – she was smaller than Donna, her face was drawn with pain, and her left hand was clutching her right shoulder – but Donna wasn't taking any chances. She needed her full attention for the woman, so she had no alternative but to leave Rufus behind.

The dog whined and strained at his lead, and Donna, much to her surprise, felt bad about leaving him behind, but she had to do it anyway. Keeping her gun trained on the woman, she took a bowl from the table and filled it with water from her canteen. 'Here you go, boy,' she said, and set the water down in front of him. As they left the room, he was drinking happily and wagging his tail. He'll be all right, she told herself.

When they got back out onto the street, Corporal Reweti called for backup. The man called him a fucking prick, and got another clip on the jaw in return. It took a couple more before he finally shut up. They waited in the deserted street in front of the abandoned house for what seemed like forever before the radio squawked again.

'Fuck,' said Corporal Reweti. 'No backup, and Anderson's other squad requisitioned the runabout. We'll have to drag these two back to base. Come on, let's go.'

Another burst of swearing, another clip across the jaw, and a chokehold around the neck. Some people never learn. Meanwhile, the woman let go a little sound of pain, and Donna put her arm almost protectively around her. They started back the way they had come, where soon a shortcut would lead them uphill and back to base. As she walked away supporting the injured woman's weight, Donna fancied she could hear Rufus whining.

✖

Nasimul Rahman was a strong swimmer. But he was a strong swimmer in the warm waters of Bangladesh: the water he had plunged into when he jumped off the *Jamalpur-2* had shocked him with its implacable desire to suck the heat from his bones.

The shallow harbour in which he now swam was nowhere near so cold but, in his weakened state, nevertheless cold enough to drain the energy from him, to make his strokes less certain, his breathing shallower. His legs began to cramp once more. If he was unable to escape the water soon, he would die here – but on this dark night, he was unable to judge the distance to shore. All he could do was to swim on.

Then the small night sounds were swept aside by a volley of barking, by voices calling, by running feet and wildly swinging beams of torchlight. Nasimul realised that he was much closer to shore than he had thought. With that realisation came the certainty that he must get out of the water and find shelter to survive. Despite the noises approaching from his left, he swam until his feet touched bottom, then pulled himself out of the water, bent as low as possible, like some ancestral lungfish reaching for new territory. He lay in the damp grasses at the water's edge and watched.

It was his misfortune that the building thirty or so metres directly ahead of him, an old and ramshackle house that would not have looked out of place on the banks of the Lakhya, was now the centre of attention. The barking dog and its human deputies had come to a halt in front of the building. A torch was played across the closed front door. Stealthy footsteps moved off to one side. Time passed. He began to shiver, clenching his teeth to prevent the noise carrying.

The scene erupted into noise and movement. The front door was kicked inwards. Boots pounded on timber. He heard a cry. Two shots rang out. A voice wailed, and was cut short.

Soon afterwards, a man and a woman were half-marched, half-dragged out the front door of the building. The man was arguing furiously with his captors, so furiously that he was backhanded across the face for his pains. The woman, and the girl guarding her, stood quietly.

He heard the squawk of a radio, voices he could not catch, more vociferous swearing. At last the lot of them moved away, voices then footsteps dwindling to his left. He waited, waited though he was beginning to feel delirious, waited a little longer still, and then climbed at last onto solid land. Ten steps, twenty, thirty. He reached the shattered front door. He was shivering harder now in the cool night air. He could choose to die of exposure on the doorstep, or he could choose to go inside. He went inside.

He heard the noise as he crept along the hallway, and the hairs rose on the back of his neck: a whining noise, the wail of an unhappy spirit …?

The wail of an unhappy dog. When it saw Nasimul peering around the corner of the bedroom in which it had been tied up, its ears lifted and it started wagging its tail: this was not a dog trying to defend its territory.

But the dog could wait. Dry clothes were more urgent, and there was a pile of them in one corner. While everything in the house was half-fallen into disrepair, the clothes were new, if dirty. They belonged to a man broader and taller than Nasimul, but they were a great deal better – an infinite deal better – than shivering. He dried himself off on the bedspread then dressed in the clothes that fitted him least badly. The dog, no longer whimpering but still not happy, watched him with liquid eyes.

Shelter, and now clothing: and someone had left their water bottle behind, with enough for a few precious sips. But with those needs satisfied, his hunger rose to the fore. He had not eaten since well before the *Jamalpur-2* sank, and even then he had been on the shortest of short rations. Surely, if people were hiding out here, there must have been food?

But if any food remained in the kitchen of this house, the rats and mice had disposed of it long since. He searched everywhere: high, low, in cupboards, on shelves. Nothing but a few bags with holes gnawed in them.

He returned to the bedroom, looked at the dog reproachfully. 'You're lucky you're haram,' he said, 'or you'd be going straight into the pot.' The dog wagged his tail enthusiastically, as if he was being praised.

The bedroom window faced the harbour. He twitched

the rotting curtains aside and looked over the water, then as far as he could see up and down the street. Nothing there, but it had started raining, and as he watched, the rain grew heavier. If he went out to forage, he would be soaked again – and the man whose clothing he had taken had not thought to leave a raincoat for him.

He found another pile of clothing besides the room's sole armchair. This was women's clothing – clothing for a small white woman, not at all what was suitable for a Bangladeshi woman to wear.

Then, as he pushed aside clothing he would never wear and would have been horrified to see Hasina wear, he felt his fingers brush against something firm but not hard and, digging in the capacious pocket of a raincoat, extracted a block of Cadbury's chocolate. He remembered his father, in a rare moment of fatherly success, buying the family one once. He remembered how it tasted.

His mouth watering, his fingers trembling, he tore open the wrapper. Then, with an effort of will, he brought himself under control. He sat down on the edge of the bed, broke off a square of the rich, dark chocolate, placed it carefully in his mouth, and chewed.

Flavour flooded his mouth, and as the sugar hit his bloodstream, he felt an intense, almost nauseating rush of energy. He had to be careful, or he would throw up every mouthful he ate. He forced himself to sit for five minutes. The dog looked up at him, whining. 'Here you go, boy,' he said: the dog did not recognise the words, but it recognised the meaning, and when he tossed it the second piece of chocolate it seized upon it with delight. One more piece for him, one more for the dog … 'You've had enough, dog,' said Nasimul, and let himself have the unimaginable luxury of cramming four squares into his mouth at once. He was almost delirious with pleasure, though his stomach roiled warningly. And the great thing, the best thing of all, is that he still had most of the block left.

He felt good, so good, better than he had since the *Jamalpur-2* began its long journey to the bottom of the globe. He was on land, and for the moment, he was safe and dry. In fact, now he had the block of chocolate, maybe he did not need to go out foraging in the rain. He decided to sit for a moment longer while he thought about what to do, and as he did, the spike in his blood sugar started its downhill slope and bone-deep tiredness rose up like the sea to claim him.

×

The problem wasn't that the guy wouldn't talk. The problem was that the guy talked too fucking much. Even a couple more clips around the jaw hadn't shut him up.

He was a good-looking guy if you liked older men, maybe in his thirties, dark curly hair, quite muscly. The muscles weren't doing him a whole lot of good, because he was firmly tied to a chair in the interrogation room … well, it was the tearoom, but they were short of space.

The interrogator was Staff Sergeant Anderson. She would never have made it onto a cop show. There were no gotcha moments, no revelation of new pieces of evidence with a dramatic flourish. She just repeated each question, sometimes with additional physical punctuation from Corporal Reweti, until the prisoner answered.

Donna and Mere were seated in the back of the room, observing. 'You might learn something,' Staff Sergeant Anderson had said. But it was late, the chair was hard, the overhead lights were bright, and although she kept telling herself to stop worrying about the damn dog, she couldn't stop worrying about the damn dog. She had already asked once whether she could go back for him, and been told to shut up and stop interrupting.

'I'm sick of this,' whispered Donna.

'Be quiet!' Mere whispered back louder.

If the guy had had some beans to spill it might all have been more interesting. But all he'd given up was his name (Brian Strong), his place of residence (West Auckland, somewhere up in the Waitakeres), his occupation (schoolteacher! Donna had snorted at that, and Staff Sergeant Anderson had turned round and fixed her with an I'm-not-telling-you-again scowl), and the fact that he had been 'visiting a friend' when they had found him, and that the friend was indeed the small, frightened Asian woman who was sitting in one of the makeshift cells down the hall. She wasn't talking because no one in this particular Shore Patrol HQ could speak her language, and they couldn't find anyone in the local Bengali community prepared to put their neck in the noose and act as her translator. 'They're all in it together,' Corporal Reweti had muttered darkly.

So the frightened woman would remain in her tiny cell until she was transferred to whichever of the detention camps could make room for her.

Staff Sergeant Anderson was starting to get to the interesting stuff – what exactly had a schoolteacher from the wild West been doing with a woman who was, let's face it, an infiltrator, in a rundown house on the edge of a Waitakere Harbour?

'I was giving her English lessons,' said the defiant Mr Strong.

'English lessons? Then how come she can't speak English?'

'We'd only just started.'

Corporal Reweti didn't even need to be told. He fetched

the prisoner a stinging backhander on the left temple. leaving him with a gash above his left eye and a trickle of blood running down his face – Corporal Reweti was a married man, and wore his wedding ring proudly.

'What the fuck?' said Brian Strong. This time, it was his right temple that started bleeding.

'Got a girlfriend, Brian?' asked Staff Sergeant Anderson. 'Boyfriend? Husband? Wife?'

'Leave her the fuck out of this.'

'If she hasn't broken the law she's got nothing to fear from us. But what you need to decide is, when is she going to see you again, and what are you going to look like when she does? Right now, you're a good-looking man who's a bit the worse for wear. Nothing a little bit of medical attention won't fix. But Corporal Reweti and I, we're just amateurs at this interrogation business, and we prefer to keep it that way. As long as people tell us what we need to know, we fall over ourselves to be helpful to them. Wounds dressed, food, water, uninterrupted sleep, that sort of thing. But when we get tough nuts – people who don't tell us what we need to know – amateurs like Corporal Reweti and I can't hope to crack them. That's when we have to hand them over to the professionals. And then we can forget about them, because we never see them again. Or if we do, we don't recognise them anymore.'

Staff Sergeant Anderson sat in silence as she let that sink in. For almost five minutes, she sat in silence, and the prisoner sat, his face downcast, dried blood clotting on his cheek. Donna shifted in her chair and wondered when the fuck she was even going to be able to get out of here, and how hungry she was getting, and how hungry Rufus must be getting too, and whether he was scared, and—

Five silent minutes, and then the prisoner looked up and

said 'All right,' and said he'd tell them what he knew. It wasn't a hell of a lot. He'd been contacted anonymously online, and told they'd heard he was against the detention camps, and told how he could help the people he insisted on calling 'the refugees': it involved going to houses for which he was given the address, and finding people there, and taking them to other houses. Besides the people he was helping, there was never anyone at the pickup house or the dropoff house.

'And how did you transport them?'

'In my car. White guy driving, no one's looking twice at me.'

'So where was your car tonight?'

'I didn't want to park it right outside – too conspicuous. So I parked it a couple of streets back, and when we went to get in it, some fucker had stolen it. We went back to the house while I tried to figure out what to do. I was still trying to figure out what to do when your goons burst through the door.'

'So what's the address of the other house you were planning to drive to?'

He gave it to them. 'But you won't find anyone there,' he said.

'Well, we'll check it out. Hey, Brian, just because I want to know: why did you let yourself get involved in all this? Why get yourself tied up with the Shepherds?'

'Why? Because everyone on these boats is a human being in desperate need of help, yet our government sinks the boats, shoots the survivors, and sticks anyone who manages to make it ashore into concentrations camps.'

'So you'd like our country to be flooded with millions of starving, illiterate peasants, would you? How are we going to feed them? Where are we going to put them? Are you going to give up your house for them?'

'They're human beings,' said Brian firmly. 'And they have just as much right to life as we have.'

Staff Sergeant Anderson stood up. 'Brian, it's been a pleasure. Thank you. Corporal Reweti, call our specialist colleagues and tell them we have a prisoner for interrogation, would you? I'm sure they can get a lot more out of Mr Strong than we've been able to.'

The man was still shouting and raving at Anderson and Reweti when the closing door cut off the sound of his voice. Donna thought it served the bastard right. He should have kept his Westie nose out of other people's business.

'Right,' said Staff Sergeant Anderson. 'It's time to check out that address in Pakuranga he gave us, although I don't believe we're going to find anybody there.'

'Maybe it was a trap,' said Mere.

'I don't think so. He was real anxious to please us when he gave us that address. But we'll make sure we're fully armed, just in case, and I'll come with you. Five should be enough. Scott, you can go and fetch that dog you left behind.'

'By myself?' squawked Donna.

'Yes, by yourself.'

'But I'll be late for work! I won't get any sleep!'

'You should have thought of that before you left the dog behind.'

'But—'

'And you should have thought of that before you interrupted my interrogation with your stupid questions and silly noises. Reflect on that while you're walking. And if picking up the dog makes you late for work, take the damn dog to work. Dismissed.'

So while the rest of them piled into the runabout to head over to Pakuranga, Donna had to walk, by herself, back down the hill to the edge of the water. The sky was growing lighter, she had her gun, and she was so furious about the unfairness of it all that she had no room to be nervous. All she'd done was snorted when the prisoner had said he was a teacher! Mere had talked, actually talked, and that bitch Anderson hadn't said a thing to her.

But all the same, it was kind of crisp to be out this early in the morning with the harbour emerging from darkness and the streets silent except for the sound of her footfalls. The city was hers, to do with as she wished – and she had certainly never felt the city was hers before. Pick up Rufus, take him back to the depot, grab a quick feed, and tell Mrs Alberts she had been held up on unavoidable Shore Patrol business, and it probably wouldn't be the last time, either. Donna could handle that. She increased her pace, swinging down the street under a brightening sky.

✖

Nasimul was roused from dreams of deep water by the dog whimpering to be set free. He woke disoriented, aching, everything wrong from the light to the place he was lying, his clothes hot upon him. He sneezed.

A face appeared over the edge of the bed: a hopeful, trusting face. It came back to him: the dog, the rich, dark chocolate, the thought that he must sit for a few moments longer to gather his energy …

And now it was morning, or becoming so: too late to go out looking for food, too late to move around the streets. What was he going to do?

The dog whined at him. What did the dog want? He led it to the back door, opened the door cautiously, and soon found out as it lavishly and messily relieved itself a foot beyond the doorstep. Was it sick? It certainly wasn't sick of his company, because when he tried to shoo it away in fierce and insistent whispers, it whined at the door until he let it back in. The dog licked at its empty bowl, then looked up at him. It wanted water. So did he.

The day grew brighter. Here he was, in a strange house in a strange city in a strange country. A country where they shot people like him, and a house where someone had been shot. But he could not think how to get away, or where he could get away to.

Food, water. He needed both. He had been stupid last night. He should have left a few sips in the water bottle, but the water bottle was empty. And as for the chocolate … it was gone. He must have dropped it when he fell asleep. Now all that was left was a few scraps of foil and paper, and a dog with a bloated stomach.

'You are a very bad dog,' he told the dog. But the dog no longer appeared to care very much, and Nasimul didn't have the energy to argue with fate. It was settled – he would have to leave the shelter of the house, and soon.

He went to use the toilet, and in finding the toilet, found a solution to his most immediate need: the cistern still had water in it. Not much, and it was rusty and for all he knew poisonous, but in that moment it was sweeter than nectar. He drank all he could, poured the rest out for the dog, then returned to the cistern to refill the bottle. He was returning to the bedroom with the second bottle when he heard the sound of a footstep behind him and turned to find a gun levelled at his face.

✹

It had been easy enough to retrace her steps to the house, the last house before the sea. The houses to either side of it had fallen apart or been cannibalised for their wood, but the house in which poor Rufus had spent the night had not quite fallen into ruin, though last night's twin assault on the front and back doors had certainly helped it in that direction.

She felt too exposed at the front of the house, visible from anywhere: the sea, the sky. She trod the narrow, muddy path from front to back door, and almost stepped straight in a messy pile of dog shit. God! But if that was Rufus's little welcome to her, how the hell had he got out? And if another dog was around, a feral dog, might it have squeezed through the big jagged hole in the door and gone after poor Rufus, who would have been tied up and completely unable to defend himself?

So she drew her gun and, with visions of finding Rufus menaced by some snarling beast or dead on the floor in a pile of blood and fur, pushed the door open as quietly as she could and entered the house.

She was so keyed up with the expectation of confronting a wild dog, or a pack of wild dogs, that she was taken completely by surprise when she saw a short, skinny brown man, wearing only a shirt many sizes too big for him, leave the toilet carrying something in his hand. She took one more step forward, a floorboard creaked, and he whirled around, saw the gun, and stopped still. From beyond him, in the bedroom, she heard Rufus whine in pain.

✖

Nasimul froze. The woman was young, dark-haired, and scared. But though she was scared, she held the gun impressively steady on him.

'What the fuck have you done to Rufus?' she said.

Though her accent was strange to his ears, he could understand her. But who was Rufus?

'No Rufus,' he said.

'The dog, you fucking arsehole!'

'The dog! I give it water.'

From behind them came a series of retching noises. Rufus was throwing up. Donna stood still a moment longer, the gun now trembling slightly in her hand. If he had tried to run when he saw her, or if he had tried to attack her, she would have shot him without feeling a moment's remorse. But now, despite how much she hated and feared him, she could not bring herself to do it.

'Move,' she said. 'Move!'

She had to prod him with the gun before he moved ahead of her into the bedroom. Rufus was standing unsteadily, looking white around the muzzle, trembling and whining. He saw her and started to wag his tail, but it was a feeble effort. Where was his lead …?

'What the fuck have you done with his lead!'

More incomprehension. She had to mime taking a dog on a walk before he understood and, moving cautiously, picked up the lead from where he had left it, beside the bed. She used it to tie the thin man's hands together, uncomfortably aware as she did so of how easy it would be for him to knock the gun from her free hand, or push it away and leap on her. He was slim, but he was wiry. She was not sure she could take him in a fight.

'Sit!' she said, and he sat on the bed, looking at her with an expression she could not fathom. Fucking foreigners, she thought. Why did there have to be so many of them?

It was hard to check out Rufus and keep an eye on the infiltrator at the same time. But she didn't need a vet degree to tell that the poor dog was very sick. He quivered against her, then heaved up again so quickly that she couldn't get her left shoe out of the way in time. What the hell was wrong with him? He had been fine when she left him last night – a little sad, but otherwise fine. God, what if this guy had some weird disease? Maybe she was infected even now.

She told herself not to be silly. She told herself to think.

'Did you feed him anything?' she asked.

'I – no, no. Some chocolate. He found it in the night.'

She stood up, walked over and backhanded him across the face with the gun before she realised what she was doing. They were both very lucky, because the gun discharged as she hit him, and the bullet punched a hole in the rotting wall behind his right ear and spanged off harmlessly. He fell back, dazed and bleeding, and toppled off the bed. She stood over him, screaming.

'You stupid fuck! Never give a dog chocolate! It kills them!'

He came to and stared up at her. Again her finger tightened on the trigger. She tried to think of him as just another infiltrator, a nameless brown figure escaping from the teeming, broiling North, floating south to overwhelm New Zealand and its way of life. Let in one, they said, and you may as well let them all in. Now she had her first chance to do her duty. Was she going to fail her country?

Yes. Yes, she was going to fail her country. All she could see before her was a man, cowering in fear of death. He was a stationary target, and she was good at shooting stationary targets, but she could not bring herself to shoot this one. She hit him across the forehead again, and he collapsed, unconscious. After making sure he was still breathing, she turned to deal with the dog.

✳

'Oh, for Christ's sake,' said the dispatcher. 'You want me to do what?'

'Send a driver out to pick me up. I've got Rufus, and he's

sick. Really sick. He needs to see a vet as soon as possible.'

'Rufus? Are you talking about that red-haired dipshit of a dog?'

'Yeah, that red-haired dipshit that led us straight to an infiltrator and the prick who was helping her last night. And now he's sick. That bastard left a block of chocolate behind, and Rufus ate it, and now he's sick.'

'Well, that's shitty luck. Where are you?'

She told him, and then she waited in the alley beside the decaying house. She hoped she had hit the brown-skinned man hard enough to keep him unconscious till well after she, the driver and Rufus had left the area. She had considered tying the man up, but then he wouldn't have been able to free himself and would presumably starve to death – it would have been kinder to shoot him.

The quicker she could get out of here, the better – having decided not to kill him, she had now become complicit in saving him. Or rather, allowing him to save himself: once she was safely away from here, he was on his own.

At last she heard the faint whirring noise of the runabout. The driver scowled at her, especially when she saw the fresh trail of vomit down Donna's top from the panting, half-delirious dog Donna held in her arms. 'In the back,' she said, 'and don't bring that mutt anywhere near me. I'm taking the pair of you to a vet. For your sake, I hope the vet has a shower.'

Donna cast one look back at the house as the driver turned around on the crumbling strip of road. She fancied that she saw eyes peering at her through the bedroom window. Then Rufus threw up again, and she had other things to worry about.

✖

This time, the headache was more intense, and there was blood. This time, Nasimul did throw up, more than once.

He was alone. No woman with a gun, no dog. But she had left him something: a water bottle, and a little yellow packet of what he took to be some sort of food: he could not read English, so he did not know it read 'Juicy Fruit.' And, next to them, some coins, though he had no idea what they were worth or what they could buy. He had read death in her face when he first saw her, but now she had offered him another day's lease on life.

He drank a few sips of water and waited for the headache to recede.

The pain was so strong that he did not hear the runabout pull up. But the sound of the voices caught his attention. Had the girl with the gun betrayed him after all, leaving the water and the yellow packet and the money because she knew it would keep him distracted long enough for soldiers to come?

He was in no shape to fight, and did not know whether he had time to flee. He crawled to the window and peered out, aware of the risk of being discovered. The girl was climbing into the runabout. The vehicle was moving down the street, turning around where the sealed surface disintegrated into gravel, gathering speed as it accelerated back past him and went out of sight. For now, at least, he was alone. Having nothing better to do, he lay down on the bed again and, though his headache continued to pound, went back to sleep.

✕

The sun crawled across the face of the day. Donna was very late to work, but Mrs Alberts did not seem to mind – indeed, she refused to let the girl get on with her usual tasks, and instead insisted that Donna tell her everything about the events of the night. 'Your commanding officer called me!' Mrs Alberts said several times.

Donna thought that if Mrs Alberts was impressed by Corporal Reweti, she would be impressed by anybody. Nevertheless, recounting her adventures to Mrs Alberts was a whole lot better than cleaning up the rest of the mess Kimmy Potiki and her boyfriend had left in the back room, so she sat nursing a coffee – a rare and precious fluid these days – and told Mrs Alberts everything, except for the really important thing.

If the guy had any sense, thought Donna, he would lay low all day and make a break for it at night. The Juicy Fruit she had left him would stave off hunger for a while. She knew there was a risk he might get caught and turn her in to try to save his own neck, but as soon as she had found him and not shot him she had stepped over a line. Now she would have to live with the consequences.

'That poor dog!' said Mrs Alberts for the fifteenth time. 'Are you sure he's going to be all right?'

'The vet said he'd eaten enough to make him very sick, but probably not enough to kill him, or he'd already be dead. There's something in chocolate that we can digest easily but dogs can't. If he's going to make it through, he'll start to come right in a couple of days.'

'Well, when you see him again, you tell him he's a very brave dog from me. I can't believe that anyone would help these people! Do they really want our country to be overrun with millions of Indians and Indonesians and Bangladeshis?'

'I can't believe it either,' said Donna.

✺

Nasimul waited until the sun had been down for several

hours before daring to move. His head still hurt, and though he rationed his water as strictly as he could, only a third of the canteen remained. The strange sweets had proved tasty but unfilling, and extraordinarily difficult to swallow.

The money was in his pocket. The men's clothing that had been left behind was far too big for him, but though the women's was much closer in size, he could not bring himself to wear it. He had ended up wearing a pair of men's trousers with the bottom of the legs rolled way up and the belt cinched to the tightest possible setting, and the over-sized shirt he had been wearing when the girl with the gun arrived. The smell of vomit had only intensified as the sun heated the house, and he was as desperate to get away from the house as he was deathly scared of what might happen when he did.

At last he could put off his departure no longer. He went out the back door into the still, muggy night. It was quiet: as far as the Shore Patrol and the regular Army knew, the ship-load of infiltrators who had arrived last night had all been either captured or killed, so patrols had been scaled back. He slipped along darkened streets and quiet alleys, looking for unlatched doors and open windows.

It was very late in the night when he found a house in which someone, reckless or restless or drunk, had left the back door unlatched. He found a bedroom in which a teen-age boy slumbered, clothes strewn all over the floor. In the dark, by feel, he discarded his ill-fitting clothes and put on new ones that fit better. He was even able to steal some jandals to protect his feet from the debris of the streets.

He was creeping down the hallway, looking for the kitchen, when a light flicked on in a bedroom down the hallway and a sleepy voice called 'Jason! Go back to sleep!' He froze until the light went off again, then left via the unlatched door, stomach rumbling.

It was a pale dawn before he found a row of shuttered shops. He sat under an awning and watched two plump shopkeepers arrive, one on foot, the other on a bicycle, and unlock their shops for whoever had money or ration cards or both.

The third shopkeeper was thin and brown, and more cautious than either of his predecessors. Nasimul watched as the heavy corrugated iron door at the front of the shop rolled up, revealing a cornucopia bathed in golden electric light from within. There was no one visible in either direction. Nasimul crossed the street and entered the shop. To him, its stock of bruised fruit and undersized vegetables seemed a paradise. He selected an apple, a banana, two more chocolate bars, and a water bottle. He approached the counter with his selection, put down his little pile of coins. 'Buy food?' he asked.

The shopkeeper looked him up and down and up again, then went to the front of the shop, rolled down the blind, locked the door, and opened another door at the back of the shop. 'No talking,' the shopkeeper said in Bengali. Nasimul followed him into the darkness beyond, devouring the apple as he went.

BREE'S DINOSAUR
AC BUCHANAN

MY HOST SISTER TAKES A BREAK FROM THE DINOSAUR TO watch me baking, sits on a stool with her knees pulled up, bare feet displaying chipped nail polish. Her name is Bree and she's not quite sixteen, but her parents still have a plan for us to become best friends. I don't tell them – and they don't ask – that I already have a best friend back home, that she's getting married in five months and I'm not sure I'll be able to be there even though we promised we'd be at each other's weddings. You can make promises like that, when you're younger, because you can still manipulate the future, compress it down to converge on whichever moment seems most important.

I've lined up the ingredients on the small strip of bench not taken up by the breadmaker, the food processor, what I think is an ice-cream maker, and two other completely un-identifiable appliances. Bree picks up one of the plantains, holds it by one end delicately as if it's hot to the touch: *what is this, some kind of deformed banana?*

I tell her that I'm making cake, and that I hope she'll enjoy it. My orientation pack says that sharing something from your culture is a good way to connect with your host family, but I think my mother would be horrified at the idea of me presenting this haphazard recipe as emblematic of my culture, and I certainly don't think it will be enough to connect with Bree.

The foreignness hits me in waves, like a recurrence of the car sickness I felt on the first night as we drove in darkness up the hills and round the tight corners of Wellington's suburbs. I measure out flour and become suddenly aware that these are not the ceramic measuring cups from the box of kitchen equipment, some of it more useful than others, which my grandmother gave me when I left home. It hits me that I'm more than three hours from Sydney, another thirteen from Hanoi where I have lived these past eight years, and then two by road to the small town where the remnants of my family still live.

The cat – Chloe – crashes backwards through the cat door, tail puffing up as she returns herself to an upright position. Bree slides down from the stool to pick her up, soothe her, as I mix ingredients together. Bree wears her blonde hair in a long plait, which I don't think is fashionable. It makes her look young, which is the opposite of what I wanted at her age – but then, I'm not sure what Bree wants. Despite Sue's determination for a friendship to form between us, I've barely spoken to her in the time I've been here.

Our bedrooms are upstairs, part of each located over the garage, with a bathroom beside them and a microwave and electric jug on a shelf across an alcove. Bree's room – where she is building the dinosaur – has been closed to me, Bree slipping out through the narrowest possible opening in the door, locking it behind her. Mine could be a model for the standard homestay room. Every item on the list has been ticked off: one bed, one set of drawers, one desk, one lamp.

I bought a navy-blue duvet cover to replace the salmon-coloured one which was there when I arrived, covered the pinboard with photos of family and friends, just like I did when I was eighteen, but it still feels generic, as if I'm a *homestay student* before I'm Cam.

Sue said that she hoped I will be a good influence, and that the arrangement will help Bree take some steps towards independence. *Besides*, she said, smiling, *Bree can help you with your English.* I don't tell her that my conversational English is very good, thank you, and that the course I'm doing is English for Business Purposes which I doubt Bree can help me with very much, and wonder if a homestay was a bad choice. Sue means well, so most of the time I say nothing.

Bree wanders off with Chloe hanging over her shoulder, back to her dinosaur. I blu-tac a vocabulary list to the cupboard and read over it as I mix, my lips forming around both familiar and unfamiliar words, the vibrations of the beater numbing my fingers.

Sue works at an intermediate school, and by the time she gets home the house smells of plantains and batter. I've worked out how to set the timer on the oven, and full of all the good guest resolutions in the world, rinsed the bowl and utensils and stacked them in the dishwasher. I can hear the sound of thumping and a whir like an electric drill coming from upstairs.

'This smells delicious,' Sue comments, negotiating the doorway with her arms around a box of papers. 'What are you making?'

'It's like … a bit like a type of banana cake. It will be ready soon if you'd like some.'

'Oh, that would be lovely,' she says. 'You're such an angel, Cam.'

We eat fish with peas and boiled potatoes which Bree immediately smothers in butter, salt, and pepper. I'm well accustomed to the weeknight ritual by now: Martin will ask each of us in turn how our day was, and Sue will bring it to a conclusion by asking *and how was your day, Martin?*

He asks me first, and I say that my day was good, thank you, that I only have morning class on Tuesdays and after that I came home and did some study and baked a cake. Sue says that it's good cake and he should have some after dinner, and that I'm very talented. Martin asks her how her day was, and she says that this government has a lot to answer for, but the kids were well enough behaved. And then it's Bree's turn. I think she's going to say that after school she watched me bake and Sue will be all approving, but instead she says: *I've been building my dinosaur.*

I chew on a mouthful of lukewarm potato and look out through the ranch slider. Bree reaches over and pours herself a glass of water, the ice cubes clinking as they hit the pinched spout. Sue turns and looks at Martin, a forced smile creasing her face.

'And how was your day, Martin?'

✱

Overnight, a storm hits. The wind rattles my windows and I'm awake, sweating uncomfortably even though it's cold. Branches thump against the walls. Over my years in Hanoi, I have become used to the sounds of an inner city, the repetition of pedestrian crossings and stalled traffic. Out here in the suburbs, the Karori wind, and then the rain, take me by surprise as they emerge amongst the silence, enveloping the house, the wooden cladding stretching and relaxing, creaking each time the weather pauses for breath. The rain drums heavy on the metal roof and I feel as if I could be alone up here, as if the rest of the world has fallen away and it's just me and the weather.

It is only wind, of course, that is roaring like some untamed beast. It sounds like it's coming from Bree's bedroom, but that must be no more than a trick of how sound carries in this old wooden house. Aching, I clench the duvet round my neck and fall into an unsatisfying sleep.

By day the air is calmer, the rain coming and going in patches. I pull on a raincoat and my most waterproof shoes, run for the bus. It's close to full and I cling to a pole as we wind our way down the hills and through the tunnel, water dripping everywhere, passengers squeezing on. In class we role-play *Informal Workplace Interactions*, discuss different workplace styles and how meanings can be misconstrued, a vague feeling of anxiety clutching at me as pitfall after potential pitfall comes to light.

After school finishes, I eat lemon syrup cake with yoghurt in a Cuba Street café with two of my classmates. Violet is an accountant from China; unlike me, she wants to stay in New Zealand permanently, just a matter of finding a job, she says. Katja is German and only taking the first part of the course. After that, she says, her girlfriend will meet her in Wellington and they will buy a second-hand van and travel for three months. We're all around the same age, and we talk about how strange it is to be studying again, to have classmates again, and yet be so far from home.

I don't talk about Bree and her dinosaur, or about how Sue wants to sort everyone's life out, or about my brother, who has been increasingly on my mind. I talk, instead, about my work as a business analyst in the energy industry, and how with increasing interest in hydroelectricity in many areas of the world I hope to find work in an international company. I'll go back to Hanoi initially, I say, but perhaps I can be transferred somewhere in a few years. I realise, as I sip my coffee, that I feel the same way I did when I first started university, the same as when I first graduated: that the whole world is open to me.

I order another coffee, dark, strong, as Katja tells Violet a story accompanied by demonstrative gestures, wide arm movements. Through the window, as I wait in line at the counter, I watch passersby, an abundance of tattoos and striped socks. A rite of passage I circumvented, though some people seem to stretch it forever, unrestrained by plans.

And yet I know from my life, and from my parents', that plans don't always work out anyway.

I look at posters over Violet's shoulder as we laugh about one of our tutors who is able, at will, to transform himself into an exaggerated American, dragging us up to the front for role-plays as we attempt, nervously, to respond to his loudness in kind.

Outside, the rain comes down heavier, pedestrians manoeuvring themselves against the windows to stay under the awnings, drops of falling water reflecting in headlamps as the darkness comes early. We look outside at the weather uncomfortably, reluctant to make a move.

As it happens, we stay there another hour, ordering coffees on a rotation so there is always something on the table, an excuse to stay inside. Eventually, though, Violet swings her red leather bag over her shoulder.

'My turn to cook,' she explains, wrapping a long scarf around her shoulders as she makes it through the glass door and out onto the street. After Katja finishes the last of the bottle of pear cider she bought when she tired of the repeated coffees, she too moves to leave, on her way to meet up with a group of German travellers she's connected with online. She tugs at her straggling dark-blonde hair, retying it in a loose pony tail, and promises to see me in class tomorrow.

So that just leaves me here at this painted, chipped table. I drink up the last of my coffee and then make a move, toes numbing up with the cold even as I'm barely out of the door, hands dug deep into my pockets. It's still apparent how few people I know here – and that the few I do know have therefore become such a big part of my life, irrespective of how little we may have in common, whether we would have made our connections in another place.

I make my way through the rain, hood pulled up tight, manage to find a seat on the crowded bus as it makes its way through the city, past the botanic gardens and up the hills to home.

Home for now, at least. The wind is loud against the wooden walls. I change into dry clothes, switch on the fan heater, and drag a blanket around my shoulders, enter a new batch of vocabulary into my flashcard app. I try not to listen to whatever is happening on the other side of the thin plasterboard wall that separates my bedroom from Bree's.

✖

There's a phrase in English: *the elephant in the room.* As far as I can tell, the only reason for it being an elephant is that it's big enough that no one can avoid seeing it. Perhaps what's happening here is something even bigger than an elephant. A dinosaur in the room.

I broach the dinosaur in the room to Sue and Martin. *Why is Bree building a dinosaur? Is it for school?*

They look at each other, Martin in the armchair and Sue on the couch, a cup of tea in his hand and a phone in hers, conversation flickering between their eyes. Simultaneously, they return their gaze to me.

'It's just something she enjoys doing, that's all,' says Sue.

'A hobby.'

'So it's art?' I run through my mental dictionary for the correct word. 'Sculpture?'

'Have you seen the dinosaur?' Martin asks me. He's wearing a polo shirt with the logo of his sailing club on the pocket, and it's quite apparent where he'd rather be.

I shake my head. 'She doesn't let me in her room.'

More eye conversation. 'We were hoping …' Sue says. 'Bree's always been a very shy girl. She doesn't have any friends, really. We were hoping that having you in the house would encourage her to talk to people a bit more.'

Bree does have friends, though. I've seen her with them from the bus with their tartan skirts hitched up, passing headphones between each other, laughing, taking up the whole width of the footpath, drinking Coke. I saw her in McDonald's once, with a group of boys and one other girl, flicking fries at each other's faces. She's not shy, but a veil descends around her in this house. She is not, to use another phrase, at home when she's at home.

'I'll try and talk with her,' I say, smiling, but there's a hint of anger creeping up inside me. I want to help, but I pay them two hundred and forty dollars a week, and I'm here to study to further my career and I have my own family who need me. Bree – Bree cannot be my responsibility. I swallow the anger. Sue and Martin have not picked up on it, and I think that is for the best. It is important to me that I'm a good guest in their home.

'What's a good recipe?' I ask Sue, moving on. 'I'd like to bake something new.'

'Edmonds,' replies Sue, pulling a spiral-bound book from the shelves and handing it to me. 'Real Kiwi icon.'

I've noticed how people emphasise things as cultural pointers but don't explain them, only serving to mystify them further. Still, I'm sure it's meant to be helpful; I take the book and thank her and she smiles in return and says it's no problem at all, that she's pleased I'm interested. Martin turns on the news and I stretch back on the sofa to flick through the recipes.

I make chocolate-coconut brownies. The recipe is easy, almost soothing – one saucepan and then into a tray, the oven. I take some time to myself while it's cooking; headphones in, idle internet browsing.

On my way back, alerted by the oven timer, I almost trip over something large and white, about the size of a soccer ball, sitting halfway down the stairs. Bree runs out, grabs it and cradles it to her chest, mouths an apology and runs back to her bedroom. I only catch a glimpse of it, so I tell myself it was most probably a rugby ball. Except one end was considerably thinner than the other. Like a giant egg.

A few minutes later she follows me down. When I cut the brownies she takes one from the rack before it's cooled, bites a chunk out of it hungrily. I think I see the hint of a smile on her face. I ask *what's your dinosaur, Bree?* and panic clutches at my chest. I want to hear her say *a sculpture*, and at the same time, I'm not sure I do.

To my surprise, her face breaks into a clear smile. She perches on a stool, talks semi-incoherently as she forces the rest of the brownie into her mouth.

'It's a Titanosaur,' she says, 'A sauropod, like the Diplodocus or Brachiosaurus, only they came a bit later.'

I struggle to process the words, cycling between the known and unknown, a repeating translation running through my head as I scrub the saucepan and wipe the silicon baking pan.

'Long neck.' It's the over-enunciation people tend to do when they underestimate my English, but it don't sound like she's being unkind – more that she's lost in her own world with the dinosaur and is unsure how to communicate with people from outside it. 'Eats plants.'

She grabs an envelope from the table behind her and starts to draw on the back of it. The outline of a dinosaur quickly emerges, a blue, long-necked creature. She finishes by drawing grass around its feet and labelling it in large, rounded capitals: *TITANOSAUR*.

She leaves after that, muttering about going to see some friends, people who understand her (though I think that's a dig at her parents rather than at me). I don't think initiating another conversation about the dinosaur will be easy – in any case, Bree's been taking up more of my headspace than she should. With study occupying the majority of my thoughts during the day, and much of my evenings spent wondering what is going on in the next room, I've had little time to relax, barely set foot in a bar since I've been here, haven't been to a concert or shopped for anything beyond necessities.

I resolve to move out of this *rut* and text Violet and we eat kebabs sitting on one of the triangular benches in Te Aro park, amongst the pigeons: thick fried falafel smothered in sweet chilli sauce. A vaguely drunk-sounding man tries to sell a pair of jeans to passers-by. Brand new, he says, and not stolen. Definitely not stolen. We giggle, watching the water bubbling up from the shallow fountain, the pigeons stalking over the blue and grey tiles around our feet. Someone a little way across from us is dropping pieces of bread, and the pigeons, along with the occasional sparrow and seagull, make for that direction.

Violet tells me that she's thinking of moving in with her boyfriend. They're serious, she says, a wedding might be on the horizon; but she looks nervously down at her fingers spread out across her dark jeans as she says it.

'But one day. Not now. He has a big room, we can share that, and get a place to ourselves later.'

I nod, drink the dregs of my apple juice. 'I think you'll want to find a job first. And things aren't so good with the economy still, you might need to search a bit.'

She pauses. 'Yes. I'll have to … what is it … *crunch numbers*.' We laugh.

'You need to *take stock* of your situation. You don't want to end up in … in a *tight spot*.'

We sit and watch the buses drive past. The commuters turn to office workers heading hurriedly home from Friday night drinks, then the party-goers beginning to emerge. I'm growing to like this city, despite its cold and wind and endless hills. I will perhaps miss it, when I leave, even though I expect I will never return. Some experiences, once over, are consigned to the past forever.

✖

I look up the Titanosaur that night, curled up in bed with my laptop, idly eating my way through a packet of M&Ms. *It includes some of the heaviest creatures ever to walk the earth,* Wikipedia says, *such as Argentinosaurus and Puertasaurus – which are estimated to have weighed up to 90 tonnes.* 90 tonnes. I'm not quite sure how much that is, but I'm pretty confident nothing of that weight would fit in anyone's bedroom. I find some small consolation in learning that they were, at least, herbivores.

I read further, bring up a news article:

One of the largest known dinosaurs, a titanosaurid, once roamed New Zealand about 80 million years ago.

The article details the identification of a bone from the spine of a dinosaur which was found in a stream in Hawke's

Bay. I flick to Google Maps. Hawke's Bay isn't so far away. Especially not in the context of a time when continents were shifting, when the land that is now New Zealand was sandwiched between Australia on one side and Antarctica on the other.

This bone, the article says, is the first evidence that titanosaurids once lived in New Zealand. It's not clear if it was from a child or an adult, but adds a lot to what is known about dinosaurs in New Zealand …

But this isn't *Jurassic Park*. Either Bree's got some slightly eccentric art project going on, or she's mentally unstable and imagining things. Either way, looking up types of dinosaurs isn't going to help and, I reiterate to myself, it's not my responsibility.

(Even if I still feel slightly relieved about it being a herbivore.)

My mother says the same thing (about responsibility, not herbivores) when I finally get hold of her on Skype. By now it's dark outside, and I talk softly to avoid waking Bree who is – for once – quiet. 'It's your own life, Cam,' she says. 'I'm sure these people are very nice. You must be polite to them and help out when asked – you do help them out?'

I nod, and see the small image of myself in the corner of my screen nod back at me. My mother's face looks dull, but I tell myself it's just the poor quality camera, and the sunlight behind her beginning to fade. There's something about time zones that always makes me vaguely uneasy, as if no matter how clearly I understand it, I still can't quite process the difference between here and there.

'But your responsibility is to yourself and your family,' she continues. 'You can't worry about everyone else – so worry about those who will worry about you in return. How is your course?'

I tell her about the topics we've been learning, that the tutors are mostly good and that I've been getting on well with my classmates. She's sipping at tea and picking at a slice of cake that is indistinguishable at this low resolution while she talks to me. She says that this is all very good, that she misses me but it sounds like I've made the right decision, and that I must remember to send a postcard to my grandmother, who paid for this after all. She catches me up on the local gossip; the son of a neighbour on his way to university, two others trapped in a dispute over the theft of a fridge.

'How do you steal a fridge?' I ask. 'Casually slip it in your pocket when you're invited round for tea?'

I tug my blankets over me even though I'm still dressed. Eventually I swallow and ask after my father, and she says he's all right, as well as can be expected, she doesn't want to wake him now but she'll make sure I can talk to him soon, and that it's good to get my emails – he reads those, or she reads them to him.

I say that I understand, because I do understand, now that I'm an adult, and we chat some more before I shut down the computer and go to sleep. Though the wind taps branches against my window, the night is relatively quiet – and Bree's room in particular does not disturb me. I sleep soundly.

×

My responsibility isn't to Bree, but I'm still looking up dinosaurs on my phone as the bus heads into town. Tuatara are living dinosaurs, say some sources, but the more reliable clarify that they are the last surviving members of the order Sphenodontia, a group of animals that were common 200 million years ago. There are Coelacanths, thought to have become extinct in the Late Cretaceous, until their rediscovery in 1938. That story is a little closer than I feel comfortable with, so I move on, but find only a controversial idea that dinosaurs lived past the asteroid impact into the Palaeocene epoch, and from then on it's all conspiracy theories.

But however ridiculous this whole thing is, I keep looking. Because I, more than most people, know that when people say the last of a kind has died, they are not always correct. There are many stories – and I look through some of them now – of creatures that have survived their seeming extinction, or are caught between myth and reality, who stalk through jungles and deserts, soar over mountains. Of giant eagles and worms thicker than a man's arm, large cats loose on moors and prehistoric relics hiding in deep lakes.

I get off the bus at Lambton Quay without stopping to think about it, walk down to the waterfront. This is the first time I've missed class but right now I can't stand the thought of other voices and the squeak of chairs and the clear enunciation of every role-played word.

For now, among the stories, there is a memory.

The overlapping of hills by the harbour's entrance makes it look closed in, as if it could be a lake. Hồ Hoàn Kiếm is much smaller – as an adult I walked its perimeter many times. But as a child, it seemed similarly endless.

The waterfront is busy with joggers and office workers, roller skaters, the occasional family out on this clear winter morning. I sit on a bench by the edge of the water and watch the ferry leave, pulling my coat around me.

1997. I was ten years old; my brother, Thanh, two years younger. We were living in the city then, though the town where my grandparents lived was still where we called home. In the city we had an apartment with no land and only a slip of a balcony, so we went to the lake often. We were afforded less freedom in the city, but going to the lake by ourselves was okay, as long as I looked after Thanh.

I liked the banks of the lake then, even though they were messy with only patches of yellow flowers in the soil. The river was murky green and it seemed as if it could be a portal to another world, the vague reflections of buildings another city entirely. Looking out we could see the red Bridge of the Rising Sun, the Turtle Tower on a small island. Sometimes there were turtles there, moving like slow lumbering rocks, but not today.

There were larger turtles there too, once. The last one died in 1967, beaten by a fisherman with a crow bar. It was stuffed and put in a glass case which we were taken to see, one Saturday, awed by its size, longer than the height of anyone we knew. But long before that, a turtle in the lake took a sword from the emperor Lê Lợi and returned it to Kim Qui, the Golden Turtle God, from whom it originally came. But the turtles were all gone now, our father said, and the gods too.

We'd never been taught to swim, and so when Thanh leaned over the shallow waters, looking at something I couldn't see, I warned him to be careful. Then he leaned forward just a little too much, and toppled in head first. I screamed.

The lake was not deep; men could stand up in it, or near enough, and two slid in after him, half swimming, half wading, as I sat on the bank wailing, more with shock than the grief which would hit later. They shook their heads as they couldn't find him, and then police and other official-looking people and eventually our father arrived, but he didn't swim determinedly like the others; instead he splashed and flailed until others dragged him, exhausted, back to shore.

He wasn't the same after that. They said it was because water had got in his lungs and stopped him breathing for a bit, and that had hurt his brain and made him sick.

It wasn't entirely a lie.

I didn't tell them everything, either. I didn't tell them how I saw the large flippers, the turtle's twisting neck, the giant shell emerging like an island, and how Thanh went with it, deep into the lake. I wasn't sure, and I'm still not sure, whether it dragged him in or if he followed it down. The turtle was long-extinct, and mostly just a legend anyway, was what people would say, so I said nothing.

Early the next year, an amateur film-maker produced footage of the giant turtle in Hoàn Kiếm lake. No longer just a legend or a creature from the past. I didn't feel vindicated, only sad. I lived with my grandmother for two years and didn't see the lake at all. Only as an adult did I become comfortable walking the path – newly landscaped – around its green waters, sit beside it eating street food, noodles or fried cake of flour and peanut powder, sweetened with honey.

I look up. The waterfront is quieter, the work day begun. A small group of teenagers are huddled around a bench, two kayakers taking on the cold harbour.

Three years ago the turtle was put in an enclosure in the middle of the lake for observation and treatment, before being released. Crowds turned up, lined the concreted banks hoping desperately for a glimpse. Depending on who you believe, it's either the last of its species or one of only four left.

They dredged the lake, to clean it as part of their effort to save the remaining turtle, and I spent weeks on edge, waiting for a phone call, notification of a discovery. There was none.

That was the year I decided to leave Hanoi. It was not a sudden decision, not a flight of terror, rather a clarification of the increasing feeling that my future lay elsewhere. That what happened in that lake was never going to be something I could predict or control, and it didn't need to be so central in my life anymore. If anything was to change, it was not going to be achieved by me staying there.

I worked, studied, researched. Calculated expenses. I made plans.

✖

The newsreader says there has been a meteor detected, heading for Earth, but *no reason to be alarmed*, she says, as her voice lifts to a type of professional urgency. I am rarely alarmed by what I see on the news, unconcerned about pandemics and train crashes and cyclones, and I laughed off my mother's earthquake worries when I bought my ticket to New Zealand, but there's something about this that brings me a slight edge of unease.

Bree perches on the arm of the chair next to me, eating half-defrosted cheesecake. 'Do you think it will hit here?'

I shrug.

'Because with the velocity they reach even a small one can kill heaps of people,' she continues. 'Mostly they explode before they hit the ground, but that explosion's like the size of hundreds of nuclear bombs.'

'The world's a big place,' I say, though I'm unsure if she wants reassurance or a co-conspirator in her excitement. 'And two thirds of it is water. It probably won't hurt anyone.'

'You never know, though, do you? It could wipe out the whole country.'

'I'm sure we'll be just fine, Bree. Sorry, but I'm behind with study.' The words emerge more abruptly than I intended, but I've no intention of apologising. I'm sick of it all, sick of the noise from her bedroom, the idea I have to somehow reassure her, save her. If I couldn't save my own brother, how could I save her?

In my bedroom I write out sentences, each using a designated word: *negotiation, trade, taxation*. I memorise the meanings of another list of seemingly impenetrable idioms: *ambulance chaser, back to the salt mines, laugh all the way to the bank*. Next, responding to an email from a former colleague, I keep my answer to the question of whether I'm coming back vague. To Hanoi, certainly, at least for a while. To my old company? Everything is *up in the air* right now, and I like that expression, as if I've just thrown all the pieces above me and am waiting for gravity to fit them in to place. No loud collision, as a meteor would make, but simply a gentle fall, blowing on a breeze, shuffling neatly together.

Bree bangs on my door and opens it without waiting for a response. 'What are you up to?' Her voice is confrontational, goading.

'Study,' I say, not making eye contact, filling in a worksheet.

'You study a lot.'

'That's what I'm here for,' I respond, aiming for monotone.

'Well, why are you baking all the time? No wonder you're fat!'

That gets me to my feet. Not because I'm particularly sensitive about the subject, but because I am twenty-seven and used to having my own apartment, and wearing a suit to work, and people being at least superficially courteous, and I have no time to be insulted by a child – a child! – who's been keeping me awake at night with some crazy imaginary *dinosaur*.

I pause, breathe, aim for calm, make my voice low. 'Bree,' I say. 'You need to go now.'

She hovers there in the doorway, momentarily, then

silently turns and walks away, each footstep, though not particularly loud, unmistakeably deliberate. I shut the door after her, shaking with rage or guilt or probably both. I'm not sure if she was crying.

Later in the evening, while Bree bashes away at something upstairs, I'm in the living room messaging a friend. Martin looks up from his laptop.

'How's Bree seemed to you lately?' he asks. I think quickly, wondering if he's heard something, but he's talking to me like another adult and doesn't seem at all annoyed.

'She's been … okay.' I choose my words carefully, worried of saying anything that will cause offence. 'She talks a lot about her dinosaur, and I think this meteor they're talking about on the news is scaring her a bit.'

Martin nods, evidently thinking. 'She's quite private from us. I guess that's just being a teenager, but we were wondering if you'd picked up on something we hadn't. I know you're not close, and we don't expect you to be, but you're a little nearer to her in age, and maybe you can see some things we can't.'

He pauses, and I say nothing in the silence. I feel lost; afraid of not measuring up when they clearly want something from me, but equally afraid of intruding.

'When Bree was two years old we lost her.'

I frown as I parse the translation. I know when people say they lost someone they usually mean they are dead, but that's clearly not the case here. But Martin continues.

'She was in the garden, the gate was shut. Sue was watching her, she was there and then she wasn't. We didn't know what had happened. All the obvious answers – abduction, running away – made no sense. She couldn't have gone far by herself, but surely Sue would have seen if someone took her. They had helicopters out with infrared and teams of volunteers searching the bush, appeals for information … but no sign of her.'

He closes his eyes, briefly, remembering.

'But then you found her?' I say. It's half a question, half a reassurance. I'm feeling slightly nauseous – the police helicopter with its infrared in this family's past, the police divers in mine. Only with a different ending.

'She just turned up. The next evening. A little muddy, but unharmed. She seemed to have been fed. She couldn't have come back on her own, but there was no sign of anyone else. The doctors told us – they told us there was no indication of abuse or anything like that.

'So the best answer we could come up with was … there's a woman down the hill, has lots of cats, you know the type. Harmless, but she doesn't like going near people, always does her own thing. We think maybe Bree wandered down there and she fed her and let her sleep, and then she realised she had to return her. But …'

'You don't believe that?'

'It's the best answer we have. Bree used to talk about it all the time when she was younger – I'm sure she didn't remember it, but she pieced together what she was told. Children like anything that makes them sound special. She hasn't spoken about it for a while. I hope she's forgotten …'

'You think it's related? To the dinosaur?'

He pauses. 'Well I sometimes wonder if it had an effect. I probably shouldn't say this to you, but they say that anything that happens before you're three has a particularly big effect. At some fundamental level. I wonder if it's … unbalanced her a little. She's a good kid.' He adds the last sentence hastily.

I shuffle uncomfortably, wanting to be anywhere but here. I think I probably need to go bake something else.

Bree's words still sting a little, antagonism hanging in the air, shadows and wisps of the petty arguments and wind-ups Thanh and I would engage in. But for now I just have to say something to try and calm the anxiety lurching in us all, even if I don't really believe it.

'I think she'll be okay. I know why you're worried … the dinosaur thing is unusual, but lots of people lose their way a bit when they're her age. I think she'll find it again.'

✖

As days go by, I'm becoming increasingly uncomfortable and distracted. Nightmares I thought long gone are flaring up inside my brain, memories surfacing at inconvenient times.

I attribute it to lack of sleep, resolving to find somewhere new to stay – even if I will forfeit a board payment – if things don't improve. I can't believe how little the constant noise bothers Sue and Martin. I may be closest to Bree's room, but the house is not particularly big; there's no wall insulation (no insulation at all, I'm increasingly suspecting) and sound carries easily. Near every night I'm woken, sometimes multiple times, by the sound of heavy footfall, growls, roars, thumping, and something that sounds like a wild animal eating. I consider, briefly, that this could all be an attempt to drive me away, that Bree's behaving like a spoiled child who can scare off any nanny, but I suspect in reality I'm just not that high on her list of concerns.

I think that when class starts again on Monday, I'll be fine, that I'll *perk up* and *put my best foot forward*, but I catch the bus in a sleep-deprived haze. By ten o'clock my head is throbbing. Katja walks me round the corner and pushes me into a taxi. Words seem to have deserted me; I barely manage to recite my address to the driver in stilted syllables.

No one is home. I let myself in, kick off my shoes, close

my bedroom curtains and collapse onto the bed, lying on my back, staring up at the ceiling in the semi-darkness. I feel more vulnerable in every respect right now, much more than I did at home. I drift into sleep over and over, but noises come from the next room, chomping, and soft growls which startle me awake. Eventually I force myself up, my vision fuzzy, knock on the door, *Bree, are you there*, but there is only silence.

I drag myself downstairs, trailing a fleece blanket with me, hoping this is not some breach of etiquette, because I can never quite work out where I fit between guest and visitor and family member and resident, let alone apply New Zealand norms to my role.

Then again, presumably building a dinosaur next to someone's room is a breach of etiquette in most countries.

I prop myself up on the sofa with my laptop, pulling the blanket over me, nibbling at a slice of ginger loaf. Everyone seems to be talking about the meteor, but I've had enough of hearing about it. I open up a season of *CSI* I downloaded a while ago but haven't yet had time to watch, telling myself it's English practice. Just in case I ever need to talk to someone about a crime scene.

A child is bawling outside. The crime scene thing is looking increasingly likely.

I'm not sure which department investigates murdered dinosaurs.

Eventually, even watching TV becomes too much. I keep closing my eyes and thinking that I'm drowning, waking from a daze as if fighting for breath. Finally, and with relief, I fall into sleep. I sleep most of the afternoon, then make some instant noodles and apologetically excuse myself from the evening meal before I clamber into bed, cold and clammy, exhausted. Sue asks if I have a fever, if I need her to take me to the doctor, but I brush away her concerns. The streetlamp is orange, a slightly eerie glow through my curtains. The cat rustles and leaps as if chasing something, but I don't get up to check, and fall into sleep.

I'm woken, later, by a loud whisper, tapping on my door. *Cam, Cam. I need your help.* I lean over to switch on my regulation desk lamp, pleased to find that my headache has cleared and I have only the usual level of just-woken-up grogginess. *One minute.* I pull on clothes, whichever I get to first. The family may walk round in their pyjamas, but I don't feel comfortable with that, not here.

Bree slides in, her blonde hair tangled and unusually frizzy, a child in her arms. She stands awkwardly by the door. Bree is fully dressed, as if she's just got home, or as if she expected something to be happening tonight. I look at my phone: almost 3am. Bree leans against the wall in tight jeans, a low-cut top, her eyes anxious beneath the mascara'd lashes. She clutches the child to her chest awkwardly. Though the girl makes no obvious signs of unhappiness, she must be uncomfortable; her arms and legs hang loose rather than clutching, as children almost instinctively do at that age.

'Sit down,' I say, because I can't bear to look at that awkward pose any longer. Bree hesitates before perching at the end of the bed, the child still in her arms. The child is dressed in pink dungarees over a white top, her hair loose but with a bow clipped in one side, a smear of mud on her right cheek.

'Where … who is she?' I ask. I reach out and put my hands under the girl's shoulders and pull her away. I have heard no sounds from her and Bree obviously has no clue (only child, I guess) how to take care of her, so I need to make sure she's okay. She turns her head, looks at me for a moment before scrunching up her face as if to cry, but mercifully thinks better of it, letting loose only a few tearless sobs. I rock her, feel her forehead, place my hand on her chest to check her breathing and scan her for injuries. She seems fine.

'I need you to help me with her,' Bree replies. 'She needs to go back home.'

'Of course she does. Who is she?' I'm aware that exasperation is showing in my voice, and that it may well be counterproductive, but at this point I've no interest in containing it.

'It's complicated.'

Teenage stubbornness at the worst possible time. I want to shake her. Who knows what she's done, what she could possibly be implicated in – or implicating me in?

'Bree, the child. Is she a relative's? Did you just find her? Do you know who her parents are?'

'She's a relative's. She got out of her garden and got lost so I'm looking after her.'

I breathe a sigh of relief. 'That's great. So they live nearby? Let's go and take her home – I'm sure they'll be relieved to have her back.' I touch Bree's hand lightly, as if to guide her up and to the door.

But Bree shakes her head. 'She can't go back to her parents yet. I kept her in the shed yesterday but I can't keep doing that – the wood's full of splinters and she cries heaps.'

I take a deep breath. Bree means well, but … I just hope it's a long time before she considers having her own children. I take a deep breath.

'Okay, Bree, listen to me. If there's something wrong, if her family have been mistreating her, you need to talk to your parents about this. I know it's hard when you're related to them, but you're fifteen years old, Bree, you can't just sort this out by yourself.'

'I can!' Her voice is still quiet, but desperately insistent. 'I'm exactly the person who needs to do this, but … I need you to help me.'

Suddenly crashing begins next to us, the sound of glass smashing and wood splintering. The house seems to shake to its foundations, the walls visibly vibrating. I duck down, my body bent over the child's as she starts to cry. The initial shock is followed by a series of loud thuds which send smaller, but still terrifying, vibrations through the house. I hear a yell, footsteps from the other end of the house. Bree grabs the child and runs, her footsteps echoing against the wind as she takes the stairs two at a time, made louder with the weight of the child still between her arms.

✖

The night wind is sharp. I'm in mismatched clothes; sneakers, knee-length cotton skirt, long-sleeved T-shirt, my hair loose. I round the corner at the end of the street, run up then downhill, making for the bush, steep land not yet surrendered to housing, muddy under foot. I push through someone's gate, climb the fence at the back of the yard Bree can't have gone far, not with a child in her arms. I use my hands to steady myself, pull my way through the thick bush. I scan the darkness; a rustling in one direction and then another as I haul myself another metre up the slope, find enough ground to stand upright on.

'Bree!' When my voice comes it is laughably faint: even with the urgency of the situation I'm afraid to shout in this darkness. A bit louder: 'Bree!' I pull out my phone, which I managed to stuff in my bra as I left, but its light is of minimal help.

I catch a movement, drag myself over. Scratches all over my bare legs. The cold air aching at my throat. Bree clinging desperately to the child.

'Bree, come on, let's go home.' I hold up my cell phone, illuminate her tear-stained face with bluish light.

'The dinosaur left,' she says, looking upwards at the hill. 'My dinosaur. I tried to look after it well. I fed it three times a day. I created it – it never would have existed without me. No one cares about it like I do.'

I take a risk. 'There was no dinosaur in your bedroom, Bree. I know this means something to you, something important, and I can help you with that, but … dinosaurs are extinct.'

Bree chokes a little, softly.

'I looked up your dinosaur. The Titanosaur? They grew to forty metres long? How long's your bedroom? A tenth of that?'

'There are other dinosaurs. Maybe it wasn't a Titanosaur after all. Besides, they're smaller when they're young. I hadn't had it very long.' Her tone is defensive, but her voice is quiet.

'What are you scared of?' I ask, gently, betraying none of my frustration.

Bree looks upwards, up at the sky, and I can tell she is desperately trying to make it clear that she fears nothing. 'Don't assume I'm scared just because you are.' She pauses. 'That meteor's going to arrive soon. It's a near-Earth asteroid not big enough to hit the ground – I've been reading about it. That's good because if they're bigger they can cause all kinds of problems. Extinctions.'

'Dinosaurs are extinct, Bree. Not us. We're going to be fine.'

'It's going to explode here. Right above us. Soon. It's …'

'You can't know that. I watched the news too – the scientists say it's not possible to predict where it will be, but most likely over ocean. We probably won't even see it at all.'

'Won't you listen to me? Just because I'm young doesn't mean I don't know things. It will be here, I can sense it …'

I bite my tongue. I'm not going to argue about the plausibility of sensing a meteor, not out here in the cold and dark. My priorities are to get the baby back to its parents (who must be frantic by now) without getting into any trouble myself, to get Bree home and ideally get her some help, because this kid is really not okay, and to get more than two hours' sleep before my test tomorrow.

Not necessarily in that order of importance.

I'm suddenly almost uncontrollably homesick. Not for Hanoi, for my small but modern apartment, or the friends I would meet up with after work. Not for speaking my own language again, rather than having to think before every word; or even for my parents and my grandmother, and the house she was born in and never left. My homesickness is for something longer ago, before the turtle and the lake, for a life I've never really mourned. Children are resilient, they said, they are used to going along with their parents' decisions, they adjust. I'd adjusted well, they said.

I'm homesick, right now, for a time when I didn't have to make decisions, because I'm tired, so tired. For the drive back to my grandparents' house, Thanh getting increasingly carsick next to me, his excited voice as he opened the door before we'd quite stopped (even though he was told not to) and charged round the vegetable plot to the front door.

But now I'm thousands of miles away, and I've embraced change – a career, a new language, any number of new countries beckoning me – because that was how I could absolve myself. By being adaptable, and not crying when we gave away Thanh's clothes, or every time my father struggled to talk.

My eyes are adjusting to the darkness. There's just the

three of us out here in the middle of the night, our breathing audible over the wind, running far too many thoughts through our heads until it seems like everything else just falls away, as if we could be standing forever, out here, in inadequate clothes against the winter air.

The explosion above throws us to the ground. Bree, with an instinct I'd never have guessed she had, falls on top of me, sandwiching the child between our bodies, sheltering her from the blast, then immediately sits up. Sounds shake through my eardrums. The light above, just for an instant, illuminates the whole suburb, the green of trees and white of houses, searing on to my eyes, red and yellow shapes lingering on my retinas against the darkness.

I hear glass smash, broken glass blown out of windows, smashing into bedrooms and onto the road, raining down and the tinkling goes on and on. Then the sirens start, one after another to form a chorus, every burglar and vehicle alarm in the suburb. Footsteps out on the street, yells rising above the sirens.

The child begins to cry, bawling at the noise surrounding her. Bree comforts her gently. Then she looks up at me.

'We're losing her.'

What do you mean losing her, I'm about to say. *She's fine, just shaken, a bit bruised at worst.* But Bree is already running, limping slightly. Lights are coming on but the sirens are still going. I make after her along the road. She's weighed down by the child, but her legs are longer than mine, and we're almost at the gate by the time I catch up with her.

The child has stopped crying. There's mud spattered up her legs. The sirens begin to shut off. Bree places her on the path and she seems unsteady for a moment, then regains her balance, toddles up the path and disappears.

✷

We don't sleep that night. We sit in the living room with blankets and cellphones, a candle on the dining table, waiting for the power to come back on. Wind whistles through the upstairs of the house.

'Well I guess it's happy birthday, Bree,' Sue says, rising from the sofa. 'Good thing I made your cake yesterday.'

Bree stretches, raising her arms in the air in an exaggerated fashion. 'I forgot.'

Texts start to come in on our phones – mostly Bree's, but I exchange messages with my few friends in the city. There's damage throughout, is the picture I'm getting, though we were at the heart of it. Windows shattered from office blocks down onto the streets. School closed until further notice.

Sue and Martin are (fortunately) under the impression that there was a smaller explosion before the main one, and their house had the misfortune of being right next to it.

'Thank god you two got out okay.'

'Bree was terrified.' I know that she'll be torn between relief at me covering her and fury at being portrayed as scared, and I'm okay with that. 'She just ran. I went after her to check she was okay.'

We eat cold meat and three kinds of cheese with bread for lunch. One wall of Bree's room is missing. A builder-friend has confirmed the structural integrity isn't at risk, and they pull a tarpaulin over to protect the remainder of the room from the elements. I've volunteered to move out, so Bree can take my room while it's being fixed. They're terribly grateful and say I don't have to, that Bree could sleep in the study, but I think it's more than time for me to move on. There's a room free in the same student hostel as Katja, just down the corridor in fact, and Martin's going to drive me there later today.

Neither of them appears to know anything about the

child. Now I have worked things out, I realise they would surely know if they saw her, and I think it's best they don't know. But I think things are going to start getting easier for them – once they get the house repaired, of course.

The cake has a thin coating of icing, and below that layers of pink, chocolate, ginger. I press my fork down, pushing up layers as I go. Bree hesitates, eyes her slice for a moment, then eats hungrily.

'You're okay now?' I ask. She nods, swallowing the mouthful of cake, eyes welling with restrained tears. She picks up her plate and walks out to the deck, balancing it on the rail, staring out at the garden. After a moment I follow her.

'She was you, wasn't she?' I ask, though I already know the answer.

'I don't remember much, but I put things together. And I think I remember the meteor as both me and her. I mean, me now and me as a kid. So when they said that it was coming I understood more.' She laughs a little. 'I don't really like kids, but I guess I had to take care of her and make sure she came back. If Mum and Dad had found her, or if she'd been too far from the house, things could have gone really wrong. So it was … self-preservation.'

I look round the corner, where the blue tarpaulin billows out above the garage. They've picked up most of the pieces of house, the big ones at least, but the concrete is still flecked with chips of white paint and the occasional sliver of glass glints in the afternoon sun.

'You're good at self-preservation,' I reply. 'Don't let anyone tell you otherwise.'

Martin and Sue don't follow us, and we stand on the deck for a while, a gangly teenager who has just met her past self, and a young woman whose past is far away, eating sugary cake with our fingers as the sun trickles through the kowhai tree that spreads between us and the road.

Sometimes, I know, things come back from the past, and sometimes they take pieces of our selves away with them. Sometimes abstractions like emotions and memories aren't enough to hold them; like everything important to us, they have to become monsters at some stage or another. Monsters not with dripping blood or giant fangs, monsters just so big they can't stay under your bed or trapped in a lake. A turtle that once took a sword from an emperor returned to take a boy from his family. A girl desperate to reconstruct a past that makes no sense has looked even deeper into the past and found a dinosaur which may once have lived on this land.

The sky is clouding over. Bree smudges up the last few crumbs of cake onto her finger and then into her mouth, picks up the fork and plate and moves to head inside.

She pauses and turns. 'About the dinosaur. You know … when you're a kid, people notice if you're gone even a few minutes, they freak out. But when you're a bit older you tell them you were at a friend's place, and you might get grounded but it's hardly a big mystery.'

'You travelled more than once, didn't you?'

But Bree is already on her way upstairs. My possessions have been packed into my suitcases, and Bree has already moved most of hers into her new room. She leaves the door open and I walk in behind her. The room is neat, with everything put in place as it was brought in. She has posters on the walls and a pinboard of photos of her and her friends pulling faces for the camera. A toy pig sits on her turquoise pillow. I stand behind her at the window. A dark shape moves over the hill and is gone.

'I can make us some cake,' Bree says. 'And bring it to your hostel after school. No deformed banana cake, though.'

THE LAST
GRANT STONE

The Toyota blew a tyre somewhere not far north of Huntly.

Rachel twisted the steering wheel and swore, squeezing the brake and aiming for the side of the road. The car stumbled to a stop in foot-high grass, barely missing a fencepost many degrees from straight.

She was not surprised to learn the rental company had not included a spare tyre. Simon had told her to expect that sort of thing. 'It's like travelling back to the seventies, especially when you get out of Auckland. Maybe that's why she picked it.'

She leaned against the cooling car and listened to the cicadas buzzing their arses off.

Her phone still had a signal, which at this point Rachel was prepared to consider a bona fide miracle. She had already dialled Simon's number before she remembered it was still three in the morning back in London. She killed the call. Simon couldn't find his reading glasses on his desk half the time. There was no chance of him finding a mechanic on the other side of the world.

Rachel reached through the window for the map Simon had printed for her. She'd just gone over a short bridge with a long name and it didn't look too far from there to where Simon had marked an *X* in blue ballpoint and written *KSJ* next to it. She grabbed her suitcase from the back and started walking.

The Toyota's tyres might have been shot but its air conditioning had been top notch. The humidity was jungle-strength. Five minutes walking and she was covered in sweat. Biggest interview of her career and she'd go into it soaked. Figured.

✖

Rachel had been at her desk in *Sounding*'s tiny Earl's Court office when the call had come in. Maria, the receptionist, had looked over the top of her magazine at the ringing phone as if it were an alien. First time it had rung in a month.

'Who was it?' Rachel asked once Maria had passed the call through to Simon's office.

Maria shrugged and mumbled something. She only enunciated on the phone.

Rachel frowned. That couldn't be right. 'Sorry? Did you say Katherine St. John?'

Simon burst out of his office so fast he nearly took the door off. 'You. Pub. Now.'

✖

'Wait, I don't – what?'

Simon sipped his pint. He was loving this, being the one with a scoop for the first time in a decade or more, having Rachel hang on his every word.

'That was Katherine St. John on the phone. She's about to release a new album and she's going to give exactly one interview. To us. Or more specifically, to you.'

'To me?'
'And only you.'
'Shit.'
'I know.'

*

Eleven-year-old Katherine St. John had come to the attention of the public in 1965. She had been camping with her parents on the edge of Bedgebury Forest in Kent when she went missing. The story held the front page for over a week. Black-and-white pictures of St. John's parents, arms around each other, stricken looks on their faces. Long lines of volunteers marching between the trees, trying to cover every square foot of a forest whose heart had been untroubled since the days of Hadrian. Then, as the days went on, rumours that the police were taking a particular interest in St. John's father. One telephoto shot of him being led up the stairs to the Maidstone police station for further questioning was published on Monday morning, a thin civil servant with a comb-over and a permanently crooked tie. The *Sunday Mirror* published a picture of a child's blue canvas shoe lying beneath a holly bush. In the opinion of the majority of the paper's readers, the man was clearly guilty, a trial just a formality on his way to the gallows.

A base of operations was established at the campsite, now deserted except for the St. John family's tent and their grey Hillman Minx, already starting to sink into the mud. On the Monday of the second week of the search, Detective Harlan Smith was eating lunch at his temporary desk in the prefab office when Katherine St. John walked in, looking as unruffled as if she had just been out for a brief stroll. No injuries, no malnutrition. Still wearing both her black leather shoes which, even scuffed and covered with mud, looked nothing like the one on the front page of the *Mirror*.

The papers printed full-page photos of the newly re-united family under headlines such as MIRACLE CHILD, but could find no more explanation for what had happened than the girl herself. In the few minutes after she reappeared she mentioned that she had been to see the 'dancing man'. But she was unable to clarify who she had meant and, as the days went on, seemed to recant even that, claiming she had no memory of her time in the forest.

Nobody remembered the lost girl who had been to see the dancing man in 1978, when Katherine St. John's first album was released. It was a revelation. Her voice rose above her own sparse piano playing, then swooped low. People compared her to Joni Mitchell, to Laura Nyro, but that wasn't quite it. She more ethereal than her contemporaries, more otherworldly. Nothing about her songs should have worked: the surreal lyrics, the unorthodox keys and time signatures – none of it suggested commercial success. And yet there she was, barely sixteen, topping album charts all over the world. Her time as a lost girl was mentioned, of course, in the initial coverage, but faded away. The music obliterated her history as it propelled her on the way to inevitable superstardom.

St. John's follow-up album two years later met middling reviews. Punk was on the rise and it seemed that St. John's unique sound was going to be consigned to the same dustbin of history as Prog Rock. She had never toured, and with the poor reception of her sophomore effort she became even more reclusive.

Rachel couldn't remember the third album at all. Her own attempt at an English degree was already in flames at that point. She had spiked her hair to look like Siouxsie Sioux and spent every weekend going to see The Damned and The Clash.

'It's a wind-up, surely. Every music magazine from here to New York would have got that call.'

Simon's hands were trembling slightly. Did they always do that? Why hadn't she noticed before? 'I don't think you're hearing me. That wasn't St. John's agent on the phone. That was her.'

'Shit.'

'I know.'

×

There was no gate, just a break in the fence. No mailbox. The number 257 had been scratched into a piece of tin and nailed to the fencepost. Rachel checked the map again and shrugged. This was the place.

The bare dirt driveway ran along a stand of trees before turning right around the side of a shed. One of the suitcase's tiny wheels had already crumbled from being dragged along the side of the road instead of a smooth airport floor, so she had to carry it. She heard a buzzing as she approached the shed. Then a smell that made her step back.

The corpse of a rabbit was balanced on the top of a fencepost, attended by a cloud of flies. It lay on its back, head lolling towards the ground, one dead eye looking at Rachel. The rabbit's belly was bloated, the blue mottled skin under its grey fur writhing with maggots.

Rachel backed away, holding a hand over her mouth and nose until she was around the corner of the shed. She leaned over, hands on knees, for a few moments, sucking in lungfuls of fresh air. The grass on the side of the driveway was long and ragged. She could see small patches of green in the middle of the bare dirt. Rachel wondered how long it would take for the grass to claim back the whole driveway.

When she picked up the suitcase again her arms were trembling.

✖

The farmhouse was small but tidy. It was surrounded by a garden that was a strange mix, English roses sitting next to native ferns and flaxes. There was no sense of untidiness; the garden had clearly been tended with great care.

The front door was pine, inset with stained glass. Rachel knocked and waited. A shadow appeared on the other side of the glass, stretched and rainbowed, so tall and wide that for a moment Rachel wondered if she'd got the wrong place after all. Then she heard footsteps in the hall and the shadow shrunk. The door opened.

Katherine St. John smiled and held out her hand. 'You must be Rachel Mackenzie. Welcome. Come in.'

She looked like someone's grandmother, which was, Rachel thought, entirely possible. Her hair wasn't completely grey yet, but there were wide streaks around her temples. The wrinkles around the corners of her mouth were beginning to deepen, like streams in sand at low tide. Rachel was only a few years younger than St. John, but looking at her now it could have been a couple of decades. Her eyes, though, were still that deep, endless green, same as they had been thirty years ago when they stared from posters on tens of thousands of suburban teenage bedroom walls.

'It's so nice to meet you, Miss St. John,' Rachel said.

St. John waved her hand. 'Just Katherine, please. I'm so glad you could come.'

The house was blessedly cool. Rachel nearly fell across the threshold.

✖

Katherine led her into a kitchen that looked out to a small

conservatory and took an old whistling kettle from the gas cooker. On the wall were paintings of English landscapes with fussy, gilt-edged frames. Bunches of dried flowers hung from the roof. There were no gold records on the wall, none of the awards St. John had won, just Devonshire granny chic. Not at all what Rachel had expected.

'Where's your car?'

'Down the road a little. Flat tire. No spare.'

Katherine pouted. 'Oh dear. To fly halfway around the world and then have that happen. I'm so sorry.'

Rachel shrugged. 'I've had worse.'

'Still. There's a garage back by the river. I'll give them a call.'

'You don't have to—'

'Please. You're my guest.'

Rachel smiled. 'I've interviewed the biggest names in rock for over thirty years and I don't think anyone's said that before.'

'Well,' Katherine said, passing over a mug of tea, 'there's always the chance of something new, on any given day.'

✗

'We can go back to the house if you want. No need to start straight away. It's a terrible flight.'

Rachel shook her hear. 'No. It's fine.'

The headache had started up while she was sipping St. John's tea, a buzzing like a badly earthed mic. Katherine had suggested they walk around the farm while they talked and Rachel had agreed, hoping the fresh country air would help clear her head.

The gumboots Katherine had given her looked ridiculous over her business slacks. Or perhaps it was the slacks that looked ridiculous out here in the country.

'We'll start over here,' Katherine said, leading the way to the milking shed.

Light through the looming black clouds rendered the land in high contrast. There was a heavy feeling in the air, as if a thunderstorm were imminent, but there was no smell of rain, just the sticky, oppressive heat.

'It's a working farm,' Katherine said, 'although I don't get up early to do the milking. That's a young person's game.'

Rachel pulled out her tape recorder. 'Do you mind if I use this?'

Katherine shook her head. 'Not at all. That's what you're here for.'

Rachel had seen many different responses to her tape recorder. Back in the day, she'd had more than one rock star refuse to speak as soon as she'd placed it on the table. Never mind that these people had a tendency to make all manner of libellous and offensive statements in the media. There had been a power in the sight of the recording device once, she supposed. Why else would a shirtless, tattooed rock god who had been arrested in Texas six months previous for exposing himself on stage clam up at the sight of the turning wheels of the tape? More than once recently she had placed the recorder before some bright young pop star and had the impression it was the first time they had seen such ancient technology. Justin Bieber had snorted and asked why she didn't just use her phone like everyone else. She'd bought the JVC KD-2 in a store on Tottenham Court Road in '82. It had cost her a fortune then, and several more since. Perhaps Bieber was right. But she liked the weight of it, the solid click of the buttons, the slow turn of the tape.

Rachel hefted the recorder. The strap dug into her shoulder. She suspected St. John might be the kind of interviewee who would just start talking without a lot of prompting.

'Milking here. I had it all upgraded last year. We've got just over a hundred Holstein-Friesians. Which isn't much by New Zealand standards, but I don't think the land would take any more.'

The milking shed was impeccably clean. The concrete floor had been hosed down recently and the shining water reflected the corrugated iron roof.

Katherine led Rachel out a smaller door on the far side of the shed. A newer building stood on the other side of a paddock, near a stand of old, gnarled trees. They trudged through knee-high grass, Katherine doing a better job of avoiding the cow shit than Rachel did. 'Some macrocarpas there,' Katherine said. 'Oldest trees in the area.'

They were an unimpressive collection, a handful of rough trees no more than fifty feet wide. They sat nearly exactly in the middle of the farm, the last remnant of a wilder time, before roads, before farms. The trees had been shaped by decades of wind, bent over as if they were trying, and failing, to support a great weight. Though the stand was thin and Rachel could see the paddock continued to either side, the trees were close enough together that she could not see anything but darkness between their trunks.

'And this,' Katherine said, tapping the side of the building, 'is my studio.'

It was tiny and looked like it belonged on a building site. There was nothing about its plain white walls to indicate that this was where Katherine St. John had recorded her first album in nearly thirty years.

Katherine shook off her boots and climbed the steps to the front door and Rachel followed.

The room was dark, apart from the red and green lights of the moderately sized mixing desk that sat in front of a glass partition halfway across the room. On the other side of the glass a mic stand was set up. Several synths were arrayed in a semicircle and an old Rickenbacker guitar leaned up against the wall. There was a large window on the far wall, but a blind was pulled down over it, so the only light was a dim glow around the edges.

Rachel had never bothered too much with the technical details of how albums were made. But she had been in enough recording studios over the years to recognise that this was very well organised. The console was new and had to be worth at least eighty thousand pounds. An expensive iMac was mounted in the corner.

'It took a lot longer to set up than I'd hoped. Then I had to learn how to drive the whole thing. But it was important to me that I do it all myself.'

'So there was nobody else here when you were recording?' Rachel couldn't see how that was possible. Surely Katherine would need at least one engineer, even for a console as small as this. Someone would need to run the board while she was in the other room.

'Nobody else. Just me and my muse. Otherwise I might have finished sooner.' She shook her head. 'No. Wouldn't have worked. My muse likes to be alone with me. He gets jealous if there are too many people about.'

Rachel looked at the Rickenbacker leaning up against the wall. One of the defining characteristics of St. John's debut album was how spare it had been – mainly just her voice and piano. The later albums had a larger sound, but that had all been studio musicians. Had she taught herself to play the guitar in addition to learning how to drive the desk and all the software?

'So,' Katherine St. John said, 'do you want to hear it?'

✖

Katherine brought up the first track on the monitors.

There was the sound of muffled footsteps so clear Rachel felt the urge to look around. The sound of a piano lid being opened, then a few notes, low down on the keyboard.

St. John's voice rose out of the mix, starting low and rising to a high C. Her singing voice was, perhaps, a little more ragged than it had been, but had lost none of its power. If anything, the more weathered tone gave her voice a stamp of authority that her first album had lacked.

He moves through the wood
Dragging the darkness like a shroud
He is the last.

There were more instruments in the mix, but so low down it took Rachel several seconds to place them. Strings and the faintest lilt of a penny whistle that filled her heart with an ache she couldn't place. It was barely there, but Rachel was sure she could hear a choir, singing the same two words over and over.

(Don't go)
(Don't go)

Katherine ran her fingers across the console, although she did not appear to be adjusting the mix at all. Rachel closed her eyes. It was possible she was the first person in the world apart from St. John to hear this. The song rose and fell, washing over her.

The dizziness returned, so quickly she opened her eyes and fell heavily into a chair. Katherine shot her a concerned glance but Rachel gave her a thumbs-up.

The song continued to build. Rachel hadn't been paying

too much attention to the words. St. John's lyrics had always been cryptic, as if they'd been designed to be pored over by generations of teenagers.

Rachel noticed the light was stronger in the studio. The blind on the window had rolled up. The window framed the trees perfectly. Something was there, in the shadows beneath the branches. There was the shape of a man, leaning against the trunk of a tree, looking directly at her. The light changed, and the shape that might be a man bled, swam, like a thumb rubbing over wet ink.

Another wave of dizziness struck her. Rachel closed her eyes and sucked in fresh air. When it had passed, she looked again at the old wood.

Nothing there but trees and shadows.

It took her some time to realise the song had finished and Katherine was speaking to her.

'—feeling any better?'

'I'm fine,' Rachel said, 'just the jet lag, I guess.'

'Why don't we continue this tomorrow?'

Rachel nodded, her head heavy.

As they returned to the house across the paddock, Rachel turned back once. Nobody was standing beneath the hunched trees. She could see through them to the paddock beyond.

But she could still see the man in her imagination. Tall and thin. No shirt. Tan trousers. And a wide, tooth-filled smile that might not have been a smile at all.

✖

Even in the age of digital downloads and piracy, Katherine St. John's first album was a solid seller. A perennial, like *Dark Side of the Moon* or *Rumours*, each new generation discovering it and claiming it for their own. But apart from the recording studio at the other end of the paddock, Rachel couldn't see any evidence of St. John's royalties.

Katherine had chatted the whole way back, then insisted on cooking dinner herself. As if Rachel and Katherine were friends who hadn't seen each other for years, finally catching up. Katherine didn't speak about the new album and Rachel didn't ask, so tired she was barely able to keep her place in the conversation. She'd feel much better after a good night's sleep.

The guest bedroom was on the second floor and decorated just as garishly as the kitchen. It had to be nearly nine, but the sun hadn't completely set. Light leaked through the thick red curtains and made her eyeballs ache.

'I'm right next door,' Katherine said, 'If you need anything during the night.'

Rachel's thanks were more yawn than word. She lay down, still dressed, and was asleep before Katherine closed the door.

✷

She opened her eyes in the darkness, no idea of the time, but suddenly wide awake. She fumbled for the phone and pressed it on. The screen was blindingly bright in the darkness. Simon would be awake now.

'So how does it sound?'

Rachel opened her mouth to speak. Closed it. Tried again. 'I've only heard the one track so far, but excellent. Her best work, no question.' She bit her tongue so she wouldn't say anything more. The room was vibrating slightly. She hoped it was just the jet lag.

'—rest of the interview?'

Rachel opened her eyes again, sat down heavily on the bed. Tried to figure out what she'd missed.

'Tomorrow,' she said, hoping that was noncommittal enough.

'Good. Good. Get some sleep. You sound terrible.'

Rachel walked over to the window and peeked through the curtains. She could barely see the milking shed or the recording studio in the darkness. But the tops of the trees behind the studio were clear, as if picked out by a shaft of moonlight. The illumination did not extend to the space between the trees, which remained resolutely dark.

The window was open just a crack. Refreshingly cold air ran over the tops of her fingers. She shouldn't have called Simon. Now she was awake she'd have a hell of a time getting back to sleep.

There was a scream from the trees.

Rachel gasped. She waited, heart pounding, but the sound didn't come again. Possum, she remembered, after a while. Simon had mentioned them. Nasty little bastards. Sound like a kid getting murdered.

As she expected, it was a very long time before she fell asleep.

✻

Rachel lifted the KD-2 and checked the cassette again. There was still a decent amount of tape on the spools. She had another couple stashed in the pockets of the oilskin Katherine had given her before they set out. It would be scorching later, she said, but it was always surprisingly cold first thing in the morning.

'Why now?'

'It was time.'

'You disappeared after your last album. It was as if you'd dropped off the face of the earth.' Rachel regretted the words as soon as they had left her mouth, thinking of the faces of

St. John's parents on the front page of *The Sunday Mirror*, but Katherine did not react.

'Money has never been important to me. Nor has fame. The music, though—'

Katherine St. John stopped walking and squinted into the sun along the fence line. The air was full of the sound of cicadas in the trees.

'My mother always used to tell me there was no point opening my mouth if I didn't have anything to say. And perhaps, for a long time, I didn't.'

'And now you do?'

'Did. This will be my last album.'

Katherine strolled off along the fence line, leaving Rachel standing, stunned.

'You can't mean that, surely,' she said, after she had caught up. 'If the rest of the songs are anything like the one you played me, this is going to be the best work of your career.'

Katherine had picked up a long stick from the grass. She swung it side to side as she walked, knocking the flowers off the clover. 'Thank you. I do hope people like it.'

'So what then? If you're retiring, what's next for you?'

Katherine shrugged. 'Just this. The farm. I could happily spend the rest of my days walking the land here. There's just something about it. It feels like home, more than anywhere else ever has. Does that make sense?'

Rachel thought about the number of years she'd spent on buses and planes, in expensive hotel rooms and seedy motels, tracking down the next story, following the latest rock god. 'Yes,' she said, 'perfect sense.'

✷

Rachel collapsed into the big couch against the wall of the recording studio. It was still early morning but the sun was already beating on her like a mallet. She had no idea how she would cope by midday.

Katherine called up another track on the console. The sound of cicadas came through the studio monitors mounted on the wall. Then St. John's voice, breathy, barely singing.

So cool
Beneath your boughs
Inside the heart of the wood

Instruments emerged slowly. Rachel heard a harpsichord being plucked somewhere to the left, while a choir sang to the right:

Don't go
Don't go

echoing the song she'd heard yesterday.

Rachel looked out at the studio, frowning. Katherine had said she recorded and engineered this alone, so where had she recorded the choir? Katherine's voice and the harpsichord were clear but the choir was so quiet she could barely hear it. Perhaps it wasn't there at all, just some acoustic trick.

Rachel closed her eyes and fell into the song. She could feel loam under her feet, the mighty, silent presence of trees. There was a snare drum in there somewhere. Rachel could see an army marching. The soldiers wore deep blue-black tunics and sabres on their hips, decorated with gold braid. At the head of the column marched a drummer boy, no more than ten, a serious expression on his face as he set the pace for the men marching behind him. The boy wore something that might have been a tunic once, but was now little more than a vest. Loose threads dangled where the arms had been torn off. It hung loose on his small frame. There were dark smudges along both his cheeks, soot perhaps, or blood.

A buzzing started in Rachel's head. It felt like the room was rolling, as if she were about to fall beneath the floor. She opened her eyes, but the light did not immediately return. When it did, it was with a sticky slowness that clawed at her face. Katherine had already half risen from her chair at the console. Rachel waved her off.

'Oh, god. I'm so sorry. I'm not coming across as very professional, am I?'

'It's fine. Maybe it's still the jet lag.'

Rachel nodded. 'Perhaps.' She closed her eyes for a second. Jerked them open again.

'Perhaps we should get out again. In the fresh air.' Katherine looked across the studio to the window. 'There's something I'd like to show you.'

✖

Steam was rising off the grass, making a knee-high haze across the paddock.

The fresh air helped a little. The buzzing in Rachel's head had died away, although her worry about what it could be did not. Rachel had spent large parts of her career flying between London and New York, Los Angeles, Sydney. This was nothing at all like jet lag.

Katherine St. John walked several paces in front of Rachel, wearing a wide straw hat she had grabbed from the hook on the back of the studio door, in the direction of the macrocarpa trees. There was an easy confidence in her walk, as if she were far younger than sixty. Rachel had a sudden flash of the eleven-year-old St. John walking in just this way towards another forest.

She only had a couple more days before the flight back to

London. Simon would be waiting for her at Heathrow, USB stick in hand. She needed to get the bulk of the interview done today. She switched on the KD-2 still hanging over her shoulder.

The fence line stopped abruptly before the trees. The last fencepost tilted to one side, as if whoever had put them in had suddenly found something more important to do.

Something was balanced on the post. Rachel's stomach began to lurch as she realised what it was.

Katherine clicked her tongue. 'Ach. Little monkey.' She picked up a stick from the ground and began poking at the little bundle of brown and red.

'Fresh,' she said. 'This morning, or last night perhaps. Birds haven't been at it yet.'

The possum's head moved from side to side as Katherine poked it. It had been slit from neck to groin, then left broken-backed on the top of the post.

'There was something like this near the gate when I came in,' Rachel said. 'A rabbit, I think.'

'Really?' Katherine frowned. 'I've never seen one on that side of the property before.' She hooked the stick deep into the possum's guts and deftly flicked it into the trees. Nothing was left on the fence post but a brown smear, drying in the sun.

Rachel's mouth was dry. 'This happens a lot?'

'More often these days. Just pests though: rabbits, possums, the occasional rat. He wouldn't dare touch the cows.'

'Who wouldn't dare touch the cows?'

Katherine cocked her head, as if trying to decide if Rachel could be trusted.

'Calls himself Slipper. He's a good boy, really. Doesn't mean any harm. I think it's kind of a tribute.'

'There's a boy doing this? Haven't you told his parents?'

Katherine sighed. 'It's not quite as simple as that. And he's keeping the vermin population down. Sometimes I wish he'd do it a little more.'

There was a prickliness to Katherine's voice. Her mouth had contracted to a thin line. She looked nothing at all like the grandmotherly type who had answered the door the day before.

Rachel forced herself to smile. 'These kinds of things happen in the country, I guess.'

Katherine was still moving towards the trees.

'Can we—' Rachel called, lowering her voice again when Katherine stopped and turned. Rachel held up the recorder 'I'd like to ask you some more questions and this doesn't do so well when we're moving. Could we go back to the house?'

Katherine looked at the trees for a few more seconds. Then she smiled. 'Of course.'

✖

Katherine sipped her tea. The teapot sat between them, a commemoration of a royal wedding that had lost much of its gilding over the years. Princess Di, faded and scratched, stared out from beneath her hair.

Rachel leaned forward across the table. Her pen and paper lay at her elbow, ready. She was lost, not really sure where to begin; the walk had cleared her head, but not entirely. Something still buzzed at the back of her mind, like a person seen from the corner of her eye.

Then Katherine began talking. Rachel clicked record and listened.

'The family changed, after Bedgebury. My father the most. Did you know the police suspected he'd murdered me?'

Rachel nodded.

'They both fell apart. Fell away from each other too. Not enough to actually separate of course. The swinging sixties took a long time to reach Surrey. My father didn't move out, but something else came in to live with us. I could feel its weight every time we sat down to dinner. The silence.

'I forgot the forest. Much as I could, though a deliberate forgetting is really no forgetting at all. But after a while I couldn't remember what had happened to cause the rift between my parents. Except in dreams. My mother would hear me, singing in my sleep. In the beginning she would shake me awake, but when she did I'd scream, loud enough to wake half the street. After a while, if she heard it she'd just close my bedroom door.'

'When you were first found, you said you'd been with the dancing man.'

'I was eleven. I explained as best I could, but every time I tried, I could see them getting agitated. My parents, the police. It was easier to say I couldn't remember. After a while it almost became true. But it never really went away.'

Rachel hesitated. She hadn't expected to talk about this at all. They were a long way from the music.

'What never went away?'

'The memory of him.' Katherine stared at Rachel over the rim of her teacup. 'The dancing man is as good a name as any, I suppose, if you need one, although he never did. He just *was*.'

'So there was someone else in the forest?'

'Not like you're thinking. I wasn't abducted by some local farmer. It was more that inside the forest there was – there was somewhere else.'

'I don't understand.'

'No. You wouldn't.' Katherine looked out the window. Rachel felt like she was failing another test, but she was lost.

Katherine St. John's lyrics had always tended towards the abstract. Rachel was not surprised to learn her conversations had a similar quality.

'Tell me about him.'

Katherine closed her eyes. 'His skin was the colour of varnished oak. I sketched him once, when I was back at school. Imagined him as Pan, drew buds of horns sprouting from his forehead, but he wasn't like that at all. I remember his eyes, more than anything. They were golden. The things they write in those terrible romance novels about falling into someone's eyes. But him – when he looked at me, it was as if there was nothing else in this world. Or other worlds. And when I looked into his eyes I knew there were many, many other places. His eyes were like doorways.'

The recorder sat in the middle of the table, the wheels of the tape still turning. Rachel felt another wave of exhaustion, found herself struggling to hide a yawn.

Katherine put down her cup. 'Oh, dear. It's not getting any better, is it?'

'I'm okay, it's—' another yawn. Rachel waved it away. '—just jetlag. 'Snothing.'

'More tea,' Katherine said. 'That's the English answer, isn't it? Or perhaps a coffee might be better?'

'No, tea's good.'

Katherine stood to pour, holding the teapot far above the cup.

Rachel blinked. What had they been discussing? She had the feeling they had wandered a long way from music, but now she couldn't remember. It would be on the tape, but she hadn't written anything down.

'There's – there's something I've been meaning to ask,' Rachel said.

'Anything. It's what you're here for.'

'Why me?'

Katherine sat back down.

'It may seem as if I'm a long way from the music business these days, but I keep up. I still read *Sounding*. Costs a fortune to get it shipped. I like your writing. And there's more. I—' she sat for a moment, considering. 'I think you and I have a lot in common.'

'In what way?'

'Well, we're very rare ducks, aren't we? There aren't many doing what we do – either of us. How many woman reporters do you know, still covering music?' *At your age*, though unspoken, hung between them.

'You may have a point, for music reporters. But not you. I can think of plenty of songwriters of your generation, some of them doing the best work of their careers: Joni Mitchell, Stevie Nicks, Rickie Lee Jones—'

Katherine raised her hand. 'All promoted to the godhead, years ago. But it's not …' she looked away, back again. 'I don't want to disparage my heroes. But the ones who are still on the tour circuit – something goes out of them, over the years. A vitality. I'm not talking about age. It's about walking the same path time and again. Singing the same lines. It eats at you. I may not have been releasing albums, but I've been writing. I had to walk a strange path to get to where I am. And I read your articles and I know you're the same. We're the last of a dying breed.'

Rachel opened her mouth to tell Katherine that she had it wrong. Reporting was just a job to her, nothing more. But she couldn't speak and while she was trying to think of the right words the world went fuzzy and slipped away.

✕

Rachel woke and found herself lying on the bed.

She sat up. There was a noise in her head, a background roar, as if she were on an airplane.

The curtains were drawn, but a thin light seeped around the sides. Rachel reached for her phone to check the time. It was past midnight. She had been sitting at the kitchen table with Katherine, then – she didn't know. She'd lost the better part of a day.

Katherine must have helped her up the stairs, though how she managed it Rachel had no idea. She wasn't fragile by any means, but Rachel was taller and heavier. Rachel didn't know if she'd be able to carry St. John if the situation had been reversed. She was still wearing the clothes she'd put on that morning.

A light was flashing on her phone. Voicemail. Simon, most probably, but she didn't check. She walked over to the window, pulled back the curtain, gasped.

The sky was wrong. It was light, far lighter than it should have been for this time of the night. There was a burnt look to it, a dark-tinted orange that made her think of fires burning in a desert at sunset. The milking shed and recording studio stood out like exhibits in a museum. The trees behind the studio remained resolutely dark.

There was movement, on the grass below her window. Someone was standing in the shadow of the house. The orange light reached tendrils into the shadow, picked him out in shards and flecks. A boy, no more than thirteen surely, wearing an old vest and threadbare trousers. He looked up to her window. Their eyes met and his teeth grinned orange.

Rachel pulled away from the window and leaned against the wall. When the hammering in her chest slowed a little, she peered around the edge of the curtain again.

The boy was strolling across the lawn, back towards the

milking shed. Slowly, as if he didn't have a care in the world. As if he wanted her to follow.

Rachel hesitated, for more than a moment. The boy disappeared around the corner of the milking shed and the orange moon shone on the empty paddock.

She turned back to the bed and fumbled for her shoes.

As she placed her foot on the first stair, a sound made her stop, turn. She listened, looking into the darkness of the hallway.

There was a whisper from Katherine's room. Rachel could not make out what Katherine said. Her voice was muted, heavy, as if she were talking in her sleep.

Another, deeper voice made a reply.

Katherine said something else, followed by a silence again. Rachel stayed where she was, almost holding her breath, but she did not hear anything else.

She began to move down the stairs, hoping each time she put a foot down that the stair wouldn't creak beneath her.

✱

There was no sign of the boy when she rounded the corner of the house. She set off across the lawn at a jog, hauled herself uncomfortably over the fence. She peered around the corner of the milking shed. She was sure the boy had been moving in this direction but there was nobody here now. Perhaps she had paused too long on the staircase, listening to Katherine and – whoever it was. She'd missed her chance.

The moonlight stained the side of the shed a burnt orange. Rachel stared at the face of the moon. Perhaps it was a mist from the river, blown across the farm. There had to be some explanation.

The moonlight surged, so bright she had to close her

eyes and turn away and as she did the buzzing came again. She steadied herself against the wall of the milking shed, closed her eyes. When she looked again the moon was just the moon, though still wrapped in that sickly orange glow. But the thought lingered that, just for a moment, it hadn't been a moon at all but a weird and malevolent sun, older and angrier by far than her own.

Rachel saw movement in the shadow of the trees. The boy stood at the edge of the forest. Something dead dangled from his right hand, blood pulsing slowly into the grass. He placed it reverentially on the top of the last fencepost. Then he looked directly at her before walking into the forest.

Rachel remained where she was. She could leave. She could go back to the house, try and get some sleep. She could leave tomorrow morning, although she might have to call a taxi. Katherine had said she'd get the car towed to a local garage, but Rachel realised she hadn't asked about it. How many days had she been here, anyway? The dizziness had played havoc with her sense of time. Surely she'd spent enough time with St. John, got enough on tape. She could go back to Auckland, type everything up in a hotel or even the airport departure lounge. It didn't matter, as long as she got away. There was something about the farm she didn't understand, but she had the feeling that the farm understood her all too well.

She could feel the dizziness again and she shook her head; she wouldn't, couldn't fall asleep now.

The blood of the thing on the fencepost was a glistening black.

She had to know.

She stepped forward.

A rat, eyes open and staring sightlessly at the orange moon, its mouth wide, almost in a grin.

She stood directly in front of the trees and from here they looked different, although she couldn't exactly say how. Larger, perhaps. There seemed to be more of them, as if it really were a forest and not just a tiny stand of trees in the middle of a paddock. She couldn't see through to the other side now. The orange moon picked out a bare patch between the trees, the path the boy must had taken. She stole one more look at the slaughtered rat, its paws brought close to its body in an attitude of prayer, then stepped beneath the trees.

She had to know.

✖

The forest was the world.

When she'd stood in the paddock (had it been yesterday? It was hard to remember) and looked at the sad stand of trees, she had wondered why they had been preserved in the middle of all that grass. There might have been ten of them, scraggly and poor, shaped through years of wind until they bent over like ancient crones. But these trees were straight-backed and tall enough to hold up the sky and there were so very many of them. She turned around. Though she hadn't taken more than a few steps, she couldn't see the paddock. Only more trees, and the trail and she knew, somehow, that if she followed it she'd walk for untold hours and never find her way back to the yellowing grass and the recording studio and the fencepost with its tribute rat.

The air smelled full and wet, like moss under ancient roots, and she could feel the inrushing energy of every breath. She should have been terrified, was, perhaps, on some level, yet she could not suppress a smile, grinning like the dead rat had grinned at the moon. It was as if a secret belief that she had held her whole life without knowing had been confirmed.

She followed the path, not bothering to look back. Any exit was ahead, not behind. If one appeared, what would she do? Would she take it? It should have been no question at all, but now there was the thought, lurking. Why would she? Why not stay?

There was music in the air, just on the edge of hearing and she recognised it immediately. The same melody she'd heard in Katherine St. John's recording studio. A choir, she had thought at the time, but there was no choir in the forest. The sound didn't come from any particular direction. It was as if the leaves of the trees were a choir, their song quiet but insistent.

Don't go.
Don't go.

Arms of trees reached out across the path, hiding the sky, but the orange moonlight found a way through, washing everything, making every shadow deeper. They looked like oak trees, but there was something about them – they seemed, somehow more real than any trees she had seen before. As if these were the models that all other trees aspired to. Their size and the deep cracks in their trunks marked them as immeasurably ancient, yet there was a youth about them, a vitality that she knew would last forever. This was the Forest Beneath, the leaves whispered to her, and it was between and beneath and around all. The forest was the world.

The boughs of the trees covered the path entirely now, so she walked in almost total darkness. Just a few small patches of orange moonlight on the path like running lights along the aisle of an airplane. She could see a larger light ahead, but she could not judge how far away it was. And still the singing, quiet still but slowly becoming louder.

Don't go.
Don't go.

Then the light was close enough to touch and then she was in it. She found herself stepping into a glade. The path ended here, giving way to a wide space of low brown grasses and nightflowers. The orange moon hung fat and full above, draining the scene of nearly all other colour. She stepped forward, walked to the centre, where a circle had been marked in white sand, too perfect to be any kind of accident. She saw now that there were several paths through the trees besides the one that had brought her here. The one directly ahead seemed to continue in a straight line, but the three to the left of her and four to the right seemed wilder. The last one on the left curved uphill somehow, though there was no hill there. The sight of that path leading impossibly up brought forth an ache, an overwhelming feeling of loss that she did not understand. *These are the paths of the Dancing Man, though he has not come these ways for an age*, said the voice in her head that was hers and yet was not.

She turned around, looking at the trees that were the perfection of all trees. Still singing, louder now—

Don't go!
Don't go!

—as if it were not just the song the leaves happened to sing. As if they were singing directly to her. In warning.

Don't! Go!
Don't! Go!

Don't—

The song stopped so suddenly that the silence rang.

The boy stepped between two trees on the other side of the clearing. He walked towards her, barefoot, stepping lightly on the balls of his feet, as if he were a ballet dancer and this was all a performance. His right hand held the dagger he had used to split the rat, long-bladed, the edge broken by dents and cuts turned rust-coloured by the moon. He stared at her and there was rage in his eyes but something deeper too, some skill or power of command that he had not mastered – but he would and when he did the world would scream.

Slipper walked towards her slowly and still she did not, could not move. She had not listened to the warning of the trees and now she would die here, in the Forest Between. She should have run, but something more than fear kept her standing in the circle of sand. *Stay*, said the voice in her head that was her voice but not and Slipper crept closer still. The rough vest he wore had once been a deep blue; time and the elements had faded it to a futile grey. The remains of a gold braid clung to one shoulder. He wore nothing beneath; the shadowed lines of his ribs stood clear on his sides. His trousers had obviously come from a far larger man; they were tied around his waist with a length of twine and hung slack to mid-calf, where they had been jaggedly hacked shorter, perhaps with the same knife he was holding out towards her, straight-armed as though it were a spear. He grinned, and his teeth were a scatter of angles. The knife was a hand-span from her eyes. With one more step he too would be standing in the white sand circle and that blade, she knew, would be at her throat.

A shout.

The boy dropped his arm and stared behind her, to where

the path opened out on the clearing.

The shout, again. Slipper whined and wrapped his arms around his stomach. His face softened, the slope of his shoulders changed and his projection of malice was swept away. He was no threat to her at all, just an emaciated and shivering boy, wrapped in the ill-fitting clothes of luckless and long-dead men.

'Arrête!'

Rachel turned. A man stepped from the trees. He was tall and moved confidently. Like the boy, he was barefoot. But the man's clothes were not old and frayed. He wore dark trousers that shone like silk and a small bolero jacket, embossed with gold braid. He looked impeccable, as if a team of tailors dogged his every step.

The man shouted something else. He spoke French, or something close enough to it that Rachel could nearly make out the words. But they danced along the edge of her mind, meaning slipping away even as she grasped for it.

Slipper hissed some more words and spat at his feet. He waved the knife dismissively, in the direction she had come, the path to the house.

The man spoke again, a hint of steel in his voice. The words remained alien to her, but this time, she caught the meaning of a handful. *She is a guest.*

She could chart the course of the conversation from the change in the boy's posture. Had the man not spoken when he did Slipper would have slit her throat. The man reached out a hand, palm down.

Slipper shook his head vehemently and did not back away. Rachel stood between them, afraid to move in case she interrupted their delicate dance.

The man took a step closer, then another. Slipper remained where he was, the knife dangling from his fingers like a favourite doll. The man had covered half the distance to the centre of the clearing now, still speaking low and calm.

Slipper hissed and raised the knife again and Rachel could not suppress a whimper of her own.

The man shouted – something. He opened his mouth and sound came out, but the sounds were older than any language. The sound hit Slipper like a blow and he stumbled back a couple of steps. The man closed his mouth and the forest fell silent. But something buzzed in Rachel's mind, as if the power of the word was still draining away, dark and slow like black oil on the surface of the world.

Slipper quivered, struggling against a force Rachel could not see. His mouth stretched wide in agony and a sound like a sob escaped him. A tear ran down his cheek. The knife tumbled from his hand.

The man resumed his quiet approach. Slipper dropped to his knees and snatched up the knife. Then he turned and ran towards the trees. Rachel could still hear his loud sobbing long after he had disappeared from view.

She let out a long breath, unaware until then she had been holding it. Her legs quivered.

The man reached her and held out a steadying hand. 'Are you hurt?'

It took Rachel a few moments to realise she had understood the words. 'No. I'm—' Another shuddering breath. 'I'm fine.'

'You should not be here. It is not safe for you.' The man's eyes were a deep brown that gave no clues to his age or origin.

'I'm sorry. I followed him. He wanted me to.'

The man gave a short laugh and looked towards the trees. 'Yes. He did. He is a rough one. He is not used to—' He paused, trying to find the words. '—gentle custom.'

She remembered Katherine's words upon finding the slaughtered possum. *Little monkey.*

The man smiled. *My muse likes to be alone with me. He gets jealous if there are too many people about.*

'Go,' he said, 'before the little monkey comes back.'

Some large part of her wanted nothing more than to stay. To walk the paths under the trees, listening to the singing of the leaves until the Dancing Man returned. But Slipper was still out there. And it was not her place to be here. Not yet, anyway, she thought, with a sense of loss that felt like a dagger.

She turned and walked towards the path that led back to the farm. Just before she slipped beneath the boughs, the man called.

'Not that way. Go the way you came.'

Rachel frowned. She was going the way she came. She—

She looked again. She was standing directly in front of the weirder way, the path that sloped upwards yet was not on a hill. She backed away. It seemed there were worse dangers than Slipper in the Forest Beneath.

She made her way around the clearing. When she reached the real path she turned and the man nodded. 'Stay on the path,' he said.

'Thank you,' Rachel said.

The sun was so bright she had to blink away tears. Rachel took another step and stopped. She did not remember the journey from the clearing to here. A heartbeat ago she had been in the clearing, deep in the Forest Beneath. It was as if she had arrived here with a single step. She thought of how close she had been to inadvertently taking the weirder way, wondered where else she might have gone with a single wrong step, and shivered.

The mighty ur-oaks of the Forest Beneath were no longer visible. Only the original trees, the wind-bent macrocarpa scratching the sky.

Morning was burning the dew from the grass. She could hear the buzzing of bees. A line of cows was being led away from the milking shed.

Rachel took a deep breath. The air was humic and smelled of grass, diesel, shit. As she breathed, she felt the memory of better air. As if she had been somewhere recently, some other, more real world.

'There you are!'

Katherine St. John was striding towards her in a pair of old, dirt-encrusted jeans, a flannel shirt and a hat that looked like it had been snatched from a cricket umpire's head. There was nothing of the ethereal musician about her; she looked as if she'd spent her whole life on this farm, walking this dry grass under the scorching southern sun.

'Wondered if you'd gone out for a walk. I love it first thing in the morning, when everything's new and the rest of the world hasn't woken up yet.'

'I – yes,' Rachel said, 'thought I'd take a stroll.' But the words felt wrong in her mouth.

She remembered sunrise striking the wall of the bedroom. She had dressed and decided to see the farm. She remembered, but there was something else, as if the memory stood in front of something else, blocking it from view. She turned and looked again at the pitiful stand of trees she had thought of as the forest for some reason. There couldn't have been more than ten of them and they looked so dry that they'd crumble in a strong wind. Hadn't there been something else, something—

'I've got the kettle on,' Katherine said. 'Let's go back to the house.'

'Have you got everything you need?' Katherine called from the kitchen.

Rachel blinked, lost in a waking dream. There had been a path, and an orange moon. 'Sorry?'

'Don't you head back to Auckland today? Or have I got the day wrong.'

Rachel pulled her phone from her pocket and checked the date. Friday. She'd spent a week on St. John's farm, although it didn't seem more than a couple of days. 'No, you're right.'

Katherine placed her royal wedding commemorative tea set on the table.

The voicemail icon was flashing on her phone. Rachel couldn't imagine who had been trying to call her, or why she hadn't heard it.

Katherine finally finished fussing in the kitchen and sat down. 'The garage called. Car's all ready to go. Tony will drop it over this morning. Was there anything else you wanted to discuss?'

Rachel struggled to remember what they'd spoken about the past few days. She remembered recording a few conversations. But had she captured anything really new? Did she have enough to put together a story? If not, it was too late to do anything about it now.

'I think I've got everything, thanks.'

✖

She was packed by the time Tony from the garage parked her rental in front of the house and refused any form of payment. 'Don't worry,' Katherine said, 'It's all taken care of. Least I can do for the last remaining female rock reporter.'

Rachel had no answer.

When she'd loaded everything into the car, Katherine

hugged her, an embrace that didn't seem to end. 'It's been fun,' Katherine said, when she finally let Rachel go. 'It's been good to have someone else to talk to.'

Rachel didn't know how to respond. 'Just doing my job.'

'Well.' Katherine looked like she was going to say something else, but didn't. The silence stretched.

Katherine waved in her rear-view mirror until the driveway curved around a stand of trees.

She smelled something when she stopped the car and got out to unhook the gate. She followed her nose. A dead possum was sitting on a fencepost, surrounded by flies. Rachel kicked the post and the possum tumbled off into the grass.

'Little monkey,' she said to herself as she climbed back into the car, then wondered why she'd said it.

She didn't remember the voicemail until she was checked in and waiting in the departure lounge. The most impatient passengers were already forming a line. Rachel accessed her inbox and joined them.

One message, two days ago, from Simon.

'Don't know what you're doing out there, if this is the kind of research you're after. But short answer, no. The oldest oak trees in New Zealand are maybe a hundred years, tops. I don't know what you're seeing but they're definitely not oaks. Must be some kind of native, although I can't imagine which one. Get back here with my story and stop messing around with trees.'

The line was moving now, people shuffling forward on to the plane. She had no recollection of calling Simon at all. There was a fuzziness around the corner of her vision. Jetlagged for the whole trip. Some kind of record.

Rachel checked her bag again. The laptop was in there, and the KD-2, buried under a pile of cassette tapes. She'd work on the story during the flight, listening to her recordings in the darkened cabin while the rest of the passengers slept. She'd have a story for Simon by the time she reached Heathrow. He probably wouldn't be happy with it. Then again, he never was.

Rachel looked down at the land as the plane rose. The roads and buildings dwindled, until there was nothing but the green of the hills and the grey blue of the sea. She looked down until the plane hit the clouds and there was nothing to see but the falling night.

When she finally turned away from the window she was surprised to find tears on her cheeks.

✖

St. John produced the album herself from her New Zealand farm, teaching herself new instruments and how to drive the mixing desk in the process. 'It was very important, I think, to do it all myself. These songs are close to me and I feel that I have a responsibility to present them as purely as I can. There's a journey I take when I'm putting them together. It's like … It's like I'm walking in an ancient wood. And I can hear the songs there, almost as if the trees themselves are singing, I—'

She stops, smiles, shakes her head. 'I'm being terribly indulgent.' She sips her tea. 'But I had to do it alone. Just me and my muse. He gets jealous when there are other people about.'

—From *The Miracle Child Returns, again,* an interview with Katherine St. John, *Sounding,* April 2014.

PROLOGUE
LAS VEGAS, 2034

ATTICUS TĀURA SHAKES HIS HEAD. 'WE HAVE TO WITH-draw it, Selwyn. We have to. It isn't ethical.'

Selwyn Bruce, CEO of B-Cell, lets the statement hang in the air. He strolls to the window of the eighteenth-storey Las Vegas boardroom, takes a moment to adjust his tie – a Daniella Cavelli in watered pink silk – and runs his hand over his stomach. Then he turns to the gathered vice-presidents.

'I think, what is important to remember here, is our original intent—'

'To improve the lives of the sufferers of diabetes,' Andi Canterell, VP of Human Resources interrupts. The CEO gives her a sharp look.

'Sorry.' Canterell picks up her pen and busies herself scribbling nervously on her legal pad.

'As Ms Canterell has pointed out, B-Cell's intent when we embarked on this line of research, was altruistic. And it still is, Atticus.' Selwyn takes a step closer and puts a hand on Atticus' shoulder. 'We have a real ability to help these people, just not in the way we originally perceived. It isn't ethical for us to withhold that help.'

'But we're responsible. We made it!'

'Well, technically, you made it,' Canterell mutters, evoking a titter from the other VPs.

'And it's not our fault that the new insulin proved unstable over time,' Selwyn asserts. 'The backlash was Nature's doing.'

'We should have foreseen it,' Atticus insists.

'We're not gods. The point is that given what we know now, we're prepared to do something about it. B-Cell is investing heavily in cybernetic prostheses, developing a whole new range of limbs, eyes – new phalange prototypes. These products will go a long, long way towards improving the lives of the afflicted.'

Atticus frowns. What's happened to Selwyn? Does the money really mean that much? There was a time, once, when Atticus could appeal to him, make him see sense.

'Selwyn, please, I just need a bit more time. I've been working on a way to revert sufferers to their original genome. It's not finished yet. I've been thinking about families, about the way we confer immunity, and how families protect themselves. There are some things—'

The CEO drops his hand. 'Tāura, I'm sorry. This company has to evolve to stay profitable, and we are doing that. But we need the development space. And, quite frankly, we need the funds. We cannot afford to support a non-profitable activity. Your group will be disbanded to make way for the robotics division.'

Atticus glares. 'What about my staff?'

'The professors left earlier today – we think they may have left the country – and the others are being … deployed …

elsewhere. It seems none of them are keen to stay with you, since your research is no longer being funded.'

Atticus is surprised. A close-knit group; he'd expected more loyalty.

'It doesn't matter,' he growls. 'If you won't do it, then I'll find someone else to fund my research!'

The CEO grimaces. 'Ms Canterell, if you wouldn't mind.'

Smiling hawkishly, Canterell hands Atticus a yellowing document.

Atticus looks at it blankly. 'This is my employment contract.'

'Yes, and if you'll turn to pages 12 and 13, you'll see the clauses about restraint of trade, non-disclosure, confidentiality, and patents. And if I could draw your attention to the bottom of the page …'

Atticus drops his eyes to the bottom margin. *Atticus Tāura*. His signature.

'Go home, Tāura. You're done here,' the CEO says as he sweeps from the room.

CHAPTER ONE
NEW YORK, 2058

The rain is coming down hard now, pummelling the windscreen in grey, almost horizontal sheets. Mika frowns. Taking one hand from the wheel, she rubs at her eyes. It's been a long trip and she's tired. She can barely see ten metres in front of her.

The waka rolls violently. Mika purses her lips and shifts the vehicle to a lower gear, struggling to control the vessel in the surging waters. A vehicle bumps her from behind, the waka lurches, and Mika is thrown forward.

'Tangaroa!' she whispers under her breath, calling on the

sea god of her ancestors for protection. The waka pitches again. Mika yanks at the steering, pulling hard to the left to get out of the queue. In the choppy water, the waka is slow to respond. Mika can do nothing more. She holds her breath, her eyes straining to penetrate the wall of rain. Another jolt. The larger transport crowding her from behind. She's in danger of being sandwiched in, her waka crushed between two hulls.

Come on!

She didn't travel first the Pacific, and then the Atlantic, to be shipwrecked arriving on the dock. She has a meeting to make. Biting back her frustration, Mika guns the accelerator. The prow of her waka touches the transport in front, the way a bull might caress the bullfighter's cape as it thunders past. Mika exhales as the waka pulls clear. The manoeuvre has prevented a goring, but she's going to have to head straight to the ramp now. Determined, she squeezes her prow through the traffic, pushing to the front like the smallest kid at a tuck shop queue.

Coming through, people.

At last, the waka's hull touches home. Quickly, Mika changes transmission, and drives the little transport up the ramp onto the land.

The Ellis Island entry point is in chaos. What Mika can see of it, in any case. Gale-force winds and driving rain have reduced visibility to next to nil.

Is this the immigration point? Mika opens the window and is immediately soaked.

A man in a flapping yellow raincoat peers in, his face ruddy from the rain. Even with the wet, Mika can smell the engine fumes. She shivers in her wet clothes, but only partly from the cold. She waits for the officer to scan her pupil.

Please don't make me go back.

The man shakes his head. 'The bio-scanner is down. Cybernetic reader, too. The console was hit by flying metal. We're back to working like cavemen. Where are you from?'

'New Zealand.'

Someone behind sounds a horn. Raincoat man pulls away from the window and roars into the wind. 'Hold your damn horses, why don't you? I'll get to you when I get to you.' He turns back to Mika. 'Where did you say?'

'New Zealand. It's an island—'

'Staten Island? You're a local? You do know you've landed at Ellis? Day like today, you should've taken the expressway, not the shortcut across the Bay. What kind of idiot are you? I suppose you wanted to see how your home-made transport handled a storm.' He shakes his head in disgust.

'No, no, you misheard me. I'm from—'

But, huddled deep in the hood of his plastic raincoat, the official either doesn't hear, or doesn't care to hear. 'All we need. Locals wasting our time, coming through the immigration line. Drive on,' he grumbles, gesturing impatiently. 'You're holding everyone up.'

'I—' But raincoat man has already turned his attention to the next vehicle in the line. Mika shrugs. If he's going to make it this easy to get in, who's she to argue? Sliding up the window, she shifts the waka into gear.

He shouldn't have called her an idiot.

'For your information, mate,' Mika mumbles to herself, 'this isn't just any old home-made transport. It's a waka. And her name is *Torua*, if you care to know.' Mika revs the engine, giving the man a good whiff of *Torua*'s engine fumes, and speeds into the gloom.

The rain hasn't abated any as Mika takes the bridge to the mainland. On the road, the visibility is even worse. There are transports everywhere. Their lights glare, the milky beams multiplying in the gloom. Mika slows, getting an earful of honking and tooting from the traffic backing up behind her.

Keep your hair on.

She turns on *Torua*'s GPS system and, doing her best to keep her eyes on the road, punches in the rendezvous point.

'Calculating.'

The message had said it wasn't too far from the bridge. Mika doesn't want to miss the turn-off, or she could end up miles out of her way. She can't afford to miss the guide.

'Left turn approaching.'

Mika peers ahead, but can't make out the intersection through the fog of lights.

'Left turn approaching in … twenty yards.'

'But I can't see anything!' she wails.

Finally, the intersection fades into view. Hang on, there are two lefts. Which one is she supposed to take: the hard left or veer left?

'Left turn approaching …'

'Which lane?!'

The middle, take the middle.

The lights change.

Mika guns the engine to get across the gap.

A vehicle screams towards her.

Oh my god, oh my god.

She stomps on the brakes, but already she knows it's too late. As the two vehicles plunge towards each other, like jousters in a medieval battle, Mika stretches her mind across the ocean to Aotearoa, to her sister.

Huia.

Mika.

The voice is weak and thready. Mika's heart clenches. Huia needs her. Needs her to get to Vegas. She has to—

There's an agonising crunch, followed by a whine that

starts in Mika's teeth and settles in her bones. *Torua* spirals out of control. Mika is flung sideways, her head glancing off the side of the waka, before she's thrust upright again in a brutal whiplash. Soundless now, torque and momentum carry the vehicle through the intersection in a slow-motion blur, the front left corner trailing something with it. Obligingly, the object allows itself to be dragged along, throwing up silent sparks and shedding debris. Resisting the urge to cover her face, Mika grips the steering wheel and gently turns *Torua* into the curve. But the waka has power yet. It hurtles through a barrier, barely slowing. Losing the foreign object, it slides another twenty metres before coming to a stop on a huge traffic island.

'Right turn approaching in twenty yards—'

Mika switches off the GPS, and hunches over the steering wheel, panting. When her pulse has slowed, she takes a deep breath and checks herself over. A few bruises. A bump the size of a small kūmara on her elbow, but otherwise all intact.

I'm okay. Alive.

Mika's heart leaps again. But what about the other driver? The other vehicle?

Flicking the compression, Mika flings open the hatch, pushing hard against howling wind. She climbs out of the waka, the hatch slamming shut as soon as she lets go. Mika squints through the rain. The bull bars, two rows of thick pipe that encircle the waka, have been scraped back to the metal, the barnacles and rust of the ocean voyage sloughed off like dead skin. But, not built to withstand playful whales and floating garbage, the other vehicle hasn't been so fortunate. Glancing off *Torua*'s bull-bars, it has struck a tree, and is a mess of broken branches, twisted steel, and glass, the driver door buckled inwards where the two vehicles collided.

Instinctively, Mika knows it can't open. Boots crunching on broken glass, she clambers onto the hood. The windscreen's gone, leaving a glass-encrusted frame. The driver is slumped forward over the dashboard, oblivious to the rain thwacking at his back. Probably concussed when his head hit the windscreen.

'Hey! Hey there! Can you hear me?' she screams over the sound of the storm. She pushes her hair out of her face. 'I'm coming. Hold on.'

Using her boot, she breaks a branch underfoot, clearing the way so she can skirt around to the other side of the vehicle, then yanks on the passenger door – which, to her surprise, opens easily.

Oh thank god.

Climbing into the cab, she brushes away the glass on the seat with a dripping sleeve, then scoots over and gently pulls the man backwards by his sweatshirt.

'Can you hear me?' But he can't hear her because he's dead, a branch buried deep in his eye socket. Mika jumps back, relieved when the man slumps forward again, the grisly eye no longer looking at her blankly.

What have I done?

Leaning back in the passenger seat, Mika lets the rain wash down her face. Then she bursts into tears.

CHAPTER TWO

Soft stroking at her hair startles Mika from her sobs. She twists in her seat and peers into the face of a child. The kid pulls its hand back, cowering. But even shied away, Mika can see that the force of the crash has caused the five-point safety harness to draws lines of blood along both sides of the child's neck.

A boy or a girl? Mika can't tell the child's gender from its appearance.

'Oh Maui, save me,' she breathes. 'Are you all right?' There's a slight bob of its head. Straw hair pokes out in all directions from underneath a black beanie, as if it has recently had a bad haircut. The clothes are not the child's. What kid would choose to wear so much black?

'It smells funny,' the child says.

At first, Mika thinks the child is referring to the stink of body odour permeating the stale air inside the vehicle. But then she smells it too: the sharp acidic smell of a sparking battery pack.

'Come on, sweetie, I have to get you out of here,' Mika says, as calmly as her voice will allow. Leaning over the seat, she unsnaps the harness, and tucks her hands under the child's armpits to pull it forward between the front seats. 'Don't look.'

Despite the warning, the child turns to look at the driver.

'I'm sorry about your papa. It was an accident. I …'

Two small hands gently push Mika out into the rain.

Outside, the wind has picked up, whipping debris from the accident into tiny tornadoes that swirl threateningly around them. The ferocity of the weather has emptied the streets of life. The child looks into the whirling sky and smiles. Long lashes and soft features.

A girl.

She lifts her arms above her head, palms outstretched. Blood trickles from welts at her neck, several blue bruises evident on her pale skin. Mika needs to get her medical attention. And not just for her injuries. That smile, her reaction, the kid's got to be in shock – she's just seen her father's head turned into a kebab on a stray branch …

Suddenly, the broken transport sends an electrical arc

into the sky. Like a backwards lightning strike, its fingers search for contact in the metal architecture of the old bridge overhead, now clearly visible.

'Quick, before it reaches my waka!'

Mika grabs the child and drags her to *Torua*, climbing up and slamming the hatch door behind them.

She thrusts the girl into the back of the vehicle, near the hatch to the lower living level. Then, leaping into the pilot seat, she starts the engine and, backing *Torua* away from the tangle of arcing metal, pulls out into the roadway.

Away from the danger, and inside *Torua*, Mika immediately feels safer. The waka was a gift from her people, all their aroha and wairua carved into its sturdy construction. Not able to accompany her on this journey, they'd done everything in their power to give her the best chance of arriving safely on the land they'd long since cut all contact with. This vehicle is her lifeline, her support when she is far from her whānau, and from Huia. When her mission is complete, *Torua* will carry Mika back to her island home.

Mika peers through the windscreen. The local residents have finally taken heed of the weather warning because there are fewer cars on the road. Or perhaps they're there, only Mika can't see them.

'Don't worry. I'm going to find someone who'll take care of you,' she calls over her shoulder as she punches at the keypad of her outdated GPS, looking for the nearest medical centre. The GPS' voice, programmed to sound like her kuia, is rich and soothing, easing some of the panic racing in Mika's veins. She caused a man's death today. She should really go to the authorities and report the accident, except that would mean delays. Immigration didn't register her entry, so they could turn her back. Send her home. Even without that complication, she's missed her meeting with the guide. Her mission is jeopardised. Mika hasn't got time for complications. *Huia* hasn't got time. But Mika can't just leave the kid.

'Come on.' Mika taps the screen with her nails, encouraging it to respond.

'Calculating … calculating … calculating.'

Even with the window wipers on full, Mika feel like she's back on the water, *Torua*'s lights barely illuminating the way ahead. She needs the GPS but, for the moment, it's having trouble orienting her. Probably some high buildings interfering with the triangulation. She risks a backwards glance at the girl. She's from here; maybe she knows her way around?

'Hey, why don't you come up here and be my navigator? Careful now.' Mutely following Mika's instructions, the girl takes the co-pilot seat.

'Strap yourself in, honey. Until my GPS kicks in, in this pea soup, I have no idea where we're going.'

When her passenger has fastened herself in the harness, Mika takes a good look at her. The girl sits impassive, her hands unmoving in her lap. She has a thin nose with sharp cheekbones set high above caved-in cheeks, and bloodless blue-tinged lips. She keeps her eyes on the screen, hypnotised as it scans for their destination. Mika shivers. It's unnerving for a child – she can't be more than ten or twelve – to behave so mechanically. It's true she's just survived a horrific trauma, perhaps even seen her father die, but it's more than that. The child has the tired, haunted, *broken* look of a victim of illness or neglect. That's what it is. It's as if long-term suffering is etched into her features. Only unlike the evocative swirls and whorls of Mika's own tattoos, there's no beauty in the story Mika reads on the child's face.

'What's your name?'

'Bree.'

'Bree. That's so pretty. I'm Mika—'

'Tree,' Bree comments calmly, pointing as a roadside tree begins to keel over, about to block their path.

'Mahuika's fingers!' No time to calculate the odds, Mika shifts into high gear, the engines straining as *Torua* gathers speed. Mika holds her breath. There's the sound of scraping as *Torua* squirts out from under the falling tree, surging forward like water squeezed from a hose pipe. They've avoided getting stuck in a permanent embrace between the tree and the road.

'Good eye, Bree! You make a great navigator.'

Mika reaches over to pat the girl on the shoulder, but Bree flinches away at the contact.

'Oh, sorry.'

Finally, the GPS speaks up: 'Exiting left in two hundred yards.' Kuia's firm voice drags Mika's attention back to the road. Mika doesn't blame Kuia for the near miss – she couldn't have known about the tree, but it'd been a close call. Without Bree's warning, Mika's voyage, and her mission, might've ended back there on the road.

Like a flattened possum.

Determined to be more cautious this time, Mika eases back on the accelerator, keeping a watch on the screen as the distance reduces.

'Turn left in twenty yards. Turn left now.'

Mika turns off the main road.

'Destination three hundred yards, on the right.'

Away from the motorway, the rain lightens, but the wipers smear intermittent drops across the windscreen, making it just as difficult to see. Nearing their destination, Mika is forced to slow, and then stop. Out of nowhere, a traffic jam has bloomed like luminescent mushrooms after a storm. Transports are lined up in both directions, everyone heading for the well-lit parking area of the 24/7 emergency clinic. So, theirs was not the only accident. Mika runs through her security lockdown procedures. This many people in one place, especially those desperate for assistance, is a precursor for trouble.

'It looks like there could be a bit of a wait. I'm just going to pull over and take a closer look at you myself, okay?' Mika says. Staring straight ahead, Bree nods like someone who's used to having no say.

Manoeuvring out of the standstill proves less difficult than Mika expects. The waka's bull bars intimidate less robust vehicles and, with the improved visibility, the markings on its hull single her out as an unknown quantity. These days, people tend to shy from things they don't know.

Mika powers down to hibernate mode; a state which conserves the amount of energy the waka consumes, but keeps the vehicle just a few switch flicks from full power. The engines change their tone from a deep rumble to a soft purr.

'Right, let's see what we've got, shall we?'

Unsnapping her own harness, Mika swivels to face the back of the bridge. Built for a crew of four, there's plenty of space to move around and Mika's made the most of it. At sea, she spent the majority of her time on the bridge, so the room is cluttered with books: some for reading, others for writing. Directly behind the pilot and co-pilot seats are additional consoles for the navigator and engineer, roles that Mika has mastered through instinct and guesswork. At the peak of the arch – the room is shaped like an old wooden door that has fallen to the ground – is a medical bay that also houses the emergency evacuation gear.

'Would you mind if we take those clothes off? I want to see if it's just a few cuts and bruises, or something worse.'

Mika takes Bree's hand and leads the girl forward. Flicking the overhead light to its brightest setting, she rummages through her medical supplies for some cotton wipes, alcohol swabs and bandages, hoping that's all she'll need. Besides a few basic painkillers, the kit doesn't contain much more. Mika's people had sent her with everything they had.

'Hat first.' Bree takes off her beanie. She holds it in her hands like a soft toy while Mika gently prods at her scalp, checking through the dirty blonde hair for signs of injury, anything that could indicate a concussion. 'Looks good. No bumps.' Bree's about to return the hat to her head, but Mika stops her. 'Let's leave that off. At least, till I've finished,' she says softly.

Cleaned up, the welts on her neck aren't too bad: the seeping blood had made them appear deeper. And the girl's scrubbing at the wounds had smeared blood everywhere. Mika holds her face by the chin, gently washing away the layers of grime with a damp cotton ball. Underneath, the girl's skin feels cool, as if the chill goes right to the bone.

'You're so cold. We need to get you warmed up. How about some soup when we're finished?' Bree nods, the movement slight.

Keeping up the one-sided chatter, Mika removes the rest of the girl's clothing, estimating the time it would take for bruising to turn from black to green – longer than the time it's taken them to travel here from the accident site. She notes the puncture marks on the insides of Bree's elbows. There are more at the widest part of the girl's arm near the shoulders, recent ones, contrasting darkly against the child's pale skin, older ones camouflaged among the faint freckles and the bruising. Someone has been taking blood and administering drugs to the girl, and over a long period of time from the looks of it. But the story on her skin is confused: Mika can't decide if the damage has been caused by an illness, or its treatment.

'All done,' Mika proclaims, cheerily. 'Apart from these welts on your neck …' she smoothes the gauze dressings '… I don't think you were hurt in the accident, at least not badly, so maybe we won't need to go to the medical clinic.' The girl shivers visibly at her words. 'Now, let's get you into some clean clothes, and then you can help me with the soup.'

Mika slips through the hatch to the living quarters. She passes through the galley, ignoring the first two smaller berths, and heads for the master's quarters. Once there, she rummages through her footlocker and withdraws a long T-shirt, a pair of short trousers and a coat and, as an after-thought, a thick band of ribbon.

Bree is waiting at the bottom of the steps, clasping her dirty clothes to her chest, the soft light down here making her appear less like a tortured waif and more like a little girl.

'This is my sister's T-shirt,' Mika says, holding out the garments. 'She was supposed to come with me …' Mika shakes her head, willing away the thought. 'Anyway. It'll be too big for you, but if we tie it at the waist, it will do. At least you'll be dry. I'll give your clothes a wash when the weather clears.'

Bree lets Mika dress her. Mika combs the girl's hair, and ties the ribbon in place. When she's finished, she shows Bree the mirror. Bree checks her reflection in the glass. It's clear she likes what she sees. Smiling faintly, the girl loosens her grip on the hat.

Ten minutes later, seated opposite Bree and eating re-heated, pre-prepared kūmara soup, Mika goes over her options. She's missed the vital rendezvous with her guide — her only contact. Now, she'll have to find her own way. But she can't go anywhere with Bree in tow.

'I should get you home, Bree. People will be worried about you. They might already be searching for you and your dad. Can you tell me where you live?'

Bree shakes her head.

'You don't know the address?'

Another shake.

'You don't know, or you don't have an address?'

'No house.'

'What about the rest of your family? Your mother? Brothers and sisters? Where are they? I know the man in the transport this morning ...' Mika breaks off. She could kick herself for bringing up the kid's father. Now Bree will be reliving those gruesome moments all over again.

The child stares into her soup. She shakes her head grimly.

'No other family?'

'No.' She tilts her body sideways.

'What about your grandparents?'

'No one.' Bree picks up her spoon and shovels soup into her mouth, effectively closing off Mika's questioning.

Mika isn't sure if Bree's revelations have reduced or added to her problems. If Bree has no people, then Mika can safely avoid the authorities, but what's she going to do with the kid?

A beep interrupts her thoughts.

'Alarm. I'd better head up and check on things,' Mika tells Bree. 'Stay here. In fact, if you've finished your soup, why don't you hop into one of those beds? You look tired.' Smiling reassuringly, Mika waits until Bree has closed the door behind her. Mika doesn't have time to worry whether the girl will keep out of sight, but if she stays true to form then Bree will continue to do what she's told.

The beeping is louder and more frequent by the time Mika has lowered the floor hatch and returned to the pilot seat. Turning off the alarm, she checks the exterior sensors for a breach in security.

'Now that's not fair,' she says under her breath. While she's been caring for Bree, the traffic jam has turned into open road rage. Impatient or desperate for medical help, people have taken it upon themselves to reduce the competition. Through sheer size, larger transports have taken out some of the smaller ones, causing a pile-up of small vehicles on the shoulder of the road. People swarm from the transports like vigilantes. One of them probably brushed past *Torua*, setting off the alarm.

Mika isn't too worried. Her waka may look outdated, but there's some ancient magic in its defences. Still, there's no point sticking around, asking for trouble. She stokes the engines back to full power and searches for the clearest way out. But she's not the only one rethinking the situation, and soon she's hedged in on all sides.

'Shit, shit, shit.' Mika aims for a narrow gap between two smaller vehicles, intending to force her way between them. Through the waka's thick armour comes the scraping of metal on metal. Mika imagines sparks flying as she increases her speed. Like a cork freed from a bottle, the pressure is released in a sudden jolt, ejecting her from the chaos.

Damn.

Mika's got herself trapped in a maze of lots, abandoned mid-construction, on the other side of the mêlée. Like a blind snake, she weaves in and around half-dug foundations and discarded materials. Intent on seeking a way out, Mika doesn't hear the return of the external sensor alarm. Not until Bree's hand settles on her forearm.

'What?' Mika says, startled.

'There's a man outside. He wants to come in,' Bree explains, as she retakes the co-pilot seat.

CHAPTER THREE

Wearing a dark blue jumpsuit, the man is tall and broad. Rain runs down his face in rivulets and his dark hair hangs in damp tendrils, wavy as if it has recently come loose from a plait. One of his eyes is a cybernetic prosthetic. An early model, it swivels jerkily, not quite fitted properly. The erratic motion of it unnerves Mika, but she takes in the man's narrow nose and skin, dark like polished rimu, and her unease reduces: he reminds her a little of Huia's partner, Hoani. Leaping one-legged, the man bangs on the windscreen, waving her down.

So, stubborn like Hoani, too.

Mika puts *Torua* into hibernation and cracks opens the window.

'What do you want?'

'I could do with a ride.'

'Why should we help you?'

The man turns his head to look at the chaos behind, then holds his hands palm-up in peace. 'Because this blasted storm has meant I've had to work three shifts in a row until even basic supplies have run out. Because my own transport, parked round the back of the emergency centre, is completely blocked in and likely to remain that way until this storm blows over – probably even longer judging by that mess you left behind.'

'Can you show us the way out?'

'Yes.'

Mika gives him a hard stare. He doesn't look like an axe murderer. But this storm has thrown the entire eastern seaboard into a state of emergency, and there are people who'd take advantage in a crisis.

'What do you think, Bree?' she says aloud. 'Can we trust him?'

Bree tugs at Mika's sleeve and, pulling her closer, whispers in her ear.

'Hmm. Bree wants to know if you wouldn't mind turning around.'

'Why?'

'Doesn't bother me, if you'd rather not …' Mika moves to restart *Torua*.

'Okay, okay.' Shrugging, he turns around, his left leg swinging out as if he has no knee, and Mika sees the letters EMT emblazoned on his jacket. At the four points of the compass, he pantomimes a little bow. 'Is that it?' he says, when he comes full circle.

'Hang on, I'm conferring with a colleague up here.'

'Yes, that's a paramedic uniform,' Bree whispers, her head ducked below the level of the dashboard. 'EMT stands for Emergency Medical Technician.'

'Well, at least that part of his story stacks up. He hasn't shaved in a while either, which fits in with the bit about him working three shifts. Shall we give him a ride?'

The girl gazes at Mika through blonde lashes. She nods.

Mika turns back to the paramedic. 'Where do you live?'

'West of here, on the other side of Newark.'

'If I drive you home can you point me to the highway out of town?'

'Sure, where are you headed?'

'Las Vegas.'

The paramedic grins. 'Planning a road trip, are you? Well, you're in luck, because the I-80 is just around the corner from my place.'

'Okay, hop in.' Mika unlocks the door.

✖

It takes most of the afternoon, and numerous detours into back roads and alleys, to reach Stan Aspen's home. On the cheap side of Newark, he said. The expected dwelling never appears. Instead, the derelict buildings begin to show signs of life: the occasional door painted white, bright curtains escaping from broken windows. Mika finds it difficult to imagine lives lived so close to the edge. When Stan nods his head towards a large warehouse, Mika hesitates. The entrance is festooned in graffiti announcing the goods and services offered within; the coded language of illicit trade is not hard to decipher.

Maybe not a place for children.

'Come in for a coffee. I owe you for the ride,' Stan insists as he swings to the ground below. He must catch her look of alarm because he says: 'It's okay. It's safe here. We're like a family. A strange, dysfunctional family of lost souls. People here look out for each other as best they can.'

Nudging Mika, her eyes open wide, Bree whispers in her ear. She wants to see inside. Mika gives in despite her urgency to get going. Besides, the word *family* pulls like Maui's hook in her heart. 'Okay, but just for a minute.'

Inside the front doors, the world sheds its shroud of grey, revealing a carnival of colour.

'Welcome to my home,' Stan says, holding his arms up like a ringmaster introducing the next act. He leads them through the warehouse. Makeshift stalls form parallel lines in front of living spaces that have the appearance of found art. Mika recognises the cast-offs: pieces of timber, tin, glass and cloth, scavenged and brought here to become a part of the covered shanty town. A place for forgotten things, for the city's forgotten people.

The banter of people buying or selling – some openly, others less so – distracts her from the oddly beautiful constructions. She holds tightly to Bree's hand, fearful the girl will be swallowed up by the crowd. They may be here with Stan, but the wary glances tell Mika that she and Bree are newcomers, and newcomers engender mistrust. At last, near the end of the thoroughfare, Stan ducks behind a stack of caged animals, guarded by a rather smug cat and an unsmiling old woman, who sits cross-legged on a woven blanket.

'Good trading, Grandmother.' Mika can't tell if it is a question or a statement, but her eyes catch the smooth exchange of something in a folded piece of paper as Stan cups the old woman's hand in his.

'This is me here.' He fumbles with the lock and then swings the door open, revealing a snug and simply decorated room. He grabs a dirty T-shirt off the couch, balls it in his hands, then throws it in a corner.

'Sorry, it's not much. My wife wouldn't come when I split the reservation after …' Mika spots the items linking him to his home: various brightly coloured tribal blankets scattered here and there, and a couple of carved wooden bowls on the bench. Several decorative weapons, wrapped in leather thongs and decorated in feathers and beads, hang on the kitchen wall. 'Well, it's all I need. I'll get the coffee on.'

Another nudge from Bree. 'Is it safe for Bree to visit the pets?'

'Pets?' Stan looks confused for a moment and Mika realises the animals in the cages outside are destined for someone's pot, not their lap. 'Oh, the animals. Sure, just don't let them out of their cages or you'll end up owning them.'

Mika nods to Bree. Stan sets about pouring coffee into the filter. There are washed dishes in the drying rack, and the toaster is out on the counter, an old piece of toast still in one of the slots. Mika enviously eyes the lonely apple in the bottom of the carved bowl; it's been a long trip and she's missed fresh fruit.

'Here. Catch.' Stan tosses it to her.

'Thanks.' Mika takes a bite and leaves him to his coffee making. Popping her head out the front door, she checks the alley. Bree is crouched beside the cages, chatting to a puppy. Satisfied that the girl is safe, Mika returns to the living-kitchen area, her finger dragging along the thickly woven blanket draped over the couch. The indigenous design is beautiful, the lines and angles so different from the curves favoured by her own people. She knows her dad liked them too – he'd brought one of these blankets back to Aotearoa with him when he fled the United States all those years ago. She's making a mental note to ask Stan about the story behind the pattern later, when she's drawn to the large window, cut in half by the wall of the adjoining bedroom. The glass is so thick with dirt that Mika can barely make out the remains of the dismantled machinery outside.

Skeletons. A graveyard of dreams.

Mika nibbles the apple to its core, swallowing the seeds in pleasure, then turns back to Stan. The paramedic has switched the machine on. He leans back against the bench.

'She's a great kid.'

'Hmm?'

'Bree.'

'Oh, yeah,' Mika agrees.

'Quiet though.'

'She has some stuff going on,' Mika says vaguely. Stan opens the tiny beer fridge. Apart from a couple of unidentifiable jars, Mika notes there's no food in there. Mind you, Stan did say he'd worked three shifts in a row. Since the storm broke, he probably hasn't had time to shop, or maybe he eats at the food stalls outside. He takes some sachets of powdered milk from a compartment in the door, pouring one into each of the cups, ready for the coffee.

'Bit of trouble with her dad, huh?'

Mika sees a flash from this morning, the man's face, and his ruined, gouged-out eye. 'Um … something like that.'

'If you don't mind me saying, you seem too young to have a daughter Bree's age.'

Mika laughs at that. 'Oh, she's not—'

A brick caves the window in, the panes shattering in a rain of glass. The fragments hit the floor, tinkling like a piwakawaka. A stray shard glances off Mika's face. She wipes it off. The back of her hand comes away bloody.

'Shit!' Stan yells as a man swings in through the gaping hole. He is dressed in black shinobi shozoko. Dark eyes scan the room for his target. Mika's breath catches in her throat.

What on earth?

She needs to get Bree, and get the hell out of here.

'Out the front!' screams Stan, as if reading her mind. 'Hurry!'

But, recovering from his Tarzan-like swing from the roof, the brute has found his feet. He raises his gun and aims it at Stan.

'Where is it, you cheating—?'

Stan doesn't wait for the rest. Two-handed, he picks up the coffee maker and pitches boiling black liquid into his aggressor's face, blinding him. The man shrieks, throwing up his hands, dropping his gun. Stooping instinctively, Mika picks it up and runs for the door.

'Mika!' Bree appears in the opening, a dog cradled in her arms. Her face pales.

'Run for the transport!' Stan urges. The scalded man hurls himself at Stan, fuelled by pain and rage. The two men wrestle violently. Stan searches for a weapon.

The stone adze.

Mika watches, paralysed, as Stan rips it from the wall, bringing it down on his aggressor's skull. It lands with a hollow crack, the noise finally wakening Mika from her stupor. She grabs Bree, and bustles her towards the door. They need to get out.

Suddenly, Mika's hair is yanked from behind. She's pulled backwards, and twisted about bodily, where she comes face to face with a *second* intruder.

'Go, Bree,' she shouts. But she's horrified to see Bree duck and run for the bedroom.

No, the transport – head for Torua!

But it's too late. Bree's in the bedroom and now Mika can't flee. Not without leaving the girl behind. They're trapped.

Seeing her anguish, Mika's captor smiles malevolently. He shows her his switch blade. It's long and curved. Mika feels her breath leave her.

She's nobody. Whatever these men are here for, Mika knows nothing about it. She's just an unfortunate witness, in the wrong place at the wrong time. But that doesn't mean her captor won't enjoy slicing her. His unhurried smile says as much.

But she has the gun, held down low, following the line of her leg. Mika feels her fingers tremble on the trigger as her aggressor steps closer.

She raises the gun and fires.

And is thrown backwards into the wall by the gun's recoil. Crashing hard, Mika has the wind knocked out of her. By the time she's scrambled to her feet, her assailant's blood is pumping red all over the concrete floor.

Panicked, Mika searches wildly for Stan. His back to her,

he's rummaging inside the fridge.

What are you doing? Forget the coffee, Mika wants to scream.

But her voice is stuck in her throat.

The first man is back on his feet, his hood slipping back, revealing a protective helmet. Not dead. Not even unconscious. The adze had bounced off the helmet, stunning him, but only briefly. Now he rushes at Stan a second time, like an enraged demon, his face and neck a mess of angry boils.

'Stan, look out!' Not expecting the assault, Stan is caught off-balance as the man slams into his stomach, ramming him backwards into the kitchen cabinets. Grunting, Stan attempts to wrench himself free, recoiling at the sight of the puckered blistering skin. Mika's jaw drops as, silently, the man pushes a knife to Stan's ribs. Stan's eyes open wide. Beads of sweat appear on his forehead.

'This is not what the Brotherhood agreed, Aspen!' the man hisses.

'It wasn't my agreement,' Stan says, his chest heaving in defiance. Over the man's shoulder, Stan's eyes swivel desperately to Mika.

'We'll see what headquarters think of that. But first, I think I can change your point of view.' Mika watches in horror as the intruder repositions his knife. 'What do you reckon, Stan, will this help you see things our way?' He draws a line of blood beneath Stan's remaining eye.

Mika supports herself against the wall. This time, when she fires, she's prepared for the recoil.

CHAPTER FOUR

Bree reaches *Torua* first. She scrambles up the side and dives through the hatch, her anxious face lingering above the rim like a watchful possum, as Mika and Stan race to catch up.

'We're here. It's okay.' Mika groans as she struggles inside. She hasn't had time to check for damage, but already she's aware she's in for some serious muscle pain tomorrow.

As Stan moves to follow her, Mika hesitates. 'I'm not sure I can help you any more than I have.'

Frozen halfway up the side of *Torua*, Stan drops his eyes, the cybernetic prosthesis wobbling. 'I'm sorry. I had no idea they'd come to my place. But I'm begging you to let me go with you.'

Behind him, the large reinforced doors of the warehouse swing closed. A heavy metal beam slides into place, securing the residents from further intrusion. There's no welcome for them here. After today, perhaps not even for Stan.

'Who were they? What did they want?'

Stan shakes his head. 'I can't tell you.'

'Then I can't let you come.' Mika moves to close the hatch.

'Wait! It's not that I don't *want* to tell you. I'm not ashamed, or anything. I do what I have to do. It's just that you'll be safer if you don't know.' A window is closed, internal shutters clicked shut, the noise quieted. The warehouse is in lockdown. 'Look, you're not from here,' Stan goes on, a hint of desperation in his voice. 'It's evident you don't know this place. I can help.'

Mika feels Bree's gentle tug on her pant leg. Sighing, she turns, leaving the hatch open, and descends into the control room.

Stan closes the hatch behind him. 'Thanks.'

'Just so you know, if taking you in means I don't complete my journey, I'll make you regret it.' Mika knows the threat is meaningless. If she doesn't complete her journey, the regret will kill *her*.

Stan sinks into one of the empty seats. Bree, still holding her small captive in one arm, grabs the first-aid kit, delivering it to Stan with a shy smile before joining Mika at the front of the waka. Ignoring her own injuries, Mika pulls *Torua* away from the warehouse, heading in no particular direction, just one she hopes will confuse anyone with plans to follow.

'Calculating …' The warm tones of Kuia's voice break the quiet. Eyes drooping low, Bree strokes her prize until it falls into a contented sleep on her lap.

'Can you take the wheel? I need to put Bree to bed.'

'No probs. Just give me a moment to screw my leg back on.' Mika tries to hide her shock as Stan gives his prosthetic a final check, ensuring there are no bent rods or clogged cogs, then twists it back into place, mid-thigh on the left side. 'Cheap parts. The joint always gives me trouble.' There's a click and a whirl, and Stan gives a satisfied grin as he rolls down his pant leg and moves to take Mika's place at the controls. 'Las Vegas, right? Mind if I let your GPS off the hook? I know the way.'

'Okay.'

Mika gathers Bree into her arms, the dog cupped in the girl's lap. She stomps to activate the lower hatch, and descends. Below, she tucks Bree into bed, the dog curled beside her. Bree's expression flickers as Mika tucks the blankets under her chin, as if she's walking somewhere between dream and nightmare.

'Sleep well, sweetie,' Mika whispers. She leaves the light on low and returns upstairs.

'So?' Stan's question reminds Mika that she's lost and alone here. Even the ghost of her kuia in the GPS is quiet.

She inhales deeply. 'My name is Mika Tāura. Mauao is my mountain, Tauranga Moana is my ocean and I am far from home. Ngāti Ranginui is my iwi, and Aotearoa is my tūrangawaewae. My people need me to get to Las Vegas. There is no choice. I have to meet someone, someone who knew my father. I have to give him a message.' Mika pulls her jacket tighter around her shoulders, and folds her arms across her chest. 'But when I arrived, the storm meant I missed my connection. And without a guide, I don't know who I'm supposed to meet.'

'Maybe your guide's still waiting for you?' Stan suggests. 'We could check, and if the person is still there, then I'll leave. But …' His voice trails off and Mika can't tell if he's making a decision about what to say next or if he needs all his attention on the road. He narrowly misses a rubbish tin rolling in the strong winds.

'You can help me get to Las Vegas?' Mika needs to be certain.

'If I can't find your guide, I promise to get you close.' Stan moves into the co-pilot chair and Mika seamlessly takes the driver's seat. She scans the saved lists in the GPS and chooses her first destination. The place where she was supposed to meet the guide.

'Calculating. Go straight five hundred yards. Take the first left,' says the confident voice of Mika's kuia. Mika doubts she would have found her way back without the GPS, the storm has caused so much damage. The rain has slowed to a continuous drizzle, but dark clouds still swarm in the heavens, leaving little chance for the last of the day's light to penetrate. When they approach the meeting point, Stan and Mika strain for a sign of her guide.

'Wow, that looks serious,' Stan says, indicating the wreckage on the traffic island. It's the transport *Torua* collided with earlier. The transport carrying Bree. The remains of the vehicle have been shunted to the side of the island. No other vehicles are in sight.

'That's where I found Bree,' she whispers, the words loud and careless in the cab.

'The little girl? She's not yours?' Stan says.

'No …' Mika pulls up, stopping the transport close enough for them to examine the wreckage. A faulty power pack. Petals of twisted metal burst outward from the centre of the hood, the fire long since extinguished by the storm, leaving a blackened husk of smouldering steel. It's a shock to see it again. Mika's relieved that Bree's asleep.

'It was an accident,' she says. 'I didn't see the vehicle in time. We collided, and their transport couldn't withstand the strength of my waka. I didn't want to leave Bree with the body of her father. I was taking her for medical treatment. I wasn't prepared for the storm. I didn't know what else to do.' The words tumble like a prayer waiting to be answered.

'No one's here.'

'That's not surprising. I'm a day late.'

'Yes, but if your guide was local, they would've known about the storm. They would have *expected* you to be late. So, why didn't they wait?'

'After we collided, and I discovered the body, and Bree, I just wanted to get the girl away from here, somewhere safe. Maybe when the guide saw the collision, he thought the same thing.'

Stan's eyes widen. 'Hey! Do you think maybe Bree's father was your guide? Maybe they were coming here to meet you?'

Mika slumps. If that's the case, not only has she destroyed Bree's life, but she may have ruined Huia's chances.

'Hey, sorry. Look, let me check it out. Maybe there's something inside the transport that will tell us.' Stan gives Mika's shoulder an awkward squeeze, and before she can protest, he's outside *Torua*, waving at her from the traffic island.

Numb, Mika watches Stan through the windscreen as he struggles against the wind. He leans inside the twisted transport and moments later the hatch clangs and he's back inside, shaking the rain from his hair and coat, and re-joining her at the front.

'Well, do you want the good news, or the bad news?' Mika looks at him, dazed. 'Right then, let's start with the bad. I think our man there was waiting for you, but not for the reason you think.' He lets his words register, then passes over a series of renditions. Faces of people about Mika's age: mostly women, some men, all of them resembling Mika, and Huia, but none of them an exact match.

'What are these pictures? Where did he get these? Why would he have them?'

'You recognise them?'

'They could be my family, but they're not, not quite.' Mika flicks through the faces, peering at each one in turn. It's as if someone has made genetic models of what Mika might look like.

'I think they wanted to be sure.'

'Sure of what?'

'That you were the right person. The person they needed taken care of.' Mika's jaw drops as understanding dawns.

'You mean, an *assassin*?'

'I'm only guessing, but I think they only wanted half the deal. Whatever it is you brought with you.'

'I didn't bring anything with me …' Mika protests. But then she has another thought. 'What about Bree?' She sucks in the name, as if to hide the girl from danger.

'A side business?' Mika's incomprehension must show in her face because Stan extrapolates: 'Organ donation. Big business here in the United States. Especially over the past couple of decades, since B-Cell's miracle cure for diabetes backfired.' Stan's face twists into a sneer. 'Of course, it's all fine and dandy if you've got money – you can replace limbs and eyes, get yourself the best prosthetics you can afford, the corporate giant does a nice line in top-end artificial limbs – but once you reach organ failure, that's it. Unless you can source a living organ, you're dead …' He trails off, his voice softening. 'Some parents, if they're down on their luck, will sell their kids on. You know, you probably saved your own life as well as that little girl's. You've both been pretty lucky. Maybe you have a guardian angel.'

Mika thinks of Huia, sending her aroha across the ocean, and nods. Right now, she feels fairly floaty herself. All this, it's unreal. Her guide sent to kill her? Bree an organ donor? How is it possible? But then, if she considers the evidence …

'I checked Bree over after the accident,' she replies. 'She's covered in needle pricks and bruises. *Old* bruises.'

'Yeah? I guess that confirms it. Explains why the kid's so quiet. Poor thing has been kept as a living spare part. Well, that settles it,' Stan announces. 'You've saved us, so now we're going to help you. Shall I drive?' Stan's enthusiasm seems slightly misplaced – doesn't he realise that Mika's killed three people today? Okay, so she did it by accident, or in self-defence, since it turns out all of them had intended to kill her, but still, it's small comfort.

Suddenly, Mika feels heavy. The voyage, her mission, Bree, Stan, even the dog. It's all too much. Mika just wants to curl into a ball and sob. Exhausted, she lets Stan take over.

The thrum of *Torua*'s heart lulls her into a fitful sleep, full of intangible images and whispered warnings. Through it all, Mika hears Huia begging her to be strong.

CHAPTER FIVE

It's a long drive across the country from New York to Nevada. For most of the first day, they jostle for space in amongst a convoy of transports escaping the storms. Stan drives, every half hour or so erupting in a fit of expletives as blocked roads and traffic jams force him to make detour after detour. Mika keeps reminding him that he shouldn't curse in front of Bree, but after the third or fourth time, she gives up. Given what they suspect of Bree's history, perhaps a few swear words aren't the end of the world. Mika imagines the girl has seen and heard far worse.

By the second day, the amount of fallen trees and strewn debris lessens and the only delays are regular comfort stops for the dog, and a layover for pizza. Finally, late afternoon on the third day, Stan drives *Torua* into an Arizona reservation.

A gaggle of children crowd around the exotic transport, impeding their progress. Stan is forced to stop in the dusty courtyard only a few yards inside the entrance.

He laughs. 'This is the end of the road.'

They clamber down, Bree with the puppy – who she's named Paddy – tucked under her arm. The children swarm her, all wanting to pet the puppy. For a second, Bree hesitates, her face full of anguish. She crushes Paddy to her, who yelps, then she takes a step towards Mika. Mika gives her shoulder a squeeze.

'It's okay. They're friends,' she reassures her. She nudges Stan for confirmation.

'Oh yes, you and Paddy are quite safe here,' Stan says, giving Bree's hair a ruffle. He turns to one of the older children, a girl. 'Arlene, why don't you take Bree down to the river? She's been stuck in the transport for three days. Show her the rope swing. Or if she's feeling brave she might try a tube ride. I'm sure she'd like that. Maybe later on, to bring her back to us? We'll be with the professors.'

The girl grins. 'Okay.' Mika watches as Bree is guided away by the children.

'She'll be fine,' Stan says, his prosthetic eye winking out of turn. 'Arlene's a good kid. She knows what it's like to be lonely. She'll look after Bree. Come on, there are some people I want you to meet.'

Mika follows Stan into the community. Clustered together at this end of the reservation, the houses are mainly traditional adobe style, and are a hodgepodge of sizes, some with wooden or corrugated iron roofs. Brightly coloured washing hangs from lines swung between the poles of the buildings. The place is busy, and many of the people know Stan.

'Hey Stan!'

'Craig!' Stan greets a man who's missing his lower legs. Craig rolls forward on a make-shift trolley made from an old push-chair, propelling himself with gloved hands.

'We weren't expecting you back for another month.'

'East coast storm caused some disruption,' Stan says, shrugging. 'So there was a sudden change of plans.'

'I can see that!' Craig ribs, staring pointedly at Mika.

Grinning, Stan pushes the trolley, sending Craig off in the other direction. 'Yeah, yeah. It's not what you think. Gotta see some people. Talk later, okay?'

They continue on in a haze of afternoon heat, a shock after the air-conditioned comfort of *Torua*. Mika notices that, like Craig, many of the people here are missing limbs, fingers, eyes. Some have prosthetics, but they're not the sophisticated appliances she's seen advertised on billboards and digital displays all across the country. These are older models, less advanced, and judging by the way the woman in front of them is weaving and tottering on hers, far less effective. Wobbling, the woman steps aside, allowing Mika and Stan to pass. In spite of her suffering, she smiles at Mika. Mika smiles back. She may be a stranger, but already the reception here has been warm and unguarded. And unlike at the warehouse, something about this community reminds her of home.

'I have some business with the elders,' Stan says, 'But first I want you to meet some friends of mine. The Adèmes are among our kikmongwi, the wise people, here.'

'Like tohunga?'

'Tohunga? Sorry, I don't know this word.'

Mika tries to explain. 'In my culture, the tohunga is mainly a spiritual leader, but also a herbalist, astronomer, strategist, story-teller, and mediator. The tohunga is a wise person who carries the knowledge of the people.'

Stan considers her definition and nods. 'Yes, I think that's a pretty good approximation.' He stops outside an adobe. It is small and unassuming, the sort of place a hermit might choose. 'This is us here.'

Stan guides Mika into the house. Inside, the dwelling is cool and clean, the pink clay decorated with a number of lively blankets like the ones at Stan's warehouse home, diamonds and triangles highlighted in stunning reds, ochre, and black.

'Lisa? Lionel?'

'Stan! What a surprise. We didn't expect to see you back so soon.'

It's the second time Mika's heard that said. Clearly, Stan returns to the reservation regularly. Something must be important to bring him all the way from New York, and it's not as if he can fly. With so little fossil fuel remaining, air travel is reserved for the spectacularly rich. Mika has seen Stan's place. There's no way he could be mistaken for someone spectacularly rich. Anyway, it doesn't matter. They'd agreed it was safer Mika not know about Stan's activities, and it won't be long until they part company.

'And who's this with you?'

'This is Mika.'

'Pleased to meet you, Mika.' Creases at her eyes. Dark olive skin. A broad genuine smile. Mika estimates that Lisa is in her late fifties, her salt and pepper ponytail hinting of long dark tresses in her youth.

'So pretty.'

Mika blushes. 'Thank you.'

'Lionel! Bring some drinks. We have guests.'

Moments later, Lionel Adème, a diminutive bird-like man, enters carrying a tray with a water jug, glasses, and some serviettes.

'Stan! Nice to see you.' He places the tray on a low table, and gives Stan a clap on the back, a gesture Mika finds odd in such a tiny man.

'This is Mika, Lionel.'

Ignoring the serviettes, Lionel wipes his hands on his trousers. He offers a hand to Mika. 'How do you do?'

'Mika *Tāura*, from *Aotearoa*,' Stan says gravely, lingering on the words.

Why the emphasis on her being foreign? So, she's from New Zealand. It's not against the law to travel. Just a bit impractical. But Lisa Adème sits bodily on the sofa, her face suddenly pale.

'Oh.'

Lionel rushes to his wife's side. 'Lisa! Are you all right?'

'I'm fine, Lionel. It's nothing serious. Don't fuss …' Lisa pats her husband's knee. 'It's just a shock to meet a person carrying that name. It's been years. Decades …' She lifts her eyes to Mika. 'Is your father Atticus?' she says.

This time, it's Mika whose knees buckle beneath her.

An hour later, both Mika and Lisa have recovered some-what from the shock. With a fresh pot of tea and a plate of cookies on the table, and Bree — her hair still wet from the river — playing with Paddy nearby on the floor, they settle down to talk.

'I'm so sorry to hear about the loss of your father,' Lisa says, shaking her head sadly. 'We worked with him on the diabetes project, Lionel and I. We were part of the native epidemiology team. Indigenous people have always been more susceptible to diabetes. Back then, about half of all the people on the reservation were affected, and each year our children were diagnosed younger and younger. I seem to remember your father telling me it's the same for the Māori. It was one of the reasons he pursued a career in science. Anyway, when B-Cell offered subsidised gene therapy for the new insulin — your father's work — people jumped at it, and for the first few years it was wonderful. The up-regula-tion delayed the onset of the disease, and there were fewer deaths. But then the gene mutated. Your father was dev-astated. He nearly killed himself trying to find out what had happened, looking for ways to reverse the change. But B-Cell weren't interested, moving up production in their spare parts division instead. And that's when your father left. He was a brilliant man, an inspired scientist. We should have supported him when he made his stand against Selwyn Bruce. We wanted to, but B-Cell ... well, the company has huge resources. Some of the other researchers who came out against their strategy ...' she trails off, dabbing at her eyes with a serviette. Composing herself.

Lionel speaks, filling the silence. 'No one knew what

happened to them, but there were rumours. We had children – all grown now – but back then we were afraid. So Lisa and I came back here to the reservation. We've been off the grid ever since.'

Lisa reaches over and puts a hand on Mika's forearm. 'Your father was our friend, and he was right to stand up against Selwyn and B-Cell. Perhaps if we'd listened to Atticus when he came to us, things might have turned out differently. We should have helped him. I'm so sorry we didn't.'

Lionel nods in agreement.

Mika can't believe it: these people knew her father and about B-Cell. Perhaps Selwyn Bruce is the person she's supposed to meet? The one who claims to have worked with her father. It seems likely. If she can find him, perhaps he'll be able to help her. Perhaps there's hope for Huia, after all.

Suddenly, a woman pushes into the building – a handsome woman with almond eyes and slender limbs. Her face is streaked with tears.

She stares at the group. At Stan. At Mika. And especially at Bree.

Then, sobbing, she turns on her heel and runs.

Mika looks at the others, puzzled. 'I hope I haven't done anything to offend.'

'No, not at all. It's not your fault. Irina's been …' She glances at Stan. '… unhappy for some time now. Not so long ago, she lost her baby girl to the disease. A wonderful vibrant little girl. We did everything we could …' Lisa dabs at her eyes with a serviette.

'Irina's your daughter?'

But now Mika sees the ripple in Stan's jaw. Even his cybernetic eye seems to dull in pain.

'No. She's my wife,' he whispers.

CHAPTER SIX

The sound of rushing water and wind bounces off the stone walls of the gorge.

Full of excitement, Bree hurries Mika along the path. 'Come on, Mika! It's just round this bend. We're nearly there.'

'I'm coming.' But Bree can hardly keep still, running up the path to the corner and back again. 'You go on and meet Arlene,' Mika says, seeing the girl's impatience. 'I'll catch you up.' Smiling, Bree skips ahead, Paddy at her heels, his tail wagging.

Around the bend, the gorge opens into a clearing where the community has its swimming hole, a bulge in the river like the eye of a needle. On one side, a false beach has been created by the shifting river bed. Already, several families are gathered there, including Lisa Adème, who's sitting with a group of women. Nearby a bunch of tyre tubes are stacked neatly in a pile. Lisa looks up and gives Mika a friendly wave. Mika waves back.

'Geromino!' shouts a child as he swings into the water. The rope swing dangles over the centre of the pool from a tree clinging to the rock face, clearly a favourite pastime of the reservation children. The rope is worn and frayed, but the children shout and jostle for a turn, each one swinging out and tumbling into the water, where they splash like otters, water streaming off their bodies. Too impatient to wait for Mika, Bree too is in the water. Mika pauses a moment to watch her. Her blonde hair – wet – has darkened to black, and her skin is racing to catch up as it sucks greedily at the sun, camouflaging her among the others.

As if she belongs here.

Mika should leave now. Bree would hardly miss her.

Not today.

She'd promised to spend the day with Bree.

Looking for a place to set down her towel, Mika notes the large flat stone near the water, where six prostheses, tiny legs mostly, old models, some of them very battered, wait while their owners take a dip. Children damaged by diabetes. Mika's heart lurches. Her father had foreseen this.

Spotting Mika, Bree breaks away from Arlene.

'Mika, look at the rope swing,' she says, raining droplets as she emerges from the water. Twisting, she points a finger at the rope. 'See it?'

'No, what rope swing? Where?' Mika teases, looking everywhere but at the swing.

Bree giggles. 'That rope swing there. *Right there.* I did it twice, yesterday,' she says proudly.

'Twice!' Mika says. 'Well, then I'll just have to make sure I have *three* swings today, won't I?'

Bree's eyes widen. 'You'll come in the water? Really?'

'Of course.' Mika feels a twinge of sadness at the joy Bree finds in tiny things. Has she never had an adult play with her before? Time to fix that. But, looking around, Mika realises there's nowhere for her get changed. She should've put her togs on earlier, back at *Torua*. Mika isn't ashamed of her body, but she doesn't want to embarrass anyone either.

'Here, let me help,' says Lisa, padding barefoot across the sand to Mika's rescue. She chuckles. 'We've been meaning to put up a changing shed, but no one wants to spoil the view, so instead we adults make screens with our towels. I'll hold yours up for you, and if Bree holds hers up too, no one will see a thing.'

'Thank you.'

But Mika is only half dressed when Bree pokes her nose over the top of the towel, peeking to see if Mika is ready yet.

'Hey,' she says, pointing with her head at the swirls on Mika's body. 'Your skin looks like a treasure map.'

Lisa takes a peek. 'Oh, my word,' she says, breathless. 'Bree, I think you're absolutely right.'

Sitting on the roof of *Torua*, Mika watches the sun rise over the village. They've been here a week now. Mika never planned on staying this long, but the professors are convinced that with some time, she might not need to go at all. So, each morning she's watched the day break and decided to stay just one more day.

Mika pulls a blanket – a welcome gift from the villagers – tighter around her shoulders, comforted by the heaviness of the weave and the scratchiness of its fibres. Like the blanket, the quiet stillness insulates her against the urgency to keep going, to get the job done and return home.

She inhales deeply, savouring the smell of wood smoke on the air. There's a beauty here, in the barrenness of the landscape, in the widely spaced homes in various stages of decomposition, half hidden in the scrub and spindly trees. On the night of their arrival, Mika had been close to tears when each person had taken the time to greet her with declarations of their lineage reaching back into the ages. Some of the families had claimed a distant kinship to her, using it as an excuse to offer her clothes for Bree, and the meal that followed included music, laughter and shared stories.

So like home, but not home.

Bree head pops into view as she climbs *Torua* to join her.

'Hey, sweetie. Did I wake you?' Mika's amazed at how quickly the child has put away her past and begun to stretch into her new identity: loving and fearless. Mika opens her blanket, like the wing of a Haast's eagle, and tucks Bree into her side. The girl snuggles closer, leaning her head against

Mika's shoulder.

'I wish we didn't have to go.'

'You don't have to if you don't want to.'

I wish I didn't.

'You're going to leave me?' The words fall like dead soldiers.

'You like it here, don't you?' Mika brushes Bree's hair out of her eyes, no longer rimmed with black smudges. 'Let's not talk about it now.'

They sit and watch the light creep over the horizon, waking man and dog as the sun climbs. Soon though, the noise of life begins to thicken and hunger calls them back inside for breakfast.

✻

'Is this all of it?' Lionel says impatiently.

He stands at a large meeting table, rearranging strips of paper covered in the script copied from the images decorating Mika's body.

'Yes.' There's nowhere else to hide them. Does he expect her to shave her head, too? Kikmongwi or not, it twists Mika's conscience to let the professors apply the images to paper for analysis. It doesn't feel right. She wishes she had better counsel than her own.

'It must have taken years to carve all this on your body. How would they know you would grow big enough to fit it all?' Lisa asks, shuffling a row of papers from top to bottom.

'Yes, it took years, but I'm not the only one in my family to wear the moko. It was the only way to keep my father's work safe.' Mika shudders at the memory of the pain as the tattoo was etched into her skin. It was pain mixed with pride, as she'd sat alongside Huia, the two of them laughing through their tears.

'It's all nonsense,' Lionel announces, and Mika catches Lisa's cutting glance in his direction. 'I'm sorry, Mika.' He softens. 'But we've been looking at these for a week and we're no closer to understanding what Atticus was getting at.' He picks up a strip. 'Look here, this is a basic protein sequence, but …' He grips another between fingertips. '… this one is a mathematical sequencing formula.' He lets the papers flutter back to the table.

'Lionel, we mustn't blame Mika for our frustration,' Lisa says. She takes Mika by the elbow, and leads her towards the door. 'Can you give us a bit more time? We need to figure this out.'

Mika turns to her. 'Okay, I guess another day or two can't hurt. But after that, I really have to go, whether or not you've deciphered the message. I hope you'll understand.'

Lisa frowns. 'We're not sure you should even go to Las Vegas. Selwyn, B-Cell, they're not to be trusted. Stan says there was an attempt on your life …'

Mika looks past Lisa, back into the room where Lionel is muttering to himself, scavenging through the papers, picking up and discarding each one in turn.

'I was told they might have some of my father's research notes – the last pieces of the puzzle.'

Lisa snorts. 'Unlikely.' She takes Mika's hand. 'Give us time, Mika. If the answer's here, Lionel and I will find it.'

Mika kisses the older woman on the cheek.

All this can wait until tomorrow.

Bree is down at the river with Lisa, so now is as good a time as any. Mika's put off asking long enough. She steps up to the old converted school bus, Stan and Irina's home on the reservation. But Irina is there, blocking Mika's way, her arms crossed across her chest.

'I'm sorry, but you can't come in.'

'I have something to ask you both, and then I'll be on my way,' Mika says, straightening her shoulders.

'You're leaving for good, then?'

Mika pauses. 'Maybe. It depends.'

'I'll tell him. We'll find you later.' The other woman hasn't moved, yet Mika feels she's being pushed away.

'That's okay. I'm happy to wait.' Mika knows a village line when she sees one; mothers keeping close eye on their children playing in the dirt, the group of elders sitting in the shade talking about the weather. Everyone here is waiting their turn to visit the bus.

At that moment, the door swings open and a teenage girl steps out, followed closely by a woman – her mother – whose smile matches her daughter's.

'What would we do without you?' the woman says as she takes a small package from Stan; but then, noting Mika's presence, she freezes.

Irina steps closer to Mika. 'Please don't judge him,' she says gently. 'You're not from here. You have no idea what we've lost, what we're forced to do to keep our families safe.'

Mika thinks of what she's left behind, what brought her to this country, heart in her hand, begging for salvation. She knows exactly what people are willing to do.

Anything.

Stan has seen her. He pulls the doors of the bus closed and, excusing himself from his customers, closes the distance to Irina and Mika. He takes his wife's hand.

'Is everything okay, here?'

'Depends on what you tell me,' Mika says, allowing herself to be guided away from the bus towards *Torua*. Turning to Stan, she takes a deep breath. 'You're a paramedic who deals drugs. Fine. I don't have a problem with that, providing you can keep Bree safe.'

'Me? Keep her safe?'

Mika looks from Stan to Irina. 'I was hoping that you and Irina would keep her here with you on the reservation.'

Irina gasps, gripping her husband's hand, but Stan says nothing. Instead, he kicks at a stone, letting it lead them to *Torua*.

After a time, he says, 'What brought this on?'

Mika swallows hard. 'You know I have to go. I would have left weeks ago, if Lisa and Lionel hadn't seen a pattern in my moko and thought they could help. And when I do go, I can't take Bree with me. You see, once I've found the professors' old boss, and made the deal, I'll need to get home to Aotearoa as quickly as I can. It's an uncertain journey …' Just asking them is hard. Mika's heart is aching. She hates the thought of leaving Bree. Their relationship may be new, but still the idea of leaving the girl is excruciating. 'So, will you do it? Will you and Irina look after Bree? Give her a family here?'

She rubs at her eyes, hoping to fool the couple into thinking that a particle of dust is the reason for her tears.

'I … I don't know,' Stan says.

'But Bree likes you. She's happy here,' Mika insists.

Irina tugs at his hand, her eyes brimming with tears. 'Stan, please, we could do this.'

Stan shakes her off.

'But I thought you liked Bree,' Mika says.

'I do. Don't get me wrong, I love Bree. She's a great kid.'

'Then why not?'

Stan doesn't say anything, but his cybernetic eye jerks crazily.

Irina speaks now, her voice dropped to a whisper. 'Stan, we could do this. We could. I know we could. You can't save them all, Stan, not singlehandedly, you can't even raise enough stealing from the Brotherhood to get all the prosthetic limbs we need. But we could help Bree: you and I could give this one little girl a chance.'

'No!'

'Is it because of Belle? We wouldn't be replacing her. We could never do that—'

Stan pushes his wife away and storms ahead.

Mika goes to follow him, but Irina puts a hand on his forearm. 'I'm sorry. I'd help you if I could. I'd love to have Bree. But Stan … since we lost Belle, he hurts so much. I don't think he can bear to risk loving another child, not while there's a chance they could get ill, too. It's why he drives himself, leaving the reservation to find the money, so other families don't have to face what we did, at least not so soon.' She sighs sadly. 'It's got so I haven't just lost my daughter, I've lost my husband, too.'

She turns and heads back up the slope to the bus.

Mika catches up with Stan, who's kicking up stones. They're on the edge of the village now, facing an endless landscape of rock, where fierce plants grip the dry soil in a battle for survival. Scooping up a stone herself, Mika hefts it from hand to hand, then hurls it into the wilderness.

'Sorry. I didn't mean to push. Irina explained. It was insensitive of me to insist.'

Stan nods. He juggles a stone in his hand.

'If not you, what about the professors?' Mika says, stopping in front of *Torua*. 'They're older, but they're kind. Do you think they'd look after her?'

Stan looks up. 'You're trying to pawn the child off to the next person in line now? Surely Bree deserves more than that!'

'Well, what am I supposed to do?' Mika raises her voice, miffed now. 'You say you won't take her, and I have to get to Las Vegas and find the man who worked with my father. I can't take Bree with me. I can't take the risk.'

But Stan is tilting his head towards the gorge, where Bree, still in her wet clothes and wrapped in a towel, skips between the two professors. Paddy, equally bedraggled, yaps at their heels. He doesn't want Bree to know that they're arguing about her.

'How was your swim, sweetie?' Mika asks Bree when the two groups come together. Rubbing the dust from her hands, she picks up the puppy, scratching vigorously behind his ears.

'It was cool. Can I go again tomorrow?' Bree says, taking the puppy from Mika, and giggling as it licks her face. Mika hesitates. Will Bree still be here tomorrow? After all she's been through, Mika can't leave her with just anyone. Stan's right: Bree deserves more.

'Let's talk about it later, shall we? Right now you should go and get changed – and mind you don't turn poor *Torua* into a swimming pool!' Mika can't resist giving the girl a tight hug before helping her and the puppy inside.

'Mika, have you got a moment to come back with us?' Lisa asks. 'Lionel thinks we've made a mistake somewhere.' Mika notes Lionel's scowl, as if he doesn't approve of the implication.

'Can I ask you something first?' Mika says, ignoring the low growl from Stan.

'What's that?'

Lisa isn't referring to Mika's question. Her brows crinkle as she stares into the distance. Following her gaze, Mika spots the irregularity on the horizon. Stan has seen it too.

'Ah shit, the Brotherhood,' he curses, his face pale.

'Oh no, Stan, you didn't!' Lisa gasps, cupping her hand to her mouth.

'I was careful,' Stan whispers, but his fists are clenched.

Lionel turns on him, suddenly thunderous. 'You can't steal from them, Stan! How could you be so stupid?' he yells. 'You've put us all at risk, you fool! So you've stolen enough money to buy us a few spare parts – the Brotherhood will make us pay with our lives. You're going to get us all killed.' He grabs for his wife, yanking her away.

'No, no, it's fine,' Stan insists, taking a step towards the professors, his palms outstretched. 'I'll leave.' He flicks a glance towards *Torua*. 'If I'm not here to find when the Brotherhood come, they'll keep on looking.'

'Great idea,' Lionel retorts. 'You *should* go. We're none of us safe while you're here,' he says coldly, still pulling on Lisa's arm.

'But Stan won't be allowed to return,' Lisa protests. 'The elders are happy enough for Stan to deal drugs to bring cash into the community, but if there's any trouble with the Brotherhood, they'll ask him to stay away.'

'Then the elders would be right,' says Lionel calmly, as if talking to a child. 'Darling, we have to let him go. The important thing is to keep the community safe, and to avoid any unnecessary attention from B-Cell.'

'Mika,' Stan says, turning to her. 'The Brotherhood will know you were with me when I stole their money and their drugs. It's not safe for you here either.'

Lisa twists out of her husband's grip. 'I'm coming too,' she says, her voice firm. 'If you'll let me.'

'No!' Lionel's face is full of anguish.

Lisa lays her hand on her husband's forearm. 'Yes, Lionel. It's time for us to face up to our mistakes. We've been hiding out here too long.'

'That's not true! All these years, we've been searching for a solution!'

'We've been *hiding*, Lionel, and you know it. Well, I'm not going to stand by and watch this disease decimate our friends any longer. If I know anything at all about Atticus Tāura, then he kept on working until he found the answer, and that answer is here for us now, written on Mika's skin. All we have to do is decipher it.'

'Please, Lisa! If the Brotherhood catch you—'

Lisa interrupts. 'Come with me, Lionel,' she pleads. 'The two of us have been asleep here all this time. But now Mika has come along – like a miracle all the way from Aotearoa, from *Atticus* – wearing the clues to his research. Come with us. Help us unlock Atticus' secret. Please.'

But Lionel just stares at her. A second later, he turns on his heel and dashes back towards the village.

Lisa sobs. She watches, her expression sad, until he disappears inside the house, then, bowing her head, she climbs the exterior of *Torua* after Bree.

Mika turns to Stan. 'What about Bree? We can't take her with us. It's too dangerous. We've already seen what those guys are prepared to do.'

'Right now, we don't have time to interview anyone for the position,' Stan says, grim. He nods towards the horizon. During their exchange, the growing silhouettes of the Brotherhood have become more distinct. There are several of them, coming at speed.

Stan's right. If they're going to leave, they have to go now. Bree will just have to come with them.

Mika spins, and climbs into *Torua*. The hatch slams behind her and she dives into the driver's seat. Hastily, she enters the embarking protocols. No time for finesse, she engages the engines, striking for the middle distance between the village and the oncoming visitors.

Stan joins her in the co-pilot seat. 'Right, let's show these guys some dust.'

CHAPTER SEVEN

They haven't gone fifty yards when Lisa squeals.

'Stop, please! It's Lionel.'

Mika checks her mirror. His shirt flapping, Lionel is running after *Torua*, waving them down. Mika brakes hard, jerking the passengers forward against their seatbelts. Then, leaving the waka idling, she and Stan push up the hatch, just as Lionel reaches them.

The fifty-yard sprint has exhausted him. Bending over, he rests a hand on his knees and breathes deeply.

'I'm coming with you,' he huffs, getting his breath back. 'But I need to find Craig first.'

'We haven't got time for you to say your goodbyes, Lionel. I haven't even got time to tell Irina,' Stan says, his good eye squinting towards the horizon. 'If you want to come, you need to get in the transport now.'

'No, no, you don't understand. It's my smoking ambition coal.' He holds up a piece of red rock half-wrapped in a grubby cloth. 'If we can get the fire-pit to the right temperature, chemicals in the smoke should pacify the Brotherhood long enough for us to get away. They might even forget why they came if they inhale enough.'

'Chemical warfare?' Stan says.

Lionel grins. 'If you like.'

'Absolutely not!' says Mika, butting in. 'What about the people? The children? I thought you cared about this community!' She can't believe Lionel would be so heartless.

But Lisa calls up from below. 'Any memory loss is only

temporary. It's perfectly safe, Mika.'

'I've been working on it for years,' Lionel goes on, unable to hear Lisa from where he's standing. 'I thought if we'd had something that would curb people's drive to achieve their goals, then maybe B-Cell might not have become so powerful. We might've stood a chance.'

'I don't like it,' Mika says, shaking her head.

'It's safe. I promise. You've been exposed to it yourself. Lisa and I have been sprinkling it in the fire pit every night for the past week. We wanted to delay your departure and give us more time to study the tattoos.'

Mika's stunned. So, *that's* why she'd found it so hard to leave! Anger creeps up from deep within her. She clenches her fingers into fists.

But Stan is throwing out a hand to Lionel. 'Right. Get in. I know where Craig is. We'll take you there.' He turns his head and calls to Mika, who's already sliding into her seat. 'He'll be at his mechno-workshop …'

Mika frowns, trying to think where that might be.

'… near my caravan,' Stan finishes.

Lionel is barely in his seat, hasn't even put on his seatbelt, when *Torua* roars to life, circling the village in just minutes and sliding to a stop outside Craig's workshop. Stan, Mika and Lionel jump down before the billow of dust has had time to settle. Stan's friend rolls himself to the front of his shop.

'What's up, man?' he says, pulling off his gloves.

'Brotherhood,' Stan says. 'Sold some drugs for them in New York and I might have forgotten to give them the money. Might have held some drugs back, too.'

'Shit!'

'Yeah, I've gotta go. Lionel and Lisa, too. The profs think they can find a way to beat the diabetes.'

Lionel steps forward, his rock in hand. 'Please, we need your help to create a diversion,' he says.

'What sort of a diversion?' Craig points to his prosthesis. 'Because, you know, leaping tall buildings in a single bound isn't my forté.'

'An Indian smoke screen.'

Lionel pulls a piece of paper – clearly torn from an exercise book – out of his shirt pocket, then he passes both the rock and the paper to Craig. 'Instructions,' he says.

Craig scans the scrap of paper. Leaning over, Lionel taps it with his index finger, giving Craig his final advice.

'Don't add too much of the chemical at once, keep to the dosage, and the timing, or the smoke will do more than stupefy, it'll asphyxiate.'

Craig nods. 'Not too much. Got it!'

'We need to hurry,' says Mika, jerking her chin at the horizon. 'That cloud can't be more than ten minutes away.'

'Ten minutes?!' exclaims Craig, who's too low to the ground to see the Brotherhood coming for himself. 'Shit. Look, I'll try, but I wouldn't count on your smoke screen if I were you.'

'But the wood's there, the pit's ready to go,' says Stan.

'Yes, but how long do you think it'll take for the fire to get to—' He reads from Lionel's instructions. '... 2200°F and a clear orange-coloured flame? This is a big dose of chemical Lionel wants heated up here.'

Mika's heart sinks. Lionel's smoke screen isn't going to work. They'll be caught, her presence here condemning not just Bree and Huia, but perhaps the entire village. Resigned, she places her hand on *Torua*, seeking comfort in the aroha her whānau stored there for her.

Torua!

It's then that Mika remembers the aroha stored in the

waka. Quickly, she runs to the front of the vehicle and pops the bonnet. Then, ignoring the heat and the grease, she reaches in and yanks out a hunk of metal shaped like a heart.

'Mika, what are you doing? We need to go,' roars Stan.

'Coming!' Slamming the bonnet down with one hand, Mika thrusts it at Craig, who tosses the warm metal from one hand to the other.

'What am I supposed to do with this?'

'I'm not sure how it works, my people designed it, but I do know that once it's torn from *Torua*, it'll self-destruct.'

'What?! When?'

'It's an ancient power source, from the heart of my people. Hurry, you have the number of beats a human heart makes in a minute.'

'Shit!' Craig rolls for the fire pit.

Mika has almost reached Lionel and Stan when she hears the boom – the timbers bursting into flames, crackling and spitting like the fire goddess herself.

'How did you do that? Is that Atticus' invention?' Lionel asks, looking past Mika, his eyes wide like a toddler's.

'Can we possibly talk about the science later, Lionel?' says Stan pushing the older man towards *Torua*.

Mika sneaks a look over her shoulder. Already the fire is burning well, the flames beginning to turn from red to orange, and the first curl of grey smoke rising. But the Brotherhood is almost upon them. Wiping the grease on her pants, she scrambles up *Torua* after Lionel.

She isn't quite through the hatch when Stan calls back to Craig. 'The weed! The recreational stuff. Safest if you burn that, too.'

'Ah, not the weed,' Craig groans, as he pulls on his gloves.

CHAPTER EIGHT

'Is it always like this?'

Once the euphoria of eluding the Brotherhood waned, the trip to Las Vegas had taken longer than Mika expected. After relinquishing the piloting to Lisa, and the navigation to Lionel, the hours were full of their raised voices, the professors arguing at length over which roads to take, their decisions more often leading to dead ends than safe passage. Mika could sense their fear as they fought for safety in logic, their tortured experience still raw even years on. Yes, she's angry at them for manipulating her. But watching them struggle to do what's right after so many years of hiding makes her soften. It takes a brave person to do what scares you, even when it's the right thing to do.

'The lights? Yeah. It's always best to arrive at night,' Stan says, joining Mika to peer out the front window over the professors' shoulders. 'All the flaws are hidden by the pretty, pretty lights.'

Mika has to agree it's pretty. Las Vegas is putting on a show to impress: spotlights roaming the skies like giants' torches and the buildings flashing in blue and gold.

'I don't like it here, Mika. Can we go home?'

Home? But Bree doesn't have a home. Does she mean the reservation? Mika should have left the little girl there, where she felt safe. The closer they've come to the city, the more withdrawn Bree's become, sinking backwards into shadow.

'Don't worry, sweetie. I just need to see a man and then we'll go. I need his help.'

A sob – her own – catches Mika by surprise.

'Mika?'

Picking Bree up, Mika notes how much she's filled out in the past week. She sits down, the child nestled on her lap.

'It's my sister. Huia. I love her so much, but you see, she's sick – she has diabetes – and she's going to have a baby.' Stan looks up sharply, staring at Mika over Bree's head, his own face full of pain. Mika buries her face in Bree's hair.

'If I can't get help for Huia, she could die, and her baby too.'

'I can help you,' Bree whispers.

Suddenly, it dawns on Mika exactly what the girl is offering.

'Oh no. No!' Mika grips her harder. 'No, Bree. You're safe. Whatever happens, you'll never be used that way. I promise.'

'Is the man going to give your sister an organ?' Bree asks.

Mika shakes her head. 'No, sweetie. I'm going to give him my father's work and he's going to make some medicine to help my sister. To help a lot of people.'

'After that, can we can go home?'

'Yes, then we'll go home.' Mika cups Bree's face in her hand, letting the little girl see the tears in her eyes as she kisses her on both cheeks.

'Okay,' Mika says. 'Let's get this over with, shall we? Where *is* B-Cell?'

With a flourish, Lionel turns *Torua* towards the towering edifice of B-Cell Technologies, glowing like an emerald at the end of the promenade.

'They're the brightest show in town.'

The argument of who would stay with *Torua* in the underground parking lot, and who would go, was short lived. *Torua* could look after herself; everyone else felt safer together.

'I guess they've gone home for the day.' Lionel doesn't sound disappointed. They'd taken the elevator to the ground floor, expecting to have to sign in at reception, only to discover the lobby deserted.

'It's not that late. Someone's bound to be here. Let's try the top floor,' Mika suggests, tapping the top listing on the directory.

B-Cell Industries. CEO Selwyn Bruce.

'Eighteenth floor it is.' Stan presses the button and they watch the numbers count down. The doors open with a ping. Stan opens his arms to usher them inside. 'Everyone in.'

With mirrors on all sides, the elevator is crammed with echoes of themselves, all diminishing in size as they repeat into infinity.

'I don't like this,' Lisa mutters.

Mika doesn't blame her. The angles are creepy. Even Paddy is unhappy, squirming in Bree's grasp.

Mika tries to inject some cheer into the group. 'Come on everyone. There's nothing to be scared about. Remember, I was *invited*.' She smiles broadly. Stan turns his head, his cybernetic eye twitching, the strain on his face repeated endlessly in the glass. Lisa and Lionel shift uneasily. Clearly, no one has forgotten the attempt on Mika's life.

At last, the elevator stops, the doors reopening with a ping. No one moves to step out.

'Now, come on, you're all just being silly. Nothing is going to happen – it's a public place.'

'WHO DARES TO ENTER?' a hollow voice booms over the building's loudspeakers.

Startled, Mika jumps back, while Stan grabs Bree, pushing the child deeper into the safety of the elevator.

'My name is Mika Tāura. I'm here to see Mr Bruce,' Mika replies, poking her head out of the elevator. 'He's expecting me,' she adds hastily.

'GO AWAY. THERE IS NO MR BRUCE HERE.'

'Paddy, no!' Bree slips out of Stan's grip, pushing past Mika after the puppy, who is racing down the corridor, snarling and barking.

Mika leaps after her.

'GET OUT OF HERE. No. Ahh – stop it!'

At the end of the corridor, Mika tumbles through a half-open door into what must be the boardroom. With a large hollow feel, it smells of dust and decay, as if untouched for decades.

'Bree, where are you?' Mika hisses.

The voice, no longer on the loudspeaker, emerges from the gloom.

'That headset is an antique! Stupid mutt. Your owners are going to have to pay for it, and it won't be cheap.' Paddy must be in here somewhere. But where is Bree?

'I'm sorry, but you frightened him,' Mika calls into the darkness.

'Well, you people frightened me first!' the voice snaps. 'How did you get in here, anyway?' A creak to Mika's left is followed by sudden brilliance, the lighting blinding her for a moment.

'Oops, forgot how bright they were. Here, wait a second, I think the dimmer still works.' The speaker fumbles about a bit, after which the lights lower to a clear soft glow. There's Bree, under the boardroom table. No longer struggling to see, Bree scrabbles after her wayward pet, who thinks it's a game and scampers off.

Mika sizes up the speaker. There's nothing to be afraid of. Their host, obviously a big man once, looks lost in his oversized clothes. They hang off him, his pants only held up by the belt at his waist.

'We came up in the elevator. Mika here has an appointment with Mr Bruce,' says Stan, who's just arrived with Lisa and Lionel.

'What? Oh yes. I asked you how you got here, didn't I?'

'Mr Bruce?'

'No. There's no Selwyn Bruce here.' The man thumbs the collar of his suit jacket with both hands, thrusting out his sunken chest with long-lost authority.

'What kind of dirty trick are you up to?' Lionel shouts. 'Mika never even mentioned the name Selwyn. It doesn't matter. I'd know you anywhere, even if a hundred years were to pass.' He leaps forward, his fists up ready for battle. Luckily, he's prevented from delivering a blow by Stan, who grabs him from behind.

'Just stop it, Lionel. He's not a threat. He's an old man.' Lisa smacks her husband's fists open. '*You're* an old man. Stop being ridiculous.'

'Lionel? Lisa?' Selwyn stumbles backwards and lands heavily in an office chair, sending out puffs of dust.

'Now, hear this, Mister. I don't know what kind of game you're playing: sending someone to kill Mika. But she's here now. She's brought the blueprint you asked for – risked her skin to carry it across the world to you – so give her what she needs, and we'll leave.' Stan looms over the old man, cowering him further into his seat.

Selwyn Bruce shakes his head emphatically. 'But I never promised her anything. I don't want anything from her, and there's nothing to give. Look around.'

'It's true,' Lisa says. 'We searched in the offices, looking for you and Bree. The building's empty, the rooms disused and dusty. No one's been here for years.'

'Then why did he reply to our message? Why did he say to come? That he could help?' Dazed, Mika throws the questions out, hoping one of them will catch an answer.

'I never received any message,' Selwyn says, drawing

himself up. But then realisation creases his face. 'It must have been the Brotherhood. They keep the lights on here for me in exchange for pieces of old research. But it's been a while since I've had anything worth trading. They must have intercepted your message, figured you had something.'

'Vultures,' Lionel growls.

'They can use my father's research to create a cure?' Mika doesn't understand. The Brotherhood don't seem like scientists, or even the type of people scientists would work with.

'Is that what they promised you? It's a lie. Everyone's dead … the scientists … all their work … gone.' A sad old man, Selwyn looks as confused as the rest of them.

'So that's what you did with your secret keepers,' Lisa says softly.

'But what am I going to do?' Mika says, stricken. 'He can't help me. He can't help anyone.'

'Mika, that light over there is flashing.' Unnoticed, Bree has returned, Paddy in her arms, the shredded remains of a headpiece dangling from his jaw. She nods at the building opposite, which is made almost entirely of glass. Reflected in its panes, the static emerald lights of B-Cell's headquarters are flashing. 'It's a pattern: three long, three short, three long,' Bree says.

'A signal? What the hell have you done, old man?' Lionel reforms his fist, ready to deliver the pounding he promised earlier.

Selwyn steps back hastily, patting his pockets, and removes a small black device. He pokes frantically at the buttons until the lights stop flashing.

'I'm sorry, I didn't know who you were. Go now. Before they get here.'

'Let's go,' Stan says.

On the run again, and still no help for Huia.

'We have to take him with us,' Lionel says. 'We can't trust this weasel not to tell the Brotherhood about Mika's tattoos.'

'I won't. I swear. It's too late for me, anyway.' It's only then that Mika notices the sallowness of his skin. So, Selwyn has the disease too. She should rejoice at the karma, that the man who championed the epidemic is a sufferer himself, but she simply feels flat.

'You're sick. You need a kidney,' she states. She draws Bree close to her side. 'You really are a wicked man.'

'I wasn't always.' Selwyn Bruce holds his hands open, imploring her to believe that what he says is true. 'Our intent at B-Cell was always altruistic. We wanted to save lives …'

Lionel and Lisa glare at him.

'Save your marketing campaign for the dust mites,' Stan says, placing a hand on Mika's back. 'Let's go.'

'No, wait.' She steps closer to Selwyn, her nose crinkling at the stench of sickness that saturates his skin. 'You're still here. The Brotherhood haven't kicked you out yet. So, what exactly were you planning on trading next?'

Selwyn flushes red. 'Nothing.'

'What have you got?!' roars Lionel, stepping forward, enraged. 'Tell her now!'

Selwyn cringes. 'You're right, I kept something,' he blurts. 'Just in case. It's not much.'

'Give it to her,' Lionel says, his expression full of menace.

Selwyn's eyes dart about. 'It's just a scrap. Something Atticus said when he was pleading for us to allow him to continue his research.'

'What was it?' Mika asks, softly now, desperate to hear her father's words, even from this man's mouth.

'He said the answer was in the healthy gene.'

'That can't be all,' says Lisa.

'The rest never made sense. Something about family

protecting family. It was a long time ago.'

'Come on, he's got nothing.' Disgusted, Stan guides them away. They depart the way they came in, leaving Selwyn alone in his tower.

CHAPTER NINE

'Here, let me help you.'

Lisa eases Mika's grip from the steering wheel and pulls her out of her seat while Stan slides over and powers down *Torua*. The transport is tucked under a rocky outcrop in a deserted byway so, for the moment, they're safe from view.

'Take her downstairs, Lisa,' Stan says, his voice full of compassion. 'We'll be safe here for the night.' Lisa helps Mika put one foot in front of the other until they reach Mika's berth. She pulls off Mika's shoes and tucks her into her bed. Mika lets her do it. She's numb. Stunned. All this way and B-Cell has nothing to offer. Nothing! No answer to Huia's illness, no chance for her baby. How can Mika go home empty-handed after her whānau placed their trust in her?

Wracked with grief and disappointment, she trembles.

'You're cold,' Lisa concludes. She starts rummaging around the berth, opening and closing cupboards, looking for another blanket. 'Hang on, honey. I'll get you another cover.' Mika is too heartsore to object.

'Here's one,' says Bree, who's been hovering at the door. She holds out the tribal blanket, the gift offered to Mika that first night on the reservation. 'Mika likes this one. She says it reminds her of one that belonged to her father.'

'Thanks.' Lisa drapes the blanket over Mika, pulling it up to her neck when she exclaims: 'Wait!' She takes a step back, her eyes wide with shock. 'That sneaky bastard,' she breathes. 'Lionel. Come quick.'

'What is it?' Mika notices that Lionel doesn't come in. He's too much of a gentleman to enter a girl's room.

'We didn't copy it wrong. Don't you see? Look at the blanket.'

Wide awake now, something in Lisa's tone tells Mika that she mustn't move.

Lisa's eyes twinkle. She runs the back of her hand from Mika's shoulder to her neck, tracing the blue-black patterns tattooed on Mika's skin, then she picks up the edge of the blanket and shakes it gently at Lionel. 'Two codes, Lionel! Two. The proof is here: the first on Mika's body, in the coils and scrolls of her ancestry, and the second one hidden in the lines and angles of *our* tribal patterns.'

Slowly Lionel's grin spreads as Lisa's revelations hit home. 'You think Atticus meant for us to see this?'

'Perhaps. Maybe he just hoped it would be us, or someone like us.'

She shakes Mika's arm, but there's no need to wake her up to tell her the news. Already, Mika is sitting up and listening, her arms curled around her pillow, her anguish dropping away in a new surge of hope.

'You really think it'll work?' Lionel says, still not fully convinced.

'I'm sure it will. I think it's what Atticus meant about families protecting families. Like a mother confers immunity to her newborn while the infant develops its own defences, in the same way, Mika's own modified beta-cells implanted in just a few of her sister's islet cells, will *teach* Huia's other defective islets how to function correctly.'

'It's too simple. Islet cell transplants have been available for over sixty years. Why didn't Atticus carry it out the transplant on the girls himself?'

'Maybe it took him a while to test the theory. Or maybe he felt Mika was too young for the transplant – she was just a baby when the family fled the United States, and Mika says he died unexpectedly.'

'Perhaps Atticus was afraid of what B-Cell might do to his family if they knew he possessed the cure. Look at us, Lisa, we were afraid too, hiding out at the reservation for years.'

Mika nods. Lionel's suggestion sounds more like it. Her father would have weighed the risks and decided that in the short term, B-Cell was the greater risk. It was safer for one of his girls to suffer the disease than to risk losing them both. She hugs the pillow to her knees, hardly daring to believe it. With Lionel and Lisa's help she might be able to bring Huia the answers she needs.

Suddenly, *Torua* vibrates abruptly as Stan stomps on the floor, opening the mid-deck hatch.

'Stan, we've found Atticus' cure!' Lionel calls up through the gap.

'Yeah, that's great guys, but right now we've got a bit of a problem,' Stan replies. 'The Brotherhood are here.'

A dozen men wearing shinobi shozoko surround the transport when the group surrender. Miles from anywhere, there's no point running: these men are trained killers. As she jumps down onto the sand beside Stan, Mika wonders who the Brotherhood are. Had they been with B-Cell from the outset, driving the company strategy from the inside? Had the company's pit bulls turned on their masters? She'll probably never know.

Lionel hands Bree down to Mika, who sets her on the ground. One arm tight around her puppy, Bree slips her hand in Stan's.

'I don't suppose you have another one of those exploding hearts, do you?' Stan mutters to Mika under his breath as a Brother – the leader of this group – steps forward.

'You can't have her,' Lisa cries defiantly, jumping down from *Torua* and flinging her arms wide in front of Mika. 'I may not have stood up to your kind when you exiled Mika's father, but I won't let you take her.' She's so petite, Mika would smile were her knees not trembling so much. These men aren't like the jaded CEO in his tower: they're warriors, fighters, sent by their order to apprehend her, to kill her so as to obliterate the secret etched on her skin. Mika smiles inside, knowing even if she's lost, Huia has her own moko, and now that Lionel and Lisa have discovered the key …

'Her? We're not interested in her anymore,' the Brother says, sneering. 'We peeled off at the reservation and followed you to B-Cell. Just had a little chat with Selwyn, in fact. We already know you haven't succeeded in reversing the defective insulin, even with the tatts on the girl's skin.'

'Well, that's where you're—' Lionel starts, but Stan shakes his head, warning the professor to keep quiet.

'It's me you want, then, is it?' Stan says quietly.

'Well, it's true the Order isn't best pleased with you, Aspen. Skiving off with our money.'

Stan's jaw twitches. 'You have plenty.'

'Yes, we have. Which is why we're willing to forgive your little trespass, but in return you're going to have to do something for us.'

'Whatever it is, don't do it, Stan,' Lionel says, evenly, his eyes fixed on the ninja.

'Be quiet!' the Brother yells, his eyes flashing red. 'You'll do it all right. You're coming to the reservation with us and when we get there, you're going to tell us why our Brothers refuse to leave.'

'They refuse to leave?' Lionel says, parroting the words.

'We've sent messengers. Only one came back. He says they're happy, thanks, but they'd prefer to stay on the reservation. I don't have a clue what's going on up there, but whatever it is, you're going to help us smoke it out.'

Mika has to hide her smile behind her hand.

Torua idles, waiting on Mika to start them on their journey. It's time to go. Past time, really. Mika hadn't thought it would be so hard. With a quick glance back at her modified beta-cells, stored safely behind her in a cooler compartment designed by Craig, Mika takes a final look over the reservation, over the mish-mash of lean-tos and adobe homes, to the drifting of wisps of smoke that keep the Order at bay, wisps that streak the morning sky.

A good day for a journey.

Mika's friends have come to see her off: Lionel, Lisa, Craig – even Irina stands alongside the transport, her arm wrapped around Bree's shoulders. It breaks Mika's heart to leave Bree, but now Stan doesn't have to save the entire world, he thinks he can find time for one little girl. He and Irina have agreed to start over, and give Bree the family she needs.

Stan lifts his hand in farewell. Bree gives her a brave smile.

Time to go.

Squaring her shoulders, Mika punches in the coordinates for home – for Aotearoa, her whānau, and Huia. And now, with Lisa and Lionel's work unravelling her father's legacy, there's hope of a healthy niece or nephew. Perhaps in time they'll be able to eradicate the disease entirely.

Mika waves a last goodbye as the warm tones of Kuia's voice break the quiet.

'Calculating …'

POCKET WIFE
IK PATERSON-HARKNESS

I FELT BEHIND MY EAR, FOUND THE LITTLE SWITCH AND TURNED it on. Jenny hadn't activated my Tiny yet, but I figured I'd lie back and wait. It pays to sit still until it happens. I leaned back against the V-shaped pillow and stared at the light shade. I couldn't help toying with the switch, and poking at the outline of the plastic disc, which lay flat beneath my skin. I'd been worried they'd have to drill through bone but when I'd expressed my concern to the technician he'd laughed. 'The sensors are highly tuned,' he'd said. 'They pick it all up from outside the skull.'

The light shade was white, round, and smooth as a pickled onion. Seems everything's getting smoother and rounder. Gone are the good old days when you could retire to your hotel after a long day at work and sink into a decent, squishy sofa. These days you sit down and slide right off. I glanced at the fridge – thought about the Indian Pale I had in there, the condensation misting the cold glass, the sound of released pressure as I popped open the top.

I felt the usual added strain on my mind as Jenny switched on my Tiny, and immediately closed my eyes and tried to focus on whatever it was I was supposed to be looking at. The little bugger's eyes aren't the best; the cameras don't swivel properly. Ah, there we go. Jenny was holding my Tiny up in front of Nico.

'Say hello to Grandpa,' she said. The image rotated back and forth vigorously.

Nico gurgled something; it was hard to tell over the sound of whooshing air.

'It's your Grandpa!' Jenny squealed. 'Your Grandpa!'

'Stop waggling me around!' I called. I could hear my own voice coming from my Tiny's speakers – the same, but not quite.

'Sorry,' she said, and the room suddenly stabilised. A monstrous baby's hand reached towards my face and I braced against the hotel pillows.

'That's right,' Jenny cooed. 'He's far, far away.'

Nico slapped the highchair tray with his palms, and Jenny pushed me right up into his snotty face.

'Christ, that's enough,' I said, opening my eyes. The onion-shaped light shade was clearly visible through the now semi-opaque image of Nico. It looked like he had a third eye, right in the middle of his forehead. I stood up and inched towards the fridge, trying to concentrate on the hard lines of the hotel room. By the time I got back to the bed my head ached. I used a pillow to stifle the sound of the beer being opened, then lay back, closed my eyes again, and took a sip.

Jenny had propped my Tiny up on top of the kitchen bench back home, facing the sink, a chopping board, and a knife the length of a cricket pitch. Outside the window the sky was a deep blue. Sparrows and wax-eyes of pterodactyl proportions flew in and out of my vision. Jenny had bought the bird feeder a few years previously, had insisted I nail it to the fence. They made a hell of a mess, those birds, but

Jenny loved to watch them. I could just make out the sound of cicadas. But I was cold. Damned cold, actually, like I was lying on snow.

'Jenny, where on earth did you put my Tiny?' I called.

She came back into view, carrying a bag of potatoes.

'I've switched myself on,' she said.

'You've got to be joking.'

'I told Rach I'd prepare some meals for Nico, which she can take home.'

'Don't be stupid. You'll chop off one of your fingers. We don't need to both be on. And why am I freezing here?'

I had a brief glimpse of the ceiling before she repositioned my Tiny.

'Sorry. Frozen peas,' she said. I presumed she'd pressed her hand against my Tiny's back, since the cold became less.

'Turn me on, Carl. You know I like to see where you are. I feel disconnected …'

I grumbled as I leaned over to the bedside drawer and pulled out her Tiny. About four inches tall, the thing had been made in her exact likeness. The brown eyes stared blankly. I carefully gripped the tiny left ankle between thumb and forefinger, starting to make the twist, then remembered the beer and quickly placed it on the floor where it couldn't be spotted. I twisted the ankle and her Tiny's eyes swivelled to look at my face.

'You haven't shaved today,' Jenny said. Twice. The voice in my mind – heard by my Tiny on the other side of the world – and the voice coming from the speaker inside her Tiny's chest. Sometimes the voices were in sync.

Her Tiny began to feel warm, and I placed it on the pillow, facing me.

'I'll shave tomorrow.'

'You know it makes a difference.'

I had the usual dilemma. Did I close my eyes and watch what Jenny was doing back home, or did I keep them open and look at her Tiny? If I closed them, I'd have the relief of only one image to focus on, but her Tiny would be staring at my closed eyes, and Jenny didn't like that. Really the whole system was flawed.

'Rach is at a job interview.'

Her Tiny was looking at me so intently. The lips didn't move, but the voice came out all the same.

'What job?'

'At the high school down the road from where she lives. They want someone to look after the plants. It's a gardening job, really. It might involve a bit of heavy lifting, which I'm worried about, but it's only fifteen hours. She wants to start Nico at day care a couple of days per week. She says she needs to get out of the house. I told her I'd look after him, but she's dead set on day care.'

I became aware of a knocking noise and closed my eyes. Jenny was chopping the potatoes with her own eyes closed.

'She's not built for heavy lifting,' she continued. Her grey-auburn hair was tied in a loose plait, her cuffs rolled up. 'I told her she should do a course. She was so good at science when she was at school. She could do pharmacology, or study to be a radiologist.'

'A radiologist?'

'Sue's niece did some courses at university, and she's a radiologist now. Rach could do so much better than gardening.'

'Let her work it out for herself.'

I opened my eyes and the thing was still looking at me. It didn't smile. Didn't move at all – no muscles, I suppose. I never properly learned the science of it. All I knew was that there were sensors on my Tiny's body, and cameras in the eyes and what-have-you, and that somehow, through satellites I suppose, the information was sent to my brain. When Jenny touched my Tiny it was like being poked through a thick blanket. The newer models can smell, and have a better sense of physical touch – or so the pop-ups claim. It's probably only a matter of time before they're walking around, creating havoc of their own.

The Tinys arrived from the manufacturers in their boxes, naked. We hadn't expected that. There's nothing more sobering that seeing your silver pubic hairs copied in minute detail. Jenny immediately took to dressing them like little dolls. You can buy accessories from the company page. Last November she dressed my Tiny in a Halloween costume and surprised me by holding it up in front of the mirror. There I was, dressed like an English schoolboy, and there was nothing much I could do about it.

'Jenny love,' I cut in. She was still complaining about Rachel. 'I'm meeting Michel soon – the Chief Financial Officer. He wants me to go over some figures with him.'

'So late?'

'He's a very busy man. I should shower.'

'Okay ...' She sighed, the noise at my end coming out like static. 'Make sure you shave. And dress warmly, dear. You don't want to catch another cold.'

'I will. See you the same time tomorrow.' I switched off the switch behind my ear and reached for her Tiny. I rubbed its back with my finger. I knew Jenny would still be in there, would be switched on right to the last second, but I couldn't speak to the thing. As soon as I'd twisted its ankle I chucked it back in the drawer, and slammed the drawer shut.

✖

I pulled my jacket collar up against the wind. People all around me hurried from one shop awning to the next, their umbrellas held out like shields, scarves flapping. The cafe terraces were deserted, the tables and chairs packed away inside the steamy restaurant interiors. Several shops were still open, music blaring, their brightness floating on the wet street. An electronics store I passed had four drift screens all playing different music at once. One of the screens followed me halfway down the block before the boy in the shop called it back. Even while at work the boy had his e-vice turned on, its holographic screen and board shimmering in the rain. I'm damned if I know how kids walk around without bumping into each other, they're always staring into their vices. Rach changed the settings on mine once, fiddled with the opacity, but then I could hardly see what was on the screen. I sometimes think I preferred that old plastic clunky thing we used to hold to our ear. You could look like crap, be half naked in bed, and you wouldn't offend anyone by not turning on your visuals.

I turned right down Rue McGill and into Old Montreal. The spring rain had washed most of the snow away, but there was still the odd slushy brown pile slumped up against a shady corner. After two wrong turns I finally found myself on the narrow cobbled lane with the wooden sign hanging beneath the street lamp.

Madame Bellarina's, written in burgundy cursive. The black door and brick wall were featureless and scrubbed clean of moss or ivy. I turned the brass knob and wiped my feet on the door mat before pushing through into the interior.

A short hallway led to the brightly lit foyer. Ornately framed mirrors lined the walls, reflecting the central chandelier. Two young women reclining on a plush red chaise longue stopped mid-conversation and turned to me, smiling.

'Bonsoir cher monsieur et bienvenue chez Madame Bellarina,' one of them said, sidling up and taking my hand in hers. Her long, dark fringe rested just above her eyes. 'Puis-je vous débarrasser de votre manteau?'

'I speak English,' I said.

'My apologies,' she said, revealing a large a gap between her teeth as she smiled. 'Welcome to Madame Bellarina's. May I take your coat? It is cold outside, but in here you will soon warm.'

She helped me shrug off my coat while the other woman positioned herself full length on the chaise longue, propped up on one elbow, watching me. She was blonde, probably naturally so, her hair falling as ringlets on her shoulders.

'I'm here to see Madame Bellarina,' I said.

'Do you have an appointment?' the first woman asked, hanging my coat on the stand. 'Madame Bellarina is most often occupied. Would you like a drink? I am certain either Anna or I can make you perfectly comfortable.'

'Please tell Madame Bellarina that Carl is here to see her. I don't have an appointment, but she'll see me.'

The woman slipped out through the door that led to the rest of the establishment, leaving me alone with the blonde. She didn't sit up but patted the space on the seat in front of her body.

'I'm good. Thanks.'

'Your accent is cute,' she said. She sounded Eastern European, and I wondered briefly if she was related to Madame Bellarina. 'I have not seen you here before.'

'I don't come often.'

'You like drink? I pour you something.'

'I'm fine. Thank you.' I shoved my thumbs into my trouser pockets and rocked on my heels. There was nothing to look at, except for mirrors.

The gap-toothed woman reappeared. 'Madame Bellarina will see you. Please follow me.'

'It's okay. I know the way.'

The passageway was dim, lit with low wattage red bulbs – as, I knew, were the adjoining rooms. Thick, velvet drapes covered each of the doors, making the passageway feel narrower than it actually was. I had always wondered about those drapes, about their exact purpose, but had never had the nerve to ask. Madame Bellarina never talked about work. At the end of the hall was a slender spiral staircase, and at the top, Madame Bellarina's private quarters. I hesitated halfway up the stairs, my hands sweating.

She opened the door before I had a chance to knock. A fire flickered in the grate and I walked straight towards it, reaching my hands out as if to warm them. I found it hard to look at her. I always did when I first arrived. I felt her move past me, towards the liquor cabinet. She smelled like cinnamon and orange with a hint of sandalwood. I heard the cabinet door open, and close. The sound of liquid filling glass. I jumped as she placed her hand on my shoulder, her fingers brushing my neck.

'It has been a while, no?' she asked, passing me the glass of port.

'Yes.' My voice was husky, and I cleared it, and took a sip. I stared down at the contents of the glass. 'I've mostly been in Asia this year. China. And India.'

'I have missed you.'

With her heels on she was as tall as me, but she took them off, one by one, and I watched her toes wriggle in the thick fur rug. Her nails were painted red, her toes slender and perfect. She grabbed my chin, and raised my eyes to her face.

'What does India have that you cannot find here?' Her thick black hair was pulled back, piled high upon her head, her dark eyes thickly outlined. She had told me once that during the Second World War her pregnant grandmother had jumped on a boat that took her unborn mother all the way across the Black Sea, to an isolated township in Russia. And on that same night she told me that her mother only lived to the young age of 18. I remember lying there, doing the maths, realising that despite all visible evidence Madame Bellarina must be at least seventy years old.

'I don't know,' I muttered.

She knelt, and began undoing my shoelaces. The fire was becoming unbearably hot, and I loosened my tie with my free hand. I stood awkwardly on one leg, then the other, as she removed each of my shoes. As she straightened up I noticed that she was wearing the diamond earrings I had bought her. But the diamond necklace – that wasn't from me.

I touched it. She brushed my hand away.

'Do you have many suitors?' I asked, feeling myself blush.

She leaned in, on tiptoes, and kissed me on the nose. 'Yes,' she whispered, taking my glass of port and placing it on the mantelpiece. 'But you, Carl, are my favourite.'

✖

Jenny smelled of soap and washing powder. Before it started going grey her hair was the colour of Old English Breakfast, brewing in the pot. She'd grow it long, then cut it short, never entirely satisfied with it. Her eyes slanted down at the edges, giving her a melancholy look. I used to think that she was lovely. We met at a book fair, in Oamaru of all places. I was down for my grandfather's funeral and she was helping her sister with a newborn baby. My nephew-to-be. She came out of the public bathroom with a piece of toilet paper stuck to her shoe, and I mentioned it to her. That was how it started. Both glad to get away from our families, we walked up and down Oamaru's long main street about five times, past the fish and chip shops and the second-hand stores, the families buying cream-filled lamingtons on a Saturday afternoon. When I finally built up the courage to ask her back to my motel her cheeks flushed a deep pink. She told me she had to get back to her sister.

Back in Auckland, a month or so later, I tracked her down online and asked her out. She was doing a kite-making course in the evenings, and we took one of her colourful beasts up Mt Eden. It flew five seconds at most, then promptly crashed into a tree. Watching Jenny back at her kitchen table amidst pottles of glue and paint, the paintbrush held between her teeth as she readjusted the dragon's goggling eyes, I fell in love with her. Like a painful blow to my chest.

Those memories have been coming back to me recently. The ones from before Rachel was born, before we bought the first house, before we had a mortgage. Before my work took me away. Back when Jenny was slim, beautiful and red-haired, and I truly believed I'd never love another woman.

Jenny was never elegant. Never breathtaking, enigmatic, or even carefree. She didn't wear perfume. The one time I tried buying her something with diamonds on it, she donated it to the Salvation Army; she obviously had no idea how much it cost. She liked to buy plain terracotta flower pots, and painted them in bright stripes. She made a terrific pavlova. In the months leading up to Nico's birth she knitted enough hats and booties to keep a nursery of little kiddies warm. And she always made a point of meeting me at the airport when I returned home. No matter what the time. Even when things weren't good between us.

They say that when you lose someone you love you lose a part of yourself. Personally I think that's sentimental bullshit. Jenny and I weren't Siamese twins; we weren't connected by the arm or hip; we didn't share a psychic bond. If anything, I've gained something these past two years she's been gone. A new piece to me that's lodged firmly inside, which I can't pick loose. Next to all those memories. It's a pointy-edged chip of guilt. Relentless, painful guilt.

×

It was dark outside, some early hour just before sunrise. Maybe after. It was hard to tell since the sky was full of clouds. I stood on Madame Bellarina's private balcony, sipping slowly from the tall glass of water I'd poured myself from the crystal jug she keeps beside her bed. I felt like shit. In the alleyway below, a man on a forklift shifted crates into the back of the small grocery store. I could see his breath. My coat was still down in the lobby, but I had one of Madame Bellarina's thick, woollen shawls wrapped around my shoulders. Cinnamon and sandalwood.

I eased myself into one of Madame Bellarina's ornate iron chairs, put the glass on the table so I could better massage my throbbing temples. This was the kind of moment when I wished I'd never given up smoking. Jenny had always believed it was her badgering that had finally done it, and would savour her victory by pointing out smokers and commenting on how dirty their habit looked, expecting me to agree. In all actuality it was because they'd made it so damn hard for us. You can't smoke in parks. You can't smoke on the street. You can't smoke within five metres of a child without a street cam picking it up. My hasty, self-conscious puff was interrupted too many times by my vice informing me of my instant fine, and so I eventually gave it up.

I was in trouble. Not catastrophically so, but still it was trouble. I had promised her a car. Last night. In the quiet before we slept, as I held her against my side and smelled her cinnamon hair and thought about the man who had given her the diamond necklace, I'd asked Madame Bellarina if there was anything I could get for her. Buy for her. She had rolled over and kissed my neck, and told me she needed a new car. But she'd been more specific than that. She'd had the exact car in mind, told me the exact street corner to meet her on during my lunch break.

I squeezed the bridge of my nose, screwing my eyes up tight. She knew my first name. She knew I worked for an international finance consultancy firm. She knew I had a wife and a grown daughter, and that I was from New Zealand. She knew I had money enough to buy her diamond earrings. I'd been careful to never tell her a lot about myself, but I bet it was more than I knew about her. Bellarina probably wasn't even her name.

I'd catch a taxi back to the hotel, I decided, sleep a few hours, try to freshen up. I could make it into the office by 9.00 if I skipped breakfast and drank coffee instead. There was a fire escape leading down to the street from Madame Bellarina's balcony. I'd freeze my nuts off looking for a taxi without my coat, but at least I wouldn't have to stumble through the maze that was Madame Bellarina's brothel in the dark. It was all doable. Everything was going to be all right. I would shuffle the accounts in some way. I'd hidden large expenditures before.

As I slipped back through the heavy velvet curtain into Madame Bellarina's room and searched for my tie beneath her cream negligee, I wondered if it was okay to kiss a sleeping woman if she wasn't your wife.

✖

The lights turned on automatically when I entered my hotel room, and I immediately dimmed them. My throat felt as dry as a cardboard tube. In the bathroom I inspected myself in the mirror. Oh hell. I looked like a grey, wrinkly old fuck. I splashed some water at myself, but it didn't much help.

As soon as I collapsed onto the bed and kicked off my shoes I heard her. Screaming. I could hear Jenny's Tiny screaming from my bedside drawer.

I tugged the drawer open and pulled it out. It was warm in my hand.

'Carl!' Jenny's voice shrieked at me. 'Where have you been? I've been calling and calling for hours!'

I could hear her sobbing, the sound breaking up and crackling through the speakers; her Tiny's face appeared as emotionless as usual. 'I've been stuck, trapped in your drawer! Where have you been?'

'I've been working all night, I just got back,' I lied. 'But what's going on, Jenny? I switched you off after we last spoke. Why are you still turned on?' It was then that I noticed her Tiny's left leg was mangled, misshapen.

'You switched me off, but you switched me straight back on again! You jammed me in your drawer, Carl, and twisted the ankle. I think you broke the leg! My leg feels all tight, like there's something tied around it. I can't make the feeling go away. And I can't turn myself off! I push my switch and nothing happens! I'm going crazy here. I couldn't look after Nico properly, Rachel had to come and pick him up. I've got a terrible headache, I feel nauseous, I feel so sick. It's been horribly dark, darkness covering everything. And why did you even put my Tiny in your drawer?' Her voice rose several pitches. 'I leave your Tiny out where I can see him at all times! I even take him in the car with me!' Her voice broke and I heard more staticky sobbing.

I turned the Tiny over in my hands, trying to see if I could straighten the leg. It was well and truly broken. The ankle flopped from side to side uselessly.

'It's 6.30am over there!' Jenny cried.

I realised I'd turned her Tiny to face my bedroom clock, and swore under my breath.

'Were you …' I heard her choke. 'Were you *drinking* again, Carl?'

I stared into her Tiny's brown eyes, and a small cement brick settled in my gut.

'Michel had a bottle of Max Walker,' I said.

'Carl, how *could* you?'

'I thought one wouldn't hurt. But one became two, became three … I'm sorry, Jenny.'

She said nothing. I couldn't even hear sniffling.

'Jenny, love?'

Her voice was icy underneath the sound of her blocked nose. 'I am not happy about this. You've let me down more than you can know. I needed you tonight. You weren't there.'

✖

Jenny had already contacted the Tiny product representatives, had spent most of her evening on her vice being transferred from this person to that, but I gave them a try anyway. No one could be of any help. Until then they'd believed it impossible for someone to become locked to their Tiny. All it takes to end the connection is for one side to be turned off – by twisting the Tiny's ankle, or by switching the ear switch off at source. Although it seemed plausible that the Tiny might get stuck in an 'on' position, no one could explain why Jenny's ear switch wasn't working. The unhelpful woman on the holo-screen advised me to send Jenny's Tiny to them in the post, so that they could forward it on to be repaired.

'Not happening,' Jenny objected. 'I'm not having half my consciousness trapped inside a courier box. The Tinys are manufactured in Sweden. It could take days, and it would be freezing inside the cargo hold of a plane. There's no way we're doing that.'

'Then I'll cut it open and crush the battery inside.'

'But that will render the lifetime warranty void,' Jenny told me. 'I'd already asked them that.'

'But isn't it the best option?'

There was a knock at the door. Room service had come with the wake-up coffee I'd ordered, meaning it was 8.30 already. I walked out into the hallway and made a quick call to Michel, apologising that I'd be in a little later than usual. He'd cleared his entire schedule for the week I was in the city, and I knew he came in to the office early, so I hoped he wouldn't be too annoyed. Halfway through the call a message popped up on the bottom left hand side of the holo-screen, from an unknown number. 'I enjoyed your company last night', it read. 'See you at half 12. MB.' I stared at it for a few seconds, stunned that she knew my number, stunned that she'd messaged me, and then realised with a shock that I'd left my business cards in the inner pocket of my coat. Now she knew as much as she needed to. Michel was looking at me as if he expected an answer to something he'd said. I apologised again and told him I'd be as quick as I could.

'I'm going to have to go to work soon, love,' I said, returning to the Tiny's side. I picked it up and carefully removed its shirt from its miniature limbs, pulling the shirt over its head. I never usually undressed it, at least not when Jenny was switched on inside of it. The breasts were too familiar. The mole on her shoulder. The scar from the Caesarian. It didn't seem right. I prodded at the chest and stomach.

'What are you doing?' Jenny coughed. 'Stop it!'

'I'm looking for the battery.'

'No, Carl, don't. Please don't. They cost us a fortune, remember?'

I remembered, all right. Remembered standing in the lab with the green walls, and the green lino floor, being scanned from top to bottom by lab technicians in green lab coats. They were all young, glossy, shipped over from Australia and working out of a private hospital in Remuera. I was naked, standing dead still while glancing down at my grey chest hairs and shrivelled cock. Why did Jenny want to duplicate this old fart? A girl drew purple lines on my skin. She kept huffing on her wrist watch before pressing her hands against me. It took hours.

Those little dolls cost me more than a year of my annual salary. Jenny had insisted that we get them, had implied that our marriage was in jeopardy. It had seemed such a frivolous waste, an extravagant novelty, even though I'd never known Jenny to be extravagant or to frivolously waste anything. She even used the same teabags more than once to save money.

I got the money back, of course. And much more. The large settlement I received from the Tiny Corp once all this business ended will be enough to take care of Jenny for the rest of her life. I'm sure that more than a few of the Tiny hardware developers were fired over the incident; they could never explain what went wrong. I realised though, later, that I'd lied in court when I'd told them that Jenny's switch had worked perfectly up until that one time when it didn't. Because, in actual fact, we'd never tested it. I always turned her Tiny off first. I could never end the conversation fast enough.

'Look, either I cut this open and smash the battery, or I

post it to Sweden, right?' I wanted to get to work. I wanted to think about the Madame Bellarina situation. I wanted to drink my coffee.

'You could take it to Sweden,' Jenny said quietly.

'Jesus Christ, Jenny, are you serious?'

'It's much cheaper than getting a new Tiny. And you'd be with me on the plane. I wouldn't be alone.'

'I've got to get to work. We'll talk about it when I get back this afternoon.'

'What? You can't just leave me here. I'm feeling utterly wretched.'

'I know, love. But what do you expect me to do about it?'

Jenny started to vomit loudly.

✖

The office they'd allocated me for my visit was on the 92nd floor, but I realised I was very close to being unpardonably late so asked the elevator to take me straight to the top.

'Express,' I added.

'Mot de passe est requis; password is required,' the female elevator voice declared softly.

'Oh damn, what was it now?' I patted my trouser pockets out of habit, as if a password might be sitting at the bottom of one. The old-style black and white analogue clock hanging in the foyer showed the time as 9.27. 'Oh Christ, just take me up. No, no! I know, it's 7. 2. 2. 3.'

The doors closed, and I felt the sudden upward movement in my stomach and knees. Once beyond the first few floors the exterior fell away, and through the floor-to-ceiling elevator window I watched the ground dropping swiftly from my feet as the panoramic view of Fleuve Saint-Laurent widened.

Montreal transforms during springtime from dirty grey

to vibrant green. The snow recedes, revealing a hidden treasure trove of trash and frozen dog shit, and the leaves unfurl. When I was in my early forties I spent a stint there during winter. It was bloody cold – cold enough for my eyeballs to freeze on the outside, causing me to stumble around the salty streets in a steamy blur, but giving me plenty of excuses to drink the mulled wine that the pub around the corner from my hotel made in huge quantities. I'd drink the wine while watching people circle the park outside, teenagers holding hands, expert skaters. At the time, Jenny was having trouble with Rach, who was going through that 'emo' stage that was all the rage with the teenagers back then. Cropped black hair, grimy thumb-holes in her sleeves, all that. Jenny would call me, tearfully re-enacting their latest row in detail. There was nothing I could do about it.

Nearing the top floor, I opened my suit jacket just enough to see Jenny's Tiny resting in the inner pocket.

'I want out of here,' she said. She must have perceived the change in light.

'I've told you,' I sighed. 'You can't come out. What happens up here is confidential, between myself and the Chief Financial Officer. It's not exactly the kind of thing I can bring my wife along to. Now be quiet. Once I've said g'day to him I'll tell him I need to go get my papers, and I'll leave you in my office.'

The elevator door opened. The receptionist, Paulette or Pauline or some name like that, threw off her headpiece when she saw me, and sprang from her seat. She immediately hurried me down the corridor and, to my dismay, led me past Michel's office to the main boardroom. As she knocked politely on the door I racked my brain, trying to figure out what Michel had told me on the phone that morning. Michel opened the door, looking more than a little peeved.

'I'm very sorry I'm late,' I said. 'There's been a bit of an emergency.'

Behind Michel twelve people sat around the long mahogany table. Their expressions were the familiar practiced neutral, except for the woman sitting nearest to the door, who turned around and smiled maliciously.

'An emergency?' Michel stepped aside to let me in. 'I hope not serious.'

The table was set with water jugs and tall glasses; each of the twelve people had a holo portfolio hovering in front of them. I now noticed the tall blonde woman sitting at the far head of the table, and instantly recognised her as Jane Frank, their CEO. She was notorious for leaving her New York office and dropping in unannounced. It was said that wherever she went, at least one person was fired. I reached up and covered the bulge in my jacket. 'Michel, can I please speak to you privately?'

Michel closed the door behind us. Like me he was in his sixties, but with a full head of brown hair. No doubt taking stimulators. He tried to look concerned. 'What is the problem?'

I hesitated, then pulled out Jenny's Tiny. Being caught at this meeting with my wife in my pocket would not only have destroyed the relationship I'd built with this company, and all those who rubbed sticky shoulders beneath the same wide umbrella, but it would also have meant an early retirement for me. With no golden handshake. Michel looked at the Tiny, confused for a few seconds, then his eyes widened.

'So you're the man who kept my husband out all night?' Jenny's voice punctured the silence.

'This is my wife, Jenny,' I said, quickly. I could feel my face growing hot and red. I'd never admitted to any of my colleagues that my wife and I had Tinys. Although they were marketed towards married couples they had the reputation of being the next step up from phone sex. And Jenny's Tiny, with its simple chequered shirt and grey-auburn hair, looked like the doll you'd keep in the doll house's laundry. The cleaning lady. With a mop and bucket. 'She's trapped in her Tiny,' I said, trying to sound like this was a normal, common incident, like chipping your tooth or rupturing your Achilles tendon. 'The ankle is broken, see? For whatever reason, she can't turn herself off. It's quite a mystery. She didn't want to be left alone when I went to work. She's feeling pretty terrible.'

Michel, eyes still wide, shook his head vehemently, unable to speak. 'Then leave *it* with the receptionist,' he finally exploded. 'Or somewhere else! I'm shocked. I don't know what to say.' He shook his head again, and blinked several times. 'I'm astonished by your inability to realise how important this meeting is. We have waited over thirty minutes. If my wife is sick I do not bring her to work with me!'

'Okay, okay.' I clapped him on the shoulder. 'You're right. I'm sorry. This is an unusual situation and I haven't dealt with it very well.'

'If you hadn't kept Carl up all night we might have dealt with it sooner,' Jenny's Tiny said coldly. 'He shouldn't even be drinking, you know. He's a diabetic.'

Michel shot me a glance, and opened the door. I closed my eyes, inwardly thanking his good Quebecois heart for abiding by that unspoken code that keeps travelling professionals all over the world out of the deepest trouble with their spouses. But then Michel changed his mind and turned back.

'I was not drinking with your husband last night,' he said. 'I was at my wife's mother's house until nine, at which point I heard wind of our visitor today and went home to prepare for today's meeting.' He very nearly slammed the door as he went back inside, leaving me clutching Jenny's Tiny, which didn't say another word.

✖

When the meeting had finished, and Jane Frank had left for lunch without firing anyone yet, Michel shook my hand. He laughed and slapped me on the back. I was in deep shit. He knew it, I knew it.

I trooped down the corridor towards reception, full of dread, half hoping that after an entire night awake back in New Zealand Jenny had succumbed to exhaustion and was now fast asleep. But no luck there. Paulette-Pauline had propped Jenny's Tiny up on a chair against the window, facing the full light of the midday sun and a ninety-eight-storey drop through clear glass.

'She never said one word,' Paulette-Pauline said, picking up Jenny's Tiny in a familiar way and stroking its head. 'She's so amazingly life-like. So soft.'

I took the Tiny from her swiftly, and put it in my jacket's inner pocket.

'I've seen them in the pop-ups, but didn't think I'd ever touch one,' Paulette-Pauline continued, staring at my chest. 'They're for beautiful movie stars. The famous and the rich. You're both so lucky!'

As the elevator took me back down to ground level I checked my vice. I had two missed calls from Madame Bellarina's number.

✖

'I just didn't want you to know I was drinking by myself.'

I'd caught a taxi back to the hotel. Jenny's Tiny was lying on my pillow, its eyes fixed on the onion-shaped light bulb on the ceiling.

'I've been drinking a bit lately. God, more than just a bit. I don't know what's happened. It's because I'm away too much. I'm finding things difficult at the moment. Jenny, please forgive me. I'm just a lonely old bugger with a drinking problem.'

'Last night, did you *think* you were meeting Michel?' Jenny's voice was emotionless as her Tiny's face.

I hesitated. 'No … I told you I was meeting him, because … well, because otherwise you'd have found out I was just going off to sit in a bar alone. Watching ice hockey on their drift screens, drinking till the cleaners came along and they booted me out.'

'So you lied to me.'

'No, I—'

'Admit it, Carl. You talked to me for only five minutes then lied to me so you could go out drinking. Only five minutes of your time, that's all I'm worth to you. I'm at home, working, keeping the house tidy, looking after our grandson, worrying about our daughter, trying to keep a brave face while my husband is away for months at a time, but you think it's acceptable to flip me off after five minutes because you feel like a beer.'

I hung my head, though her Tiny still wasn't looking at me. 'I'm sorry. I don't know what's going on with me. I need to come home where you can keep an eye on me.'

She made a doubtful snorting noise.

I felt my vice vibrating in my pocket, informing me of an incoming call.

'Jenny. Love. I know I've screwed up here, big time. I want to try and make it up to you. It's our anniversary next week. Forty years, did you remember?'

Silence.

'Well, I've been meaning to buy you something special. I

didn't want to tell you, I wanted it to be a surprise.' The vice started vibrating again. 'But I'd like to go get it for you, now, so I can bring it back to show you. We could both do with some time to breathe and cool down. Please, it will mean a lot to me. It must be, what, 7am back home? You need sleep. I'll lie your Tiny down in my bed, nice and warm, and cover its eyes with something. You'll feel much better after a rest.'

'I'd feel much better if I could trust my husband.' The Tiny's glassy eyes swivelled madly until they finally found me. 'If I could trust him not to lie to me, not to flip me off so he could go watch fucking ice hockey at some fucking bar! If that was even what you were doing.'

'I'm sorry! But you must agree you could do with the rest …'

'Oh no you don't, Carl. You're not leaving me again for some other stranger to pick me up and fondle me. You're not leaving my sight unless you want this marriage to end right this minute.' I heard her wheezing through the Tiny's speakers – she sounded like she was in pain, or maybe she was crying. 'And book a flight to Sweden! You owe me that if nothing else.'

'Shh, okay, okay.' I reached over and patted the Tiny's head. If it had been the real Jenny sitting there she would have recoiled. 'We'll go to Sweden.'

I turned away so that my back faced her, and switched my vice to active. I opened the holo-board only, hoping that from her angle Jenny wouldn't notice the shimmer. I sent a hasty message to Madame Bellarina, telling her that I still intended to meet her, I just wasn't sure when.

✖

There's something strange that happens inside your conscience when you cheat on your partner. You take the bit of the lie that's true and focus on that until all the rest of the story seems inconsequential, just superfluous detail. You admit to yourself some lesser crime, something you know you shouldn't have done, and then you wallow in the shame of it. You roll around in that shame until you're covered in it. And only when you're covered, dripping, and stinking with the smell of it do you feel justified, like you've somehow paid your dues. And then you move on.

The real crime, the big, fat, ugly, thorny fact of my infidelity, I easily ignored. It was too massive and dark to see while I was shining a torch with practiced precision on the petty detail in the foreground. I drank. See, that was the problem. That was always the problem. Because, I reasoned with myself, if I didn't drink none of the rest of it would ever happen.

Jenny caught me only once. It nearly ruined us, and I made a pact with myself afterwards to never again have an affair with a woman inside New Zealand. At the time I'd recently secured a senior position in a new Wellington-based firm. I was only thirty-five and my salary had suddenly doubled. I commuted, while Jenny stayed in Auckland with Rach, and tried to sell the house.

I was out after work with my new colleagues. One of their sisters was an artist, and it was her exhibition opening that night. We were all dragged along. The art was average, but the booze was free. That's the good thing about art exhibitions: they never fully disappoint. I'd been there an hour and had had just about enough of staring at pastel-coloured squares on sand-textured backdrops when a woman in emerald stockings and knee-high scarlet boots walked through the door. Her blonde hair was pulled up into a beehive, and her leopard-print blouse was pulled tight above her black mini-skirt. Needless to say, I stayed longer and downed at least another three free wines. Her kitchen floor tiles dug deep grooves into my buttocks that night.

Her name was Jasmine. She was interesting, charismatic, and sexy as hell. She ran a bed and breakfast in Roseneath, overlooking Oriental Bay. She'd eat her toast and morning coffee naked on her porch. I saw her too many times. After a year she called Jenny.

I think if Rach had been just a few years older Jenny would have left me. Instead she dragged my great-grandmother's antique hope chest into the middle of our lawn and built a fire inside it. She was good with fires, and it was winter at the time. She screwed up the balls of newspaper and packed them tightly inside, then took our hatchet and chopped a small stack of kindling. After she'd lit the paper, she waited calmly for the fire to grow hot before she added the firewood. Rach had run up into her room, and peered like a ghost from her window. My shirts, ties, books, childhood paintings, chessboards, tennis racket, bicycle helmet, wallet, favourite mug, every belonging I seemed to own, were one by one sacrificed to the flames. Jenny had drilled holes through the denser objects to make sure they burned. I just watched. I knew by then that Jenny wasn't going to leave me, realised that this was my punishment, so I felt miserable – yet relaxed. For probably two whole years after that Jenny wouldn't let me touch her.

Six years later, Rach read the wrong email and blackmailed me. She was sixteen. I bought her a second-hand Honda, and then two months later paid for a weekend holiday to Sydney for her and her best friend. I told her that if she brought it up a third time her inheritance would go to Oxfam. Jenny, unaware of the deal that had been struck, was furious. She told me that I was just encouraging Rach's difficult behaviour by spoiling her.

✱

'No, I don't want your postal address!' I snapped. I could feel my blood pressure rising. For all the tens of thousands of dollars I'd spent on those damn Tinys, you'd have thought they could have spent some of it training their call centre staff. I took a deep breath. 'I am coming *myself*, delivering it to you *by hand*. And I need it fixed immediately. Whatever the cost.'

'If you are local, sir, then I'll be pleased to order a courier—'

'No, I am not local! Jesus Christ, don't you people keep a record of your calls? My name is Carl Edmond. Both my wife and I have called you numerous times within the last 24 hours. My wife's Tiny has malfunctioned. She is trapped inside the stupid thing and is severely distressed. Now please, tell me where I can take her Tiny to be repaired. I will be arriving first thing tomorrow morning, and will be leaving by late afternoon.'

Eventually, when a physical address had been sent through to my vice, I called Michel. He wasn't overly impressed by my timing, but didn't make an issue of it. To my relief, Jenny perked up a bit. She told me she'd made herself a cup of green tea and she was lying in our bed back home with the curtains drawn. It was another beautiful early autumn morning. She could hear the school kids walking to school. The mail lady had just dropped letters through the door. I asked her again if she'd like me to cover her Tiny's eyes, but she told me she wouldn't like the heaviness on her face. It would be suffocating.

I was slowly stroking her Tiny's little forehead and speaking to her softly about the baby squirrels I'd seen hopping through the trees on Mont Royal, when the hotel phone rang.

'Just a moment, love,' I told her, and tapped it to my vice, opening the holo-screen. The hotel receptionist's well-shaven face appeared.

'Mr Edmond, you have a call. Will you take it now?'

'Sure,' I answered, believing it must be someone from the Auckland office. I searched inside my pocket for my headphones.

The screen disappeared, which surprised me. Most people consider it rude to turn off your visuals.

'Hello, Carl.'

Madame Bellarina's voice poured into the room like mercury. I jumped from the bed like I'd been bitten, yanked my headphones from my pocket and slammed them into the side of my vice. Shit, holy hell. Heart thundering, I strode to the bathroom and closed the door.

'You can't call me here!' I hissed. 'I've told you I'll meet you later. Tomorrow – no, the next day, it'll have to be. There's been an emergency back home, quite serious. Look, I've really got to go.'

'My girls have been very busy today,' she said. 'They called every hotel in town until they found you.'

'I'll make it up to you, I promise. Just not right now.'

'You missed our date.'

'Look, I'm sorry,' I whispered. 'But I've had one hell of a day. And now I have to fly to Sweden tomorrow morning, because my wife is sick—'

'Mr Carl Edmond, CA BCom (Hon),' she cut me off. 'I am not a prostitute. If I was, I would charge you for your visits. For your *many* visits, all of which I have welcomed. I have good friends who will be very unhappy to hear of a man who came uninvited to my home, used me, then skulked away like a thief without saying goodbye. My good friends have good friends all over the world.'

'What? You know it's not like that! I … I care for you, Madame Bellarina. I didn't use you.' I felt out of breath. The bathroom light was too bright. It didn't make sense; I'd always left Madame Bellarina before she awoke. I'd never wanted to impose on her, never wanted the awkward breakfast conversations.

'I'm going to buy you that car,' I said. 'I was always going to. Look, I'll leave right now! I'll meet you at the car yard in thirty minutes.'

'Idiot man. I am already on my way to you.'

The quality of the sound changed and I knew she'd disconnected the conversation.

I stood, sagging against the bathroom sink. She was on her way. There. To my hotel room. To Jenny. I looked into the mirror and shook my head at the reflection. What a loser. A joke. A pathetic, slithering thing. A mosquito maggot wiggling whitely in a pond. A tape worm.

I ignored Jenny's silent Tiny on my pillow, and sat down on the hotel's hard, slippery couch to pull on my shoes. I hoped that between my three personal credit cards and my work card I could cover the cost of a car. I squeezed my temples between my palms, trying not to groan out loud. Surely Madame Bellarina would understand my position. I couldn't buy the newest, most expensive car with no warning. I stood up, shakily, and grabbed my briefcase.

'Jenny,' I said.

'Fuck off.'

'Look, I need to go out for an hour,' I said, looking down at the little doll that looked like my wife. 'I *need* to do this, trust me. But then I'll be back, and I'll explain. It's not as it seems.'

There was a knock at the door.

I felt the blood drain instantly from my face. My hands went numb and I dropped my briefcase.

And then I panicked.

I went straight to the room's kitchenette and flung open the solitary kitchen drawer. Hotel kitchenettes are notorious for being under-equipped, but this was the first time I'd actually cared. In the drawer I found both types of bottle opener – beer and wine – but the sharpest knife I could find was a butter knife. I grabbed both the knife and the wine bottle opener, and hurried over to the bed.

'What are you doing?' Jenny cried, as I snatched her from my pillow. 'You're squeezing me too tight!'

'I'll pay for a new Tiny,' I gasped, setting the Tiny on the bench and tearing off the little Tiny clothes. 'This is ridiculous. You can't stay in there. I'm going to get you out.'

There was another knock on the door, louder this time.

'Hang on!' I screamed. 'Just give me one damned minute!'

I hesitated, my hand hovering over the knife and bottle opener. Should I saw, or should I puncture? I chose the bottle opener because it looked sharpest. I prodded at the Tiny's chest, trying to feel for the battery. Jenny was crying.

'I'll do it quickly,' I said. Sweat dripped from my nose on to the bench beside the Tiny's head. When I lifted the bottle opener into Jenny's view, she screamed. A long, drawn-out static hiss.

I raised my fist, then slammed it down, smashing the point of the bottle opener into the Tiny's chest as hard as I could. The Tiny's skin, tough as leather, didn't even dent. I could hear Jenny gasping and coughing, probably rolling about in pain on the other side of the world, while the Tiny lay motionless on the bench. Swearing, I stepped backwards and nearly fell over my briefcase.

I still can't explain why I did what I did next. Why, in that moment, my mind flew to such a solution. In the court hearing I told them it had been Jenny's idea. The whole thing. They had all the recordings from when she'd called the Tiny helpline, they knew how desperate she'd been to get out of the damn thing. I actually wasn't going to lie, but Rach convinced me. She said we could do with the money.

I upended the contents of my briefcase, and snatched up my small roll of cellotape. It was ancient, gone yellow, barely ever used. I savagely attacked it with my nails until I found where the tape began, and then I took Jenny's Tiny and I rolled it, rolled it, rolled it until the entire body and head were covered. I was panting. My hands shook. But she was covered. Silent. Blind.

I opened the door. It was the hotel attendant who had brought me my coffee. He handed me a large bouquet of flowers, then held out his hand expectantly. I shut the door.

The card on the flowers read, 'To Jenny. We all hope for your speedy recovery. Michel and Team.'

I dropped the flowers on to the bench next to Jenny's mummified Tiny and left. On the elevator down I sent a message to Madame Bellarina's number, informing her that I'd meet her outside the hotel. As I passed through the hotel's foyer I saw her, standing next to a taxi outside. She looked old and haggard in the daylight.

✖

Two hours later and a good deal poorer than I'd have liked to have been, I sat on the toilet in my hotel room and slowly unwound the cellotape from Jenny's Tiny. Through the thick yellow cocoon she looked like a sleeping pixie, her features smudged, hard to define. The cellotape's colour reminded me of a condom. When I was down to the last few winds the tape stuck in the Tiny's hair, and I had to tug hard to get it off.

'Jenny?' I asked, hoping like hell that she wouldn't reply.

And, she didn't. I prodded the Tiny's chest hard, but not a sound. She was gone.

The Tiny was still disconcertingly warm. I reminded myself that it wasn't Jenny that made it warm, it was the fact that it was turned on.

I thought of calling Jenny, or at least sending a message to her vice, but decided against it. I'd be home in four days. Four days till the shit hit that fan, four days to prepare myself. I wondered which vessel she'd choose to burn my things in this time. I cringed, thinking that my newest golf set was likely to cop it first; titanium-infused steel wouldn't deter Jenny. I made the decision to take some time off work, take her somewhere nice. We went to Fiji for our twentieth anniversary, stayed in a resort run by a local village. I couldn't remember the resort's name, or even the name of the village, but figured it probably still existed.

✖

I avoided Rach's calls for two days. Either she was calling to chastise me, and perhaps blackmail me – I wouldn't have put it past her to suddenly bring up my older crime, 24 years later – or she was calling to inform me that all of my possessions had been expertly destroyed. I even imagined her there with Jenny, the flames illuminating their faces orange, cackling as they once more reduced my life to ash. But eventually she sent me a text message.

'Mum is in a coma,' is all it said.

I flew straight home. I waited outside the terminal for twenty minutes before I finally made my way to the taxi stand. I'd told Rach my flight details; I thought she might come. When I arrived at the hospital she was there, swollen eyed. She'd spread a colourful blanket over the hospital bed, and Nico was curled up on top of it, beside Jenny's knees, sleeping. I gave Rach a hug but I wanted her and Nico to leave. I wanted to be alone with my wife. I pulled another chair in from the hallway and sat, silent. Watching Jenny's chest rise and fall.

In those first few weeks the doctors thought Jenny might soon come out of the coma. She still had flecks of paint beneath her nails. She still smelled of soap and washing powder. Her grey-auburn hair spilled across the pillow. Her brown eyes were closed, but seemed like they could open at any time. Life-sized eyelids. Life-sized lips. When I arrived back at our house, the night after I'd come home to Auckland, I found my Tiny in the bed, next to where she'd been lying. It was wearing pyjamas.

I held Jenny's dry hand, while doctors rolled in and out, giving me conflicting hypotheses about what had happened. Some believed that although her body hadn't suffered any physical damage the brain had believed that it had, and so had shut itself down. Others, as far as I could tell, believed that sheer fright had made her mind turn off.

'What did you expect?' one nurse asked me. She was overweight and her shoes made sucking noises on the floor. 'Putting things into your head? Transmitting images into your mind? It's not natural. I'm surprised things like this don't happen more often.'

✖

Fourteen months after her admittance to hospital, I won the settlement and had Jenny installed in a luxury suite overlooking the Parnell Rose Gardens, where she now lies in plush comfort on a king-sized bed, receiving therapeutic, aromatic massages each morning.

The day she was transferred there I was due to fly to Sydney, and before I left I propped up my Tiny next to her hospital bed, against a blue vase. I should have bought her some flowers, but I didn't think.

That was two years ago. And so far, there's been no change to her condition. Her nurses humour me by always keeping the battery charged on my Tiny, always keeping it switched on at Jenny's end. I switch myself on most nights, to check on her.

The Ghost of Matter
Octavia Cade

CAMBRIDGE, 1930

He had become a man with grandchildren. A grandfather, and that in its way was easier than fatherhood, and more rewarding. Eileen had been a beautiful baby – Ernest remembered writing to his mother upon her birth, praising the infant's marvellous qualities – but the older his daughter got, the more difficult he found it to connect with her. Eileen moved in fast sets, and Ernest – so well versed in physics, in atoms and magnetism – could not understand what drew her to those parts of others that were so different to himself.

There were times when that difference was a delight to him. He remembered the pretty little girl she'd been, the way she'd sung and skipped about the garden on small dimpled legs. How she'd taken her dolls so seriously, brought them to him for stories and tea parties.

He'd been so glad she was a girl, during the War. Would never have said so, not to colleagues and friends who had their own loved ones posted out of reach, in the trenches, at the Somme. Eileen would never find herself on the end of a bayonet, with a grenade being thrown towards her, in a field hospital with her life leaking away from dysentery. Ernest knew he had a reputation as a slow thinker. Powerful, but slow – a bright giant glacier of a mind, one that pinned down and ground all boulders before it. There'd been four years of war to watch other people's children die, four years to try to understand, to focus the cold strength of his concentration on finding the factor that made sense of it all, that put organisation into grief. Four years, and at the end of it all he could find was relief – relief that it was over, and that his girl wasn't part of it. Relief that he'd never be one of those parents, those poor grey miserable creatures that had to bury their children. That had to *see* them buried and gone on to a place different than theirs, and unreachable.

He'd been lucky. Eileen had been there all along, bright and difficult and spoilt, too – yes, he could say that and say it with honesty, for he was her father and half the spoiling could be laid at his feet. But for all he'd been irked sometimes, confused and frustrated at the growing distance between them, he'd never stopped feeling grateful for her life.

His only child, and he found it easier now to talk to her children, to entertain them, for the little ones would listen without rolling their eyes, found him fascinating, found him *not-wanting*. There were three of them.

No, four.

Four now, although the fourth was but new born and brought death with it, perhaps, for his daughter who was so full of life and rebellion (for all that she had married a physicist like her father) was failing in her strength, failing after labour.

He was never very good at waiting. Feet together, back straight, hands clasped together in his lap so that he wouldn't fidget, wouldn't have the temptation to smoke. It would have been easier to smoke. He wouldn't have felt so much like a schoolboy then, waiting primly for news of a lesson he couldn't hope to understand. There had been so few of those – an early life of success in scholarship had given Ernest the expectation of understanding – but he couldn't find anything to understand in this, the long deep quiet while he waited to be informed of his daughter's death.

Ernest had seen what burying children had done to his mother. He didn't want any part of it. His two young brothers had drowned in the Sounds, drowned at Pelorus, and all he had of them now were the wet little footprints that followed him about sometimes, the salt smell of the sea in the corners of his laboratories. He would have liked to see the boys now – the ghosts of their presence, at least. The ghosts of their matter. He had said that once: *I have broken the machine and touched the ghost of matter*. It had been a joke, a private joke. One his brothers might have appreciated, had they lived, though no doubt they would have corrected him, or tried to. 'You didn't break anything, Ern. We were broken before you knew,' with their lungs all torn apart from water, with their bellies stuffed round with it. 'And I couldn't put you back together,' he would have said. No more than he could put Eileen back together. If it had been cancer, maybe. There were promising results with radioactivity, with radiation therapy. He could have helped then. Done something that wasn't waiting like the boy he no longer was, hoping for the presence of other boys that no longer were.

It would have been a comfort to have them beside him. To sit so upright in his chair, with little pools of salt water welling up on either side in solidarity. He wouldn't even mind if they got his boots wet. Wouldn't step around the damp patches, wouldn't look away. He was an old man now, set in his principles and his successes, the medals, the authority. Surely old men should not look away so easily.

'Charles,' he said. 'Herbert. Are you there?' He'd cringed from the sound of them once, the little ghost cries, the eerie giggles come out of the dark when the curtains were all closed about, when he was trying to adjust his eyes for radiant sparks and luminescence. There was a reason he'd taken to leaving the labs before dark, and it was different from the reason he used to encourage everyone else to leave as well. 'You need time away from the instruments, time just to *think*,' he'd said. It was a good reason, and one he believed whole-heartedly regardless, but it wasn't the truth of it. Not the whole truth, at least. That he couldn't give: ghosts in the lab, spectres in the glass, the reflections of past lives.

'They'd have thought I was telling a practical joke,' he confided – to thin air, to the absence and the presence. 'They'd have said "Rutherford's gone round the bend, the old crocodile. Can't see his tail any longer, spends too much time in his own head. That's what trying to crack your teeth on physics gets you; that's the taste of atoms. Too much time breathing fumes, too much time around the radium. D'you think it's made him mad? Could be, could be. They say the Curie woman's strange as well …"'

No. Much easier to insist on proper rest, on time spent in consideration rather than at experiment. The greatest experimentalist of the age, they called him; but he *thought* about what he did and it was that which made the difference.

What would they have said if they'd known?

MANCHESTER, 1909

Contamination was the bane of his life. The experiments, the vacuum chambers … even the tiniest bit of dust could throw the whole thing off. And it wasn't just the dirt – light was just as bad. Ernest would have to sit in the dark for half an hour sometimes, until his eyes were adjusted so he could see the scintillations that marked the little sparks of matter. Even then there was squinting and relays, as he and the other members of his team took turns in search of alpha particles.

Contamination could ruin experiments. It could ruin, too, the *ideas* come from experiments, when the outcomes given were false and nobody knew why. Ernest's strength was his experimentation: the way that he could track down and expose every probability, the way that he could cross them off until only one practical result remained. Even when he worked in teams, this was his method.

Only once had he failed to explain away the source of the intrusion – the voice in the waves, the one that could only be heard by himself, whether there were others listening or he was alone and tinkering. Ernest still thought about it sometimes, still turned that enormous brain to shadows and the inexplicable presence of sound, but he had never come to a satisfactory conclusion.

But years had passed since then and if he had not forgotten, Ernest had at least pushed that girl's voice to the back of his mind, to uncommon areas where problems of little import were stalled and sorted. That was why, when he was washing his hands in the laboratory's WC and found himself washing with salt water instead of fresh, he thought it was something he could explain.

It was the texture he noticed first. The extra softness of the water, the way it felt a little more slippery under soap. The colour was different too, but colour change in tap water was something that could be attributed to old pipes and bad plumbing … or at least it could have been, if only the shading were different. If the water were tinted red or brown, Ernest would have explained it as a result of rusted piping. Yet the soft slippery water in the basin was unusually cool in colour, reminiscent of the blue-green waters of the Sounds under cloud.

They were so different, the colours of his home. The blues and greens more vivid, undiluted by constant rain. He missed it, missed them. Missed the smell of mānuka and lemonwood and five finger, missed the bright colours of kōwhai and rātā, the way the tui would glisten in the trees, the thick plump bodies of wood pigeons. He missed winters where all the trees weren't bare. It had taken a long time, that first winter in a foreign land, to understand what was so uncomfortable about the landscape of the place his mother called Home – how skeletal and dead it all was, with frozen mud underneath instead of humus, instead of red beeches where all the leaves stayed on.

Science had taken him away, and necessarily so, for the small settlements at Brightwater and then Havelock held no mysteries for him, and the damp half-cellar of Canterbury was a depth he had already plumbed. Still, for all the excitement that came with being at the centre of physics there were times when Ernest missed his home with an intensity that was almost painful, that lodged beneath his breastbone in stutter-silence, and when he leaned over the basin to examine that strange, sad water he breathed in the scent of it, and knew it.

It was sea water, salt water, and no lad who had ever grown up on coasts, within the reach of tidal swell, would ever mistake it. More than that, though, it was the salt water of the Sounds, the salt water of too-many-thousands of miles away. Ernest wouldn't have thought he could have recognised it, but the mix of salt and sand and colour was different to the British beaches. Different, too, to the coast of Canterbury.

'It can't be,' he said. 'You're imagining things, you silly fool.' He wasn't in the Sounds now, or even in New Zealand. He was in a closed-up washroom of a physics laboratory on the other side of the world from what he smelled, and the coast was nowhere near him. 'It must be the pipes,' he said, knowing as he said it that it was a foolish thing to say, for all the water piped here was fresh.

'Damned imagination.' And yet Ernest knew that it wasn't. He was imaginative enough for a scientist – not as flashy with it as Einstein, or with the deep melancholic imagery of Bohr – but his thoughts had meaning. They didn't pop out of the depths of his brain for no good reason. There must be connections he was making that he didn't realise yet. Something to do with sea and salt, and that's why he was thinking of them – thinking that he felt them, smelled them. Signposts, that's what they were. He'd turn the tap off and it would all go away and sooner or later – probably later – the link would spark within him and he'd know what, and why. That was the way it worked for him.

And yet when Ernest turned off the tap, saw the absence of spouting, he did not see the absence of water. It bubbled up out of the plughole, blue and green and with beech leaves in it – bubbled over the edge of the basin and onto the floor, and there was nothing he could do to stop the flood.

Later, looking back, he would think he heard the echo of giggles coming from the drain. Little noises, and echoing like rat scratches in the pipes, but the bubbles were so loud and so many that Ernest told himself again he was imagining it.

HAVELOCK, 1886

Martha sat at the Broadwood piano that was the pride of her house, the favoured instrument of her life. Her feet were placed carefully together as if at parlour, and her hands were clasped in her lap. She stared at the keys as if they were waves, as if they were boards bound together as boat ribs, and unsinking.

'Mum?' said Ern, standing awkward in the door and not used, yet, to looking down on the woman who had birthed him and raised him to competence in the midst of farm and flax and reed. He was growing up now, would be a man before long and not the first she had raised. One day soon, he hoped, he'd go away to school – but he'd come back again to the house where he still felt like a child, because that was where his family was. 'Mum?'

'It came all the way over from Home,' said Martha. 'Like I did.' In the room that smelt always of lanolin and polished wood, her voice had lost all its shine. She spoke in flats. 'I was going to teach my children music. I thought it was important.'

'You did teach us,' said Ern, halfway across the room now with his quick, heavy strides and his boots still damp with dirt from last night's searching. His mother's boots were neat. Polished, even. She must have cleaned them during the night, he thought, in the few hideous hours before dawn, the first night her boys were lost.

She *had* taught them. Ern remembered, all too well, the nights when they sang together: his mother on the piano, his father on the violin and the voices of their children not nearly as tuneful but trying for all that and happy with it. Charles and Herbert, singing.

'I should have spent more time letting you swim,' said

Martha. 'Letting you learn that better, in the shallows while you still could.' Letting them learn *those* notes – the slap of flesh on water, the fountain of kicks coming up behind. As if they hadn't learned to swim, all of them, out in the Sound and on the river, when they'd gone to the Pelorus for fishing and for eeling and found themselves scaring away the fish and the eels for the pleasure of cool water in summer.

'They'll be fine, Mum,' said Ern. 'They probably got caught out too late and pulled in for the night. There are plenty of bays round here, you know that. They'll be back before you know it.'

'I should never have let them go out alone,' said Martha. 'Not in that boat. Not by themselves.'

'They've done it before,' said Ern. 'We all have. They're not little kids anymore.' Because if they weren't then he wasn't either, and Ern had a horrible cold feeling deep down in his stomach that he couldn't be a child himself now. That his parents needed him to be more. That his brothers did.

They were ten and twelve. It wasn't so very young, after all. It wasn't as if they were both small children. His brothers. His *little* brothers – and Ern away from them, with his books and extra tutoring and with no room in his head for anything apart from the excitement of science and wasn't that useless now, when he might have gone with them instead. What use was being good at books and tests, what use was knowing how to count the seconds between lightning and thunder if he couldn't stop the storms when they came upon his family, when they tore out his mother's heart in front of him?

'Even if the boat did sink,' he said, 'they know how to swim. They've probably washed up on shore somewhere. They'll follow it till they've found someone to pester for breakfast, don't worry.'

It was a picture that made him smile, he who'd had experience enough of that pestering. Charlie wanting to come shoot pigeons with him in the little grove of miro trees out back, and Ern at his shoulder, warning him not to shoot until the pigeons were about to fly off, their wings spread out all the better for targets. Herbert swinging those pigeons over his shoulder to take home, laughing and talking of roast bird, of digging potatoes to go with them, and carrots. They'd never let themselves go hungry, would bail up some poor bastard before he'd so much as washed the crust from his eyes and there'd be blankets and warm tea and bacon while someone was sent for their father, while their mother cooked them both a second breakfast and better salted.

Martha did not smile. Her face contorted, briefly, and if he hadn't been looking at that exact moment Ern would never have seen it. Then it was over; her jaw stiffened and her cheeks smoothed and the hands she'd suddenly put over her eyes were allowed to drop.

He hadn't been able to reach her. It was still there: the same sense of dislocation, the same impossibility of communication that Ern had felt when he came to her, just a few moments before. Bad enough to tramp the sides of the Sound and call with no response, but with his hand on his mother's shoulder and no distance between them he couldn't even make *her* hear him. Such a practical boy, he was, but this wasn't any practice he was used to, or any of the instruments he took such pleasure in. This was a little wooden house very far from science and there was no longer any comfort to be had inside it.

'I'll find them,' he said. 'Safe and sound.' When Martha's face didn't change at all, quiet as the surface of a still pond, a stagnant stretch of river, he knew that she didn't believe him. Knew then that there were connections other than his and that sometime during the night she had felt the breaking off of them and was merely waiting now for others to confirm the absence she had already heard. Knew too that he'd just made a promise that he couldn't keep and the breaking of it would haunt his future, taint it always with silence and salt water and the memory of failure.

'You're a good boy, Ernest,' said his mother. She did not look at him but brought her hand up to squeeze his as it rested on her shoulder. It was a brief grip, and anaemic, and Ern, come to give comfort, found his taken away.

Martha brought her hand down again to the keys before her, an automatic motion almost, and her ring was bright against the black and white keys. Bright gold, for marriage and children and bringing together. Gold that was now for breaking apart, for fragments and family shattering.

She rested her hand on the keys and did not play. When Ernest left, Martha set her hand back in her lap, clasped together neatly with the other and waited with a straight back for news that would never come, for children that would never be found.

✖

It was quite the most incredible event that has ever happened to me in my life. It was almost as incredible as if you fired a 15-inch shell at a piece of tissue paper and it came back and hit you. On consideration, I realized that this scattering backward must be the result of a single collision, and when I made calculations I saw that it was impossible to get anything of that order of magnitude unless you took a system in which the greater part of the mass of the atom was concentrated in a minute nucleus. It was then that I had the idea of an atom with a minute massive centre, carrying a charge. (Ernest Rutherford, on the gold foil experiment.)

MANCHESTER, 1909

The gold was beaten very thin, into leaf. It shimmered even as the room went dark around it, shimmered like the sea surface under sunset and Ernest held his breath, hoped for the absence of salt.

It was dark in the laboratory cellar, with pipes above and below. Whenever he heard voices on the stair, at the door, he'd have to warn them to duck their heads for the hot-water pipe, to take care when stepping over the other two water pipes just beyond. If they slipped in puddles and injured themselves, the experiment would have to be put off while they patched themselves up. Then the readjustment would have to start all over again, for it took half an hour in the dark to be able to see the scintillations, to not miss their presence with eyes too used to light. The worst of it was if they slipped, Ernest couldn't even be certain what it was they'd slipped in. The puddles might have come from leaky pipes, but he'd gone over them all himself and never found a single leak. Those puddles that appeared in the dark, smelling of salt, would magically vanish when the lights turned on. It made the cellar floor untrustworthy.

Ernest was so careful, stepping down there himself. His knee had never been the same since those first days in London, when he'd fallen and damaged it. On a banana skin, too, and that made it worse. Such a ridiculous accident. He didn't quite trust it to hold him if he skidded in water, if one leg shot out from under him and bent awkwardly. He always watched out for water, and the presence of gold always reminded him.

'Half an hour, lads,' he said. Adjusting to the darkness enough to see the scintillations, the scattered particles, could be tedious, a forced delay but a necessary one in a method that strained sight and patience both. They worked in relays, searching by turns and in single minutes for particles that wandered off-track, that rebounded in directions they were not supposed to go.

Ernest hunched over the microscope, blind and squeezed into position. He had to move slowly – they all did – to avoid stumbling, to keep the experiment from knocking over. He was looking for the little flashes that indicated radioactive particles shot through the leaf had hit the target: a phosphorescent plate, painted with zinc sulphide. Radon particles that by all rights should have hit dead on, like a boat headed straight for home.

The line wasn't straight. Instead, a fuzziness, as if the particles had lost their way, and Ernest ordered the experiment reconfigured to search further, to see if the scattering was wider than they thought.

'Do you see that?' said Geiger, said Marsden, pressed up against him like brothers and the three of them crammed together in a little space and wondering. 'I think some of them are coming back.'

One in eight thousand, they were: the little particles that hit the gold foil and rebounded back to where they came, as if returning to the source. Some scattered off to the sides, as much as ninety degrees off, but for Ernest it was the rebounders that caught him about the throat, that made his eyes squint and smart in the dark.

(Sitting in the church with Martha, with his father and his brothers and sisters, those that remained, sitting in front of an empty space where the coffins would be if they'd ever found bodies to put in them, listening to the priest talk as gently as he could of souls returned to God, and watching his mother twist a loose ring on fingers grown thin from grief.)

'Professor!' said Geiger (said Marsden and Charlie and Herbert). 'Do you see that?'

'I see it,' said Ernest, of the strange, hard scatter that could only come if the foil was solid somehow and at the same time not, as if the gold united and fragmented at once. 'I see it!' he said again, and the thrill in his voice was from more than science, more than scatter – for while there had been no puddles on the floor, no salt water and no scent, the sight of scattering had come with a cold small hand, brief and damp on the back of his neck.

'Don't jump,' said Geiger, laughing. 'You don't want to tip it all over.'

'I'll jump if I want to,' said Ernest, quick and gruff and absolutely prepared to have his chilly, goose-bump flesh excused by a more tangible mystery, by results and equipment he could reach out and touch.

'They're punching through,' said Marsden, and his breath in the dark was excited, as if he had run a race and come home first. 'Most of them, anyway.'

HAVELOCK, 1886

'I'm sorry,' said Ern. 'Do I know you?'

It was a small settlement, where they lived on the Sound. Ern couldn't say that he was on close terms with everyone, but he knew most of them by sight and this was a woman he'd never seen before. She didn't look local either, what with her light slipper shoes so unsuitable for coastal walking, but there was something about her – the turn of her head, perhaps, or the way that she watched him – that made Ern think that he knew her.

It was the colour of her dress that struck him the most, though Ern had never had an interest in fashion, had never paid much notice to what his sisters wore. This dress was different. The deep bright blue of it, so vivid in the afternoon it almost hurt him to look at it … It was the blue of the Sounds under sunlight, the colour of the water when the light hit the waves just right, just before the shallows turned deep and the surface was sheer and sharp and reflective. It was too ostentatious a colour for a day dress, Ern thought, at least in Havelock. Even without an eye for style he knew it would be noticed, would be seen as forward. Inappropriate. Not a dress for doing in; too fine for kitchen work and liable to show the dirt.

Her back was to the sun. Her hair was haloed against it, her face a little fuzzy, fraying around the edges. It made it hard to look at her without squinting and screwing his face up. Ern didn't want to be rude, to make her think he was pulling faces at her. He was too tired for horseplay, had too much of worry about him to joke on a deserted beach in Marlborough while he looked for his brothers (looked for their bodies) in old clothes and without his books, his boots damp with sand and soil and heavy on his feet.

'Excuse me, ma'am,' he said. 'Have you seen my father? James Rutherford, he is, about so tall. He should have some men with him.' Their neighbours, their friends, the village acquaintances come out to search with him, to look for boys who could have been their own. There'd been women in the first searches too, the Rutherford house being too small for all those who had come to comfort his mother – but none were impractical enough to wear dresses like this for searching, and certainly none would have been tactless enough to wear a dress the colour of celebration, the colour of happiness and sunlight on the waters those boys might have (must have?) drowned in.

'Ma'am?' he said again, but the girl just stared at him,

silent. Ern felt his temper slipping and bit his tongue so he wouldn't explode at her, rail against bad manners – but though hers were inexcusable, it wouldn't really be her he was screaming at. Grief hadn't submerged all his sense of fairness yet. He couldn't help but think her foolish, yet there was nothing of malice in her expression. Just distance, like the far-off sound of sea gulls, like the moment of silence that he imagined must surely take place in laboratories, while the experimenters watched and waited for their results.

Still, it was difficult not to sound clipped as he bade her good day and moved on, in the direction he believed the search party had taken. Ern didn't know why he looked back. The girl made no sound. She didn't call out for him to stop, didn't cry for his attention. There were no thin footsteps on the beach behind him, their weight muted by sand and shuffling. There was no reason for him to look back – and yet he did, the hairs on the back of his neck prickling, rising, and the sense of familiarity coming over him again as a wave.

The girl was staring at him. *At* him, with none of the distance or absence of her earlier self, and one of her arms was stretched out parallel to the ground. She pointed in the direction he would have gone and Ern felt himself step back, just ever so slightly, for even though he was a big lad there was something in her that gave him goose bumps, that both underlined the feeling that he knew her and reinforced the distance between them. She stared at him, unmoving, and her outstretched arm didn't waver or dip. She was still as iron, still as statues if statues had sleeves that gleamed at the edges, if they wore dresses that frayed around a figure and let the light through.

'I'm seeing things,' he said, eyes screwed up and they were so heavy in his head that what he saw had to be a result of exhaustion, of poor sleep and hallucination. Yet when Ern opened his eyes again the girl was still there, still pointing … and so he turned, quickly, unwilling to turn his back on her but compelled to follow the sightline of those insubstantial fingers—

And there was his father, returning from the day's search, stooped and stubborn in the distance. There were fewer people around him than there had been last month, and more would fall away over the coming weeks, Ern knew, if they didn't find what most of them must suspect by now that they would never find. Still, he was grateful for their presence, their support, and not only for Herbert's sake, and Charles'. Not only for his father's. Ern had always known what to say to him before but now the silences between them were uncomfortable, full of things that Ern didn't know how to say and James didn't know how to hear.

When he looked back, the girl was gone. The sands were empty, and held no trace of passage.

×

While the overall efficiency of the process rises with increase of energy of the bombarding particle, there seems to be little hope of gaining useful energy from atoms by such methods. On the other hand, the recent discovery of the neutron and the proof of its extraordinary effectiveness in producing transformations at very low velocities opens up new possibilities, if only a method could be found of producing slow neutrons in quantity with little expenditure of energy. At the moment, however, the natural radioactive bodies are the only known source for generating energy from atomic nuclei, but this is on far too small a scale to be useful for technical purposes. (Ernest Rutherford, Henry Sidgwick Memorial Lecture, November 1936.)

CAMBRIDGE, 1932

Ernest knew his strengths. Patience wasn't one of them, nor stillness, nor silence. And with his bad knee, cramming himself into the tea-chest hut in the lab was becoming ever more embarrassing. He'd been able to manage it well enough once, with Geiger and Marsden, when youth had somewhat compensated for bulk, but Ernest had always been a big man and compressing himself into small spaces was difficult.

Now, decades later, Cockcroft and Walton were making *allowances* for him. There was something they wanted him to see, scintillations from the new experiment, and they were so determined he wouldn't stumble that they actually shut the machines off before they'd allow him to stump across the laboratory floor and into the hut. Ernest knew he was developing a reputation for clumsiness, knew the equipment in the workroom was expensive and often fragile, but still … it was humiliating to be so couched in care.

'All right, all right,' he said, aware that irritation was clouding his tone and trying to hide it. 'I'm ready. Get on with it now, I can't stay like this forever.' And he'd only been there moments, really, but already he could feel his knee stiffening, feel the coming on of headaches because he'd never had patience for this sort of thing, the squinting at scintillations, and his eyesight was less than it had been.

'I'm getting too old for this,' he grumbled.

'I'm sorry, Professor, what was that?' said Walton from outside the hut, waiting on him, on his pronouncement.

'Nothing,' said Ernest. 'Nothing.' Just talking to himself, that was it. God, but he was getting old. Not that he'd ever admit it, but he could see the reactions, the sympathy from others. It had started from Eileen's death, the idea that he was something to be careful with. Not so much from

Cockcroft, who had lost a lad of his own not much before Ernest had lost Eileen – and Cockcroft's boy had been little more than a baby, a chubby-cheeked, chubby-legged young thing who Ernest had seen running about at full-tilt …

He had that to be grateful for, at least. He'd had decades with his daughter, and there were grandchildren now to remind him of her, to keep her alive in the turn of their heads, the lines of their mouths and cheeks.

Something hit the side of the little wooden hut then, hit quick and sharply, as if it were knocking. 'What's the problem?' he said, his voice loud in the confines of the chest, of the laboratory. Not for nothing had signs been put around the Cavendish encouraging people to speak softly, lest they upset delicate equipment. Ernest knew by 'people' they meant him, but he had never been one for quiet. 'Why are you rattling at me? Has that damn contraption gone off again?'

'There's no problem, Professor,' said Walton, and though Ernest couldn't see his face there was puzzlement in his tone. 'Can't you see them?'

'Of course I can see them!' said Ernest, withering. His eyesight might not be as sharp as a younger man's but he could still make out the little flashes, the bright scintillations. 'Why are you rapping on the hut?'

There was a small silence. 'We're not,' said Cockcroft. 'Professor, are you all right?'

Ernest stared at the scintillations, pursing his lips. And it happened again, on the wood just beside his head, as if someone were pressed up against the box behind him, their fist just two inches from his head.

'Professor?'

'Nothing,' he said. 'Don't worry about it. I must have knocked something myself. Easy enough to do, crammed in here.' And for once the reputation he had for quick temper and easy explosion was a useful thing, for the other men made no mention and went on as before.

The knocking continued. Fast and slow, erratic as far as he could tell – if there was a pattern behind it then Ernest could not fathom it. There were moments when he thought it had gone entirely, before an especially loud knock dragged his attention back, dragged it away from scintillations and science. He didn't let on, of course, but there was room for his attention to be divided. Ernest knew what he was seeing. He'd known from the first moment. Those scintillations were alpha particles, the result of an experiment to see lithium disintegrate, to see its atom split down into parts. Ernest would be ten years in his grave before he couldn't identify an alpha particle scintillation. He'd been there at their birth – or the birth of their discovery, at least. He knew those scintillations better than any man living or dead.

Yet he was an experimentalist at heart and it was an automatic reaction for him to tinker, to hunt down and modify and adjust. It was a skill that served him well – and with the tea chest and the lithium and the knocking, it served him twice. For the knocking had itself disintegrated, had tuned and simplified down to the final form, and it was a form that he recognised. A child's knocking game, a simple signalling rhythm that he had played with Charles and Herbert, that he had taught to Eileen.

The gruff instructions to change the current, to alter the voltage – there was necessity to them, and science. But they were also an excuse to stay within the hut, to keep staring at scintillations that he couldn't see any longer because his eyes were full of salt water. It kept his face turned away, from Walton who would have felt pity for him and Cockcroft who would have understood.

Ernest stayed in the little cramped hut until he couldn't hear the knocking anymore. When his eyes were dry he inched himself out into the comparative space of the laboratory, stiff and straining and with his knee screaming from confinement, and the success was bittersweet; for he knew more of splitting, he thought, than anyone alive.

HAVELOCK, 1887

'Dad,' said Ern. 'Dad.' It was a hopeless bid for attention, he knew, the words too short and blunt to have any effect, to penetrate the callus that had grown up over the open wound of loss. It was the only thing that he could think to say that didn't have cruelty in its bones, that wasn't sharp and terrible and indistinguishable from kindness. What else was there to say? He'd tried talking of rugby, of his school work, of the gossip he'd heard down at the local store when his mother had sent him down there to get supplies. It all sloughed off, as if magnetic: the poles of his father's misery in opposition to his own, the one directed inside, the other able to step back a little, to look outside himself.

'Dad,' Ern wanted to say. 'It's been a year. They're gone. Dead. They drowned and they're gone. You're not going to find them.' It was the cruellest he'd ever felt. Ern knew he had a temper, knew that it exploded sometimes into snapping and hard jabs but he cooled quickly, apologised easily and without sulking. This deliberate, considered infliction of pain was another thing entirely, especially when James was so pained already. His father had always been a strong man, fit from years of physical labour in a frontier environment, but the past year had thinned him further, had left him sinewy and stone-mouthed and with an expression so whippet-thin that Ern could hardly bear to look at him.

There were times that he looked at his father and James would appear so *old*. Fragile, almost, and Ern had always felt able to go to him before but the gulf between them was widening and he didn't know how to bridge it.

'He's still going out there,' Martha had confided to him when he'd come in with a pile of wood for stocking the box by the fire, come with the grim and constant expectation of comfort, of being the comforter and being inadequate to the task. Her piano was polished; it gleamed in the afternoon sun. She never played it. That was her punishment, as James found his on the empty shores and river banks. 'He's still looking for them.' For Charles and Herbert, missing for nearly a year now and drowned, everyone thought, as they boated on the Sounds. She clutched his arm. 'Ernest.' As if he could reach out, put back together what had broken so cleanly and so finally into fractures. And he was the clever one, the clever son, and he knew about pulling things apart and building them back up again, didn't he?

She didn't say anything else. It wasn't his mother's way to talk about it anymore, and Ern didn't know if it ever would be again. She communicated silently now; the waves about her were quiet and lacked the salt of early grief. She didn't say, 'I want him to give it up,' because that would have been betrayal. She didn't say, 'We need him here, me and the kids,' – the ones that were still young, still at home. That would have been guilt, and Martha knew enough of guilt now to not wish more of it on the only person who could truly understand her loss.

She didn't say, 'I hope he never finds them,' for it had been close to a year now. A year, and what remained of her little boys would be bloated and ragged, gnawed on by rats and sharks and just recognisable enough to give their father screaming dreams for the rest of his life. Worse still if he found one and not the other, because that would give a bitter hope and would also be the death of the one thin comfort they had: that their boys had been together at the end, that they hadn't died and drowned alone.

Better to never find them than that. Better to give them over to the ocean for good, to believe that they lay at rest in a place that they loved, in the sea where they'd splashed and swum and fished, ten and twelve years old forever.

'I'll find him,' said Ern. 'I could do with a walk anyway.' There were things that he didn't say as well. Like how his promises were hollow ones, sometimes, because he had once promised his mother that he'd find that which he never did, though she never reminded him of it. Never told him that he failed her, not just by breaking the promise but by making it in the first place. He didn't say anything about the guilt either – that he longed to escape the grief-pull of Havelock, that he wanted to leave the suffering behind him, to try in his own way to forget. To find problems that he could solve, and have pleasure in the solving.

He wondered what it would be like, to have a child with a woman. Whether he would ever have to see in that woman's face what he saw in his mother's. Whether he would ever have to face in mirrors what he saw in his father's. And there was a certain savage pleasure in it too, the thought of breaking out of that thin veneer of misery, in finding a way to shatter and split until a new reality could rise to the surface.

'You think I don't know that?' said James, out far along the shoreline, his big hands empty and fisting at nothing. Ern almost would have preferred if his father hit him, if he had thrown a punch or lost his rag and tried to beat what he couldn't bear instead of staring out to see, to sea. 'It's the first thing I think when I get up in the morning. There's not a moment goes past I can't feel it crouching on top of me.

The weight of it, Ernest. The *weight*.

'You can't know how it feels,' he said.

'No,' said Ernest. 'I can't. But if you keep this up you'll go mad, Dad. Think of Mum. Think of the rest of us. Think of Charles and Herbert. They'd never want this for you.'

'You don't know what you're asking,' said his father.

CAMBRIDGE, 1896

Ern had decided to give up radio work. It had been good to him: got him the Exhibition scholarship, brought him to the Cavendish and he'd made a good impression there with the detector he'd brought all the way from New Zealand, with the improvements he'd made since then.

There'd been another demonstration, even – the kind he had dreamed of in Canterbury's half-cellar. 'One day I'll be demonstrating from the finest lab in the world,' he said, and he'd done it too, more than once, though there'd been hurdles and hiccups. He'd even delivered a paper to the Royal Society – quite the coup for the boy from Brightwater. Clearly, there was room for him in radio; room to make a name for himself, to research and present and publish. Room to invent, but though Ern imagined for himself a lifetime of laboratory work he could not imagine that work being radio. Any possible commercial application was beyond his reach. Lord Kelvin, approached by J.J. Thomson, Ern's supervisor and support, had told him it would cost as much as a hundred thousand pounds to make Ern's radio work commercially profitable. Ern, subsisting on a student lifestyle of several hundred pounds per year, found such sums barely conceivable. 'We need money to get married on,' he wrote to Mary, back in New Zealand. 'I'm not sure that I can cover both.'

Besides, there were far more exciting fields open to him: radioactivity, and atoms.

'If you think that the work will get any easier then think again,' said J.J. 'This is a whole new field for you. You'll have to start nearly from scratch.'

'I don't care,' said Ern. He wasn't interested in radio or profit; he was interested in atoms and silence. Building a radio wave detector was a very fine thing, and it had been admired tremendously and that was good for his ego, coming as he was from the colonies and dismissed, initially, as only provincially intellectual.

It just hadn't fixed his interest. Ern was used to concentration, to thinking through and hunting down. He'd never been the type of scatterbrain to jump from one thought to the next, undisciplined, chaotic. He'd seen men like that, heard of them through gossip at the labs and while it worked for some it was not Ern's way. His mind, he knew, was heavy. It relied upon inertia, and once set on a path forward it would go slowly, a glacier – but glaciers drove down all before them, given time. Ern could feel the glacial weight, the monumental movement, when he was faced with radioactivity, with its prospects and potential and the giant undiscovered landscapes before him.

He didn't feel that way about radio waves. They made him flippant, somehow, unfocused in his science. That was the only explanation. There was no other reason why late in his lab at night he'd work on his receiver and hear things that weren't there. It just wasn't possible. His vibrating detector could work through walls and distances, find the waves and advertise the finding, but it didn't transmit what Ern heard. A voice, very distant, and the sound of waves he thought, although it could have been some sort of static, like a badly playing phonograph.

At first he'd thought it contamination. That he was hearing things from another source – a conversation through an open window, a tap left running. Ern closed up his space as best he could, worked to eliminate any outside influence, and still he heard it. There was no failure of the equipment – he took it all apart and rebuilt it many times, and it was only occasionally after rebuilding that he'd hear the sounds again. They seemed to come and go, although the voice became sharper occasionally, as if coming into focus. It was quick and light and feminine, but past that Ern could make nothing out.

He even worked with friends, with other students in the lab, but when they couldn't hear what he did Ern stopped asking. He didn't think it was a practical joke. He knew that some people heard ringing in their ears sometimes, but he'd never had that problem and it never happened to him at all outside of his work on radio waves.

'You don't seem as interested anymore,' said J.J.

'I'm not,' said Ern, and perhaps that was it. Perhaps his mind was wandering because there was something else out there for him, the new science of radioactivity that drew him as a magnet. He didn't like to give up on a puzzle but this seemed such a solution – his own brain distracting him, when without distraction he might have stayed on the same path, remained with radio waves when radioactivity was where his potential lay.

'Trust your gut,' his father had told him.

Ernest trusted.

CAMBRIDGE, 1933

'Over my dead body,' said Ernest. It wasn't his way to publicise disputes, to drag the disagreements of science into the public sphere and hold others up for ridicule – but he wouldn't support everything either, at least not blindly, and this was safe. He was alone with J.J., a private conversation over tea with the man who had been his mentor. There was nothing he could say here that would leave the room, nothing that would embarrass another person or himself.

'You worked in the war as well,' J.J. said to him mildly, and Ernest snorted so that tea slopped into his saucer.

'That was different,' he said, who had worked on submarines and sonar and the detection of both. He didn't bother to explain. J.J. had heard his rants before: on how terrible organisation had limited even that, on how the Navy had looked down on science and made it less of a priority than they could have done. His war work had come in fits and starts, when he was able to do it at all, when it didn't take second place to his own. And it wasn't vicious, any of it. He remembered being out on the Firth of Forth, on the HMS *Vernon*, holding on to Paget's legs while the other man had his head underwater, trying to detect different frequencies through the cold sea. 'If that's the price of having perfect pitch, rather you than me,' he'd said to Paget, after hauling him up half-frozen and with his eyes screwed shut from salt.

'It *was* different,' he said again. 'I didn't go making poison gas to throw into the trenches!'

That's what Haber had done, and Ernest had never forgiven him. It was such a betrayal – of humanity, of science. Of his wife.

'Chlorine gas,' said Ernest, and he could feel his face getting redder, feel his voice rising. 'He made chlorine gas for one conflict, and now he's on the losing side of another he wants help! Well he's not getting it from me, he isn't.' The situation in Germany was becoming dire. Jewish scientists were being fired from their positions, fired from universities and research centres, and Ernest had been asked to involve himself. He was a busy man – too busy for it, in truth – but he'd done his best to get his displaced fellow scientists to jobs in Europe, in America, in the colonies. Places where they could teach and think and experiment without fear of repercussion. But Haber … Haber with his poison patriotism no longer enough to counter his ancestry was a step too far. It was violent prejudice, deep-seated – and perhaps he should be a better man, Ernest thought. Perhaps he should take the higher ground, but he couldn't. He just couldn't.

'Haber knew what he created,' said Ernest. Knew the results, knew what it would be like to breathe and burn and choke and did it anyway. Did it because he thought it would shorten a war, perhaps, but Ernest couldn't get past the price of shortening. His revulsion had been immediate and long-lasting. He was entrenched with it.

'Do we?' said J.J.

'Of course not,' said Ernest. He wasn't H.G. Wells, or the authors of that awful play where some halfwit excuse for an atomic scientist threatened to blow up as much as he could. *Wings Over Europe*, that was it. Talk about a nightmare. He hated to think of the impression it was leaving. It was Haber all over again, Haber working with atoms instead of gas.

'Sometimes I dream,' said J.J. 'And then the next day, the next week, I find myself at my bench or my desk, or talking to a friend, and I think – *I've done this before*. It all seems so familiar. Déjà vu, you understand?'

'I do,' said Ernest. 'I think most people know what that feels like, but I don't believe it's anything more than coincidence. I don't think people really can see the future. There's no basis in science for it.' He knew what the older man was getting at, regardless. There were some men, and women too, who seemed to see further ahead than others. Who seemed to be able to tease out future paths of research, to predict things that weren't there. He'd done it himself, with the neutron. He'd felt it was there, felt it for years, but it wasn't until Chadwick proved its existence via experimentation that Ernest had been shown correct.

'Just because a man's done it once doesn't mean he can always do it,' he said. 'Or that he knows he's done it at all.' There'd been a number of ideas he'd had over the years that had come to nothing. Some that had, of course, and some he'd thought nothing of had been made successful by others. In all cases there had been something he'd been all but certain of – but there was always a gap. Ideas that hung about, created from past experience and Ernest never knowing if they were true or not, if there were any validity to them.

He'd always thought it took a really imaginative man to see the future, to be able to pick out patterns, to look ahead.

'You're an imaginative man, Ernest,' said J.J.

'I know,' said Ernest, but he never knew if he were imaginative enough. He'd never have Haber's culpability, which was something to be grateful for, but did he have any of his own? What could there be that he had missed? What consequences might be laid upon his head?

'I've done the best I can,' he said.

✖

It may be possible for an electron to combine much more closely with the hydrogen nucleus, forming a kind of neutral doublet. Such an atom would have very novel properties. Its external field would be practically zero, except very close to the nucleus, and in consequence it should be able to move very freely through matter. Its presence would probably be difficult to detect by spectroscope, and it may be impossible to contain it in a sealed vessel. (Ernest Rutherford, Bakerian lecture, 1920.)

CAMBRIDGE, 1930

It might have been the most awful Christmas that Ernest had ever had. He couldn't think of a worse. There was nothing of celebration in it, even with the new baby. 'A Christmas baby,' Eileen had said, not two months before, round and waddling with her fourth child while the other three played about her. 'My little winter baby.' She herself had been born into spring – or autumn, depending on the hemisphere, but she had been born in the north, so there were no kōwhai about her.

She had been born into spring, and had died in winter. Died giving birth to her winter baby, two days before Christmas and Ernest couldn't believe it still, couldn't understand the world in which his only child died in the season of gifts and gratitude.

He and Ralph had taken the children outside, while Mary stayed with the baby. The kids had looked so stunned, so uncomprehending and the way that they sat around the tree, listless, had forced Ernest up out of his chair.

'Come on,' he said. 'Grab your jackets. Hats, scarves, mittens. Mush! You too, Ralph.' His daughter's husband, a physicist as well, a close companion at Cavendish even though he was a theoretician at heart, and even more stupefied than Ernest. 'You can't sit here all day.' Watching the children pretend to play with their gifts, trying to answer questions that had no answer. 'You'll feel better with some fresh air, some exercise.' And didn't that just sound hollow. Ernest didn't want fresh air and exercise himself. He wanted to go to his lab, to forget his grief in experiments, to break glass and rage and have a reason for the raging. Failing that, he wanted to go to bed. To try and dream, to try and forget. Almost the very last thing he wanted was to tramp through a frozen garden on a bum leg. But someone needed to try to warm his grandchildren out of apathy, the ones that couldn't be soothed with milk and rocking, and the house had become oppressive. Too many visitors, too much sympathy. Too much food, too, spread over every surface – brought by friends and colleagues and it was all Christmas food because that was all anyone had in their larders.

Ernest could quite happily have thrown all the mince pies into the Cam before he ate another. Fruit and citrus and pastry … there was nothing about any of them that tasted of separation. He would have been happier if all that had been brought tasted like ashes in his mouth – at least that would have been fitting. It would have been suitably funereal. Instead, the tastes were so *vivid* – it was a cruelty, to eat and feel so alive. Even the children felt it. He'd put tangerines in their stockings, as he always did, but they hadn't been eaten. He'd have to peel one when they got back, share it around, and smile at the kids so that they ate it. He'd have to eat some segments himself, to show it was all right. He'd have to swallow that bright, sweet taste and not vomit.

At last they were ready. Mary was helping with boots and scarves, and the poor little things were as round as they were high, she'd wrapped them up so well. If all else failed, Ernest thought, he could roll them round the garden – but once he got them out in the snow, helped them to pack balls together in preparation for fights and snowmen, their cheeks pinked up and the lethargy fell back a little.

'I know it's hard, my boy,' he said to Ralph, quiet in a corner and watching, his breath steaming out in clouds. 'But you've got to find a way to carry on.'

'You don't know what you're asking,' said Ralph, and Ernest nearly laughed it was that terrible.

'I know,' he said. His father's face had been in the mirror

that morning.

'I don't even know why we're celebrating,' said Ralph. 'It's nothing but a farce, that tree. All the food, and the presents. As though it'll make up for anything.'

'For their sake,' said Ernest, and the two of them watched the children run around, watched them fall down in the snow.

'They won't remember,' said Ralph. 'They're so young, still. They won't remember this Christmas. So what does it matter?'

'It matters,' said Ernest. 'And it's what Eileen would have wanted. You know how she loved parties.' It was true, too, and made him smile though the smile felt like glass after he'd managed to shatter it over the floor. He remembered the way she had been last Christmas, the way she had greeted him at the door, how flushed her cheeks had been in the cold. She'd been carrying her youngest and wearing a blue dress – bright and fine and celebratory. Mary's eyebrows had risen at it but all Ernest could think when he saw his daughter was that she was the colour of the Sounds under sunlight. Her dress was the shining blue of coastal water, clear and brilliant, and he had been struck with the sudden desire for home. Not the home he had come to think of as England, as the Cavendish, but the warm waters and summer Christmases of his childhood, with cricket in place of sledding and the red rata flowers against the sunshine, more vivid than fir and mistletoe and fog.

'My dear,' he had said, 'you look beautiful. You look like summer.' She looked like his sisters, he thought, when they had been young. There were lines of them in the shape of her mouth, in her forehead and her face.

'It doesn't much feel like summer,' said Eileen. 'Merry Christmas, Papa.'

✖

It is not in the nature of things for any one man to make a sudden violent discovery; science goes step by step, and every man depends on the work of his predecessors. When you hear of a sudden unexpected discovery — a bolt from the blue, as it were — you can always be sure that it has grown up by the influence of one man on another, and it is this mutual influence which makes the enormous possibility of scientific advance. Scientists are not dependent on the ideas of a single man, but on the combined wisdom of thousands of men, all thinking of the same problem, and each doing his little bit to add to the great structure of knowledge which is gradually being erected. (Ernest Rutherford, on science.)

MANCHESTER, 1910

It was surprising how much thinking Ernest got done at table. There were the meals with colleagues, of course, when he'd get so caught up in debate he'd start to shovel his food, and Mary would remind him he was dropping it in his lap, or dribbling in his haste to talk. And that was stimulating, the dagger cut and thrust of it, the little scalpel lines between relationships, between theories. The way that they built upon each other, the giants beneath them and the giants to come. Even without company he could think and link things together, the bites a counterpoint to the testing, the tasting of theory and ideas. The sense-memory of his experiments — the clean smell of apparatus, the dry glass and the stench of chemicals, the absent sensation of distilled water. The way the laboratory benches felt under his fingers, so different than the polished dining table, the burst of colour that came from cut flowers, from filled vases with their own scents so much sweeter, so much less vivid than those of his own work.

Mary's gift was gardening. The house was always full of flowers, and if she didn't grow all their fruit, all their vegetables, there were at least none in the house that weren't worth eating. Ernest would often end his meals with the fruit she provided, a practice grown more and more common since fingerprints had started appearing on the apples, since salt water started pooling in the fruit bowl.

'That's enough of that,' he'd hiss, afraid to be heard, afraid that if he were, his wife wouldn't see what he did: the weeping palm prints on the glasses, the wet salt smudges on the linen. They followed him around a lot now, Charles and Herbert – or what was left of them. What he assumed was left of them, for Ernest had no other explanation and no way of testing. He'd heard of ghosts, of course; more so since coming to a country heavy with history, weighted down with it, but even in New Zealand there'd been talk of spirits from Māori and Europeans both. Ernest had always disdained it, put it down to soft heads and soft science but he was stuck with them now, his own spectres come to life between vacuum chambers and gold leaf and alpha particles. He'd classified them reluctantly, silently, as ghosts and/or hallucinatory images, but if they were hallucinations they were confined to salt and water, brief giggles in tones he could barely remember. It didn't seem worth going to the doctors for that, making a fuss that could, possibly, get out.

Still, the possibility that they were a figment of his own brain, disturbing as it might be, was still better than ghosts, than the dead come back to life. The dead come back to haunt the living. *Disturbing, yes. That was the word.* Ernest talked to them sometimes, testing out loud, as much to work through his own ideas as to concentrate his attention, for silence made it easier to notice small splashes, the lacy leavings of salt.

'Punching through what, though?' he said. 'Through plum pudding?' That model of the atom as an indivisible thing, studded with charges like raisins, like plums sinking in the bake. Ernest had been raised on that model, had learned the physics of it, the basis of the natural world. It didn't match his observations. It didn't match his experiments. 'I don't know that I'm seeing any of that. You'd think there'd be some pudding chunks come out if particles punched though it, no matter how small.' The same way that bullets could exit a pigeon with a small shower of blood, of deep and gamey flesh – the same pigeons that Ern had killed, as a young man, as they took flight. As Herbert and Charles had watched and cheered and brought them home with him for cooking. 'No,' he said. 'It's as if it hit nothing. *Nothing.*'

He sliced through the skin of an apple. Peeled carefully, where once he would have bitten through the skin with relish, but he was afraid to taste salt in his biting now, and it wasn't like him to avoid experiments – but Ernest's field was physics, not metaphysics, and some things were beyond him.

'Perhaps,' he said, the taste of apple on his tongue, 'perhaps the atom is not a plum pudding after all, a solid little lump shot through with electron raisins. Perhaps there *is* absence in it, a place where we thought matter would be, and that pudding is the ghost of the matter we expect to see.'

('We have to stick together,' said his father. 'Now more than ever. We're still a family. Some of us might be gone, and there might be gaps and I don't think we'll ever stop feeling them Ern, and maybe we shouldn't. But we're still a family …')

'Still a unit,' said Ern, said *Ernest,* 'but a unit made up of *parts.* Something that can be divided.'

He could see it then: the structure of it, the atom in pieces around him. It had been near two years since the gold leaf and the cellar and Geiger and Marsden, but no one had ever called Ernest's mind quick. No, it was powerful they called it. Always powerful, and he felt that power now, in the understanding that would change the field and focus of his life.

Felt more, too, in the breath against the back of his neck, the quick ghost breaths of one or the other, he couldn't tell. Charles and Herbert, his brothers – and then the breath had more than cold in it.

'*Daddy,*' it said behind him, in his ear, light and eerie and too close to him, too far away, and the apple fell from nerveless fingers.

✳

Some very fine steel wire was taken, glass-hard, and cut up into lengths of 1cm. Twenty-four of these little needles were then built up into one, each being first dipped in paraffin to prevent eddy-currents passing from one wire to the other. This little collection of needles formed a compound magnet, and offered considerable surface to the action of rapidly-varying magnetizing forces. The detector was fixed in the end of a thin glass tube for convenience of handling.

This detector only retained about one-third of its magnetism, on account of the demagnetizing influence of its ends. When magnetized and placed in a solenoid of two or three turns it supplied an extremely sensitive means of detecting and measuring oscillatory currents of high frequency. (Ernest Rutherford, 'Magnetization of Iron by High Frequency Discharges', 1894.)

CHRISTCHURCH, 1894

He'd put up with a lot worse than the Den for science. Ern found it hard to refer to the Den, his place of experiment in Christchurch, as a laboratory. It was closer to a cellar – cold and damp and other students stored their hats and gowns there. And the problem of power … each day he had to spend time cleaning electrodes, making batteries from acid and that was an endless chore in itself, but necessary before he could start on the real work, the work that caught his imagination, opened up the universe.

(*One day I'll be in a real laboratory*, he told himself. *One that doesn't smell of damp cloth, that doesn't shiver in the Christchurch winter. One with decent light and a floor that isn't frigid underfoot.*)

But even the Den – even the eternal, blasted batteries – couldn't dampen his enthusiasm for physics. And when Ern demonstrated his work to the Science Society, with two friends to help, the Den where he prepared and thought and practiced was almost worth it. At least he didn't have to present there, though the site of his demonstration was not a great deal more elegant. The Den had been swapped for the Old Tin Shed, as Ern had been allowed the use of a professor's laboratory to demonstrate his work with radio waves. Neither name had been bestowed with a great deal of love behind it.

'One day,' he said to Page, who was helping him to set up, 'One day I'll be demonstrating like this in a great laboratory, one of the finest in the world.' It was a dream, and an ill-pictured one at that for Ern had never left the country, had never experienced a lab with decent resources and excellent equipment. New Zealand was as far from the centre of physics as it was possible to be. What with Canterbury set as it was in an agricultural colony at the bottom of the world, Ern didn't know of any university more distant from the great European institutes of science. 'We don't have the money, so we have to think,' he said.

Ern didn't know, then, that one day he'd be demonstrating far more difficult experiments to far more prestigious audiences. He suspected it, he hoped for it, but he didn't *know*, and the prospect was a spectre before him. Something almost tangible, something he could nearly grip. Christchurch was far from the Royal Society, and he was a student still, journeying north for his holidays and helping with the garden, digging potatoes, taking his brothers shooting and trying to teach his sisters, though they weren't always that willing to be taught. He had to tie pig-tails together to keep their attention aligned, and he tried hard not to think of that before the demonstration. Ern wasn't usually nervy; public speaking never bothered him and he knew his subject well, knew it would be of interest … but once he'd thought of his current audience – men, most of them, with short hair and some bald besides – in braided wigs, latched onto each other with ribbons, he couldn't picture them otherwise. He had to go out behind the building and laugh until he choked on it before he could quiet his breathing and squash down humour with thoughts of batteries and corrosion and electrodes, of contamination.

'You want to get a hold of yourself,' said Page when Ern came back in, having wedged his mouth into something resembling respect and concern for his audience and the compliment of their time. 'They'll think you're not taking it seriously. They'll think that you're laughing at them.'

'I am,' said Ern. 'I can't help it!' But he busied himself checking the equipment, keeping his face away until the feel of experimentation in his fingers, in his palms, calmed his mind. He could look at them then, at the sober faces and neat jackets, at the hats and gloves and the bright unexpected blue of a dress that was perhaps too formal for the occasion, and too daring. If his mother had seen one of her daughters in that – the odd style, the too-short skirts – she would have smacked her bottom and confined her to the house. Still, he had bigger things to worry about: the demonstration, the detection of radio waves through walls and buildings, over sixty feet, and then there were the questions, the congratulations; and the girl with the blue dress seemed to fade away, and Ern forgot about her.

'That went well,' said Page, afterwards. 'I think you impressed them.'

'I hope so,' said Ern, for that was his way out, to bigger and brighter labs, less clammy in their cellars; and if he could impress enough to publish papers, to win scholarships and fellowships and chances come from exhibition, then his physics could expand in circles greater than Christchurch, and for more than magnetism.

CAMBRIDGE, 1929

It had been a long time since Ernest had been to the Den. A long time, and he couldn't quite understand how it was he was back there.

He was sure that, just a few moments ago, he'd been at the Cavendish. In Cambridge, in England – half a world away from that damp half-cellar. He'd been in the workroom, where Cockcroft and Walton had set up their new transformer – and he'd been there alone. The whole building was silent, and when Ernest checked his watch he saw that it was past six.

'I should be at home,' he said, for that was leading by

example. It was his firm belief that the Cavendish should shut at six, that experiments should be turned off regardless of their ready state, and regardless of the feelings of the experimenters.

'Can't I just have another hour?'

He'd heard it more than once from the students too new to know any better, and he always refused them. 'I'll not have anyone burning out in this lab,' he said. 'Now go home and think. Think! It's what you're here for, isn't it?' And he'd watch to see which of them bit their tongues, and which were silly enough to argue. Ernest was no theoretician; his strength was experimentalism, and the young people who came to work with him were experimentalists, mostly – in love with gadgets, with the ability to press science into their fingertips, to explore it in ways that didn't involve ink. Some would stay all night if they were allowed, puttering about the labs, fiddling with their vacuums and their pumps, the liquid air, the glass and gas and vessels. Ernest couldn't blame them. He'd done the same himself, when he was young – but he'd learned more than measurements from a different approach, one that had a place for mulling, for imagination.

And yet there he'd been, after hours, breaking his own rule. It wasn't acceptable. How could the young men and women at the Cavendish take his strictures seriously if he couldn't do the same? Ernest couldn't understand why he'd stayed so long. He supposed he must have wandered off, somehow, into the atom paths and byways of his brain, lost track of time. Yes, that was it.

His knee had stiffened under him, and he had felt the ache deep within the joint as he moved to the door, felt the handle in his palm. And then it had changed under his palm – that plain, sturdy door handle had changed to something as plain and as sturdy, but different. Ernest had looked down and seen the workroom door, seen the Den door, and when he turned around to see if the changes had come up behind him as well as in front, as well as in flesh – there were imprints in his palm, one layered over the other where he had clenched down out of shock – there were two laboratories in front of him.

They seemed to occupy the same space, and all the matter was translucent. He could see through a pump to a desk, and through that desk to a wall that shimmered with brick, with plaster. For one heady, horrifying moment Ernest wasn't sure which of them was the ghost – whether he was waking up from a dream of Cavendish to the reality of a young man, whether he had never left New Zealand, never left the Den.

There were the same old gowns and cloaks, the same poor light, the same dampness in the air and walls. There, too, were the old batteries that had been the bane of his existence as a student – the same smell of acid, the same irritation. And it was all so *real*. It wasn't just the hallucinations, the spectres of old shapes. He could taste the musty atmosphere when he breathed in, and the acid stung his nose.

And overlapping the Den was the Cavendish workroom, the new transformer. Ernest could see the difference in the floor – they'd had to reinforce it so it could take the weight. There was a vacuum pump and an accelerator tube. There were metal shields and large glass bulbs – the rectifier bulbs – and though their glass was smooth and clear, all that Ernest could see behind them was the equipment of another time. Even his watch flickered back and forth, from the cheap plain one he'd had to the newer, more expensive model.

He was backing away, backing towards that two-handled laboratory door when the Den began to flood. There was no clanking, broken pipe, no susurrus sound of water. Instead it filled in silence – filled rapidly, as the water first spread across the floor to puddle around his shoes and rose with his breath to his ankles, spilling through the cellar.

Ernest would have lurched forward, even with his bad knee, if the water was affecting the transformer, the electrics of the new workshop, but though the water was rising now to the level of the desk in the Den, his old papers floating up off the rough surface, there was no reflection in the rectifier bulbs, no disturbance in the Cavendish lab – no sparks, and no damage.

Then, too, was the smell. More than the battery acid of his early years, Ernest recognised the smell of salt. It was salt water rising through the Den now, rising above his waist, ocean-green even in the half-light of early evening. Ernest fumbled with the door then, with the handle wet and slippery in his hand, the drag of wet cloth on his sleeves, and he wrenched the door open and stumbled out of the workroom, stumbled into a hallway where his watch solidified on his wrist and his clothes were dry.

When he opened the door back to the room, opened it in a small strip to peek through, the workroom was as it should be: stable, absent of swelling and unencumbered with history. Ernest blinked, rubbed at his eyes with the rough material of his jacket, and he had himself almost convinced it was a funny turn, a dream of memory, until he checked the new transformer and found in the odd corners and creases of its carcass the faint, lacy tracings of salt after evaporation

TASMAN SEA, 1895

Letters of introduction were kept safely in his cabin, tucked in with the radio wave detector he'd worked on and demonstrated at Canterbury, all packed up in a box, and all he could think of was the opportunity for presenting them. Ern stood at the railings until the last of the coast was out of sight. He didn't know when he'd see New Zealand again, when next he'd see his family, or Mary, but he didn't feel yet the sadness he thought he would. There was too much excitement to be sad.

He'd got the Exhibition scholarship, the one that would allow him to go to study in England, to leave Christchurch for, he hoped, the Cavendish. It still wasn't quite enough to live on, but George had lent him money enough to escape the orbit of provincial laboratories. 'Let's face it,' George had said, 'you're the bright one of the family, Ern. You can't miss this.' And he'd pressed the money on him – not a fortune, for George didn't have a fortune, but as much as he could spare and it was enough, barely. Ern would have felt worse about taking it if George weren't his elder, if he didn't see in his brother's face the desire to help at least one of his little brothers, when there were two of those young ones he hadn't been able to help.

'Thank you,' Ern had said. 'George, thank you.'

'You're good for it,' George replied, gripping Ern's right hand with both his own. 'I know you'll make us proud.'

'It's a great chance for you,' his father had said, and Ern had laughed and agreed, had swung his little sisters round and talked of science to his mother so she wouldn't speak of shipping. She was leery now of boats.

'Of course it's not the same,' she had said, on his last day, straightening his collar like she had when he was small. 'It's a big strong vessel you're going in.' Nothing like the little boat that had failed his brothers, failed them in local waters while Ern was heading off to far deeper seas, far stronger tides and the potential for ocean waves. 'But you be careful. I don't want to hear of any accidents because you've had some silly ideas.'

'He's going to climb the rigging,' said one of his little sisters, giggling. 'He's going to climb it all the way to the *top*.'

'He is *not*,' said Martha, severely. 'Are you, Ernest?'

'Of course not,' he said, because that was an easy enough promise to make if it took the shadows from her eyes, if it resigned her to his going and the manner of it. And now she was out of sight — not just her but the country of his birth, the kōwhai and kauri and miro, the colour of the bush against the sea.

He thought he might wish for it, one day, but for now the horizon was clear and the wind was on his face and Ern left his place at the stern and ran to the front, to find a place to look ahead. His feet echoed on the deck, and for a moment it sounded as if there were others running with him. He could have sworn that there were. It wasn't just the footsteps. He stood at the railings, his eyes closed and face tilted up, the sun on his skin and he could feel them either side, his fellow travellers. They would be just as excited as he was, no doubt, some of them leaving their new country for the first time. Like him, they were sailing over the world to where the stars were different, where the Southern Cross was just a memory, and imprinted before all other constellations.

'This is going to be the most wonderful voyage,' said Ern, hoping to make friends, but when he opened his eyes he was alone at the railing. 'Well, don't you look a right idiot, talking to yourself,' he said, but he laughed as he said it. He was too giddy to feel embarrassed, too drunk on opportunity and ozone to be anything but happy. Ern turned against the railing, leaning back against it to look down the length of the ship — at the vessel itself, at the sailors and the other passengers. Some of the last looked a little green, and Ern felt for them. He'd had a touch of seasickness himself, but even a short time on board had taught him that fresh air got rid of the worst of it, so he spent much of his time on deck. There was too much going on to bother with seasickness.

There was someone beside him, then, and Ern knew it for more than fancy because a shadow fell across his face, blocking out the sun. He shivered a little – it was still winter, and he was in his coat even on the sunniest of days – and beneath his elbows the railings were unaccountably cold, as if ice had been run across the iron. He could feel the sudden chill even through his jacket.

The woman next to him seemed strangely familiar. She didn't look very much older than him and there was something in her face that reminded him of his sisters, though her hair was innocent of pig-tails. His mother would never let one of her daughters out like this, though – in a too-fine dress, a pretty bright blue for all that it was completely unsuitable, unserviceable for shipboard life. It was a colour he'd seen before, once on a Marlborough beach and in Christchurch too, at the university.

The woman next to him now, the one in the extraordinary dress, wore no hat. Granted it was a winter sun, but with skin as pale as hers, Ern judged she'd be in for a nasty burn if she weren't careful.

'Are you off to London too?' he said, but the girl never answered him, only stared at him from a distance just out of reach, and there was in her colour and stance something that reminded him of … of …

Ern couldn't place it, but before he could enquire further a small girl ran past him, spinning a hoop and giggling, her parents keeping a careful eye from further up the deck. Ern grinned at the child and she grinned back and he heard her little feet on the deck and there was that echo again, as if there were others with her, other little feet running and skipping after the hoop and when he turned back to the young lady she was gone.

CAMBRIDGE, 1930

He had become a man with grandchildren. He was afraid he was going to become a man with *only* grandchildren.

Ernest sat with his feet together, with his back straight and his hands clasped tight so that they didn't show the shaking. It was no use trying to keep busy through the wait – as distracted as he was, his hands would be clumsy at experiments. Clumsiness meant contamination and temper, poor results. He had little stomach for it, for the potential glass-breaking, the shattering of instruments. Little stomach too for salt water, for the rising tides of basins and bad pipes, the nausea that came with thoughts of drowning. The water of the Sounds, the water of his home, stank of death to him now.

Ernest suspected he was about to become all too familiar with death, familiar in a visceral, gut-deep and wrenching way that had little to do with shadows and all too much with the silence of pianos, with empty beaches and broken promises. After Herbert, after Charles, he'd never heard his mother play again. The piano had remained, polished still and the wood warm in the afternoon sun as it shone through the windows; but all the joy in playing had gone out of her, and none of Martha's children had kept her knack.

She'd tried to teach them, to teach all of them. Ernest remembered sitting on the bench beside her when his legs were still too short to touch the ground, to reach the pedals. He remembered his mother's hands on his own as she taught him the keys, how hard it was to get his fingers to cooperate. How he'd learned the knack eventually – quick enough, for he'd been a bright lad, but his preference had never been for music, for the long hours of practice. His practice, his patience, was reserved for radiation, for laboratories and experiments and science. Music lessons were marking time, a pleasant diversion, and his fingers had never developed fluidity in timing and notes. He'd never been the musician his mother was. None of them had been, really, though she'd tried with all her children, the sons and daughters both – until two of the sons were gone and took her music with them for drowning.

He wondered if she would have taken it up again for Eileen, if they hadn't lived half a world apart, if he'd raised his daughter in southern waters, with the red beeches and the wood pigeons and the bright terrible blue of the Sounds, the way the water wrapped around. Perhaps she would have sat the little girl beside her and picked out the keys, would have made a reconciliation with them that way, but his daughter had been brought up far from her grandmother and her catalytic potential had been undermined by distance.

Now, it seemed likely that it would be undermined by something else entirely, by a labour gone bad, an unlucky and unmusical thing. Still, if he closed his eyes Ernest could hear, perhaps, what his daughter would have sounded like had those early lessons been a reality, had the relationship between generations not been divided by continents and the oceans between. And there it was, at the edge of hearing: the picking of notes, the awkward, ungainly keys, the timing all wrong, the pressure unreliable. Some notes were louder than they should have been, some a bare presence that was repeated as the key was pressed harder, was slammed down on, and the scales were mutilated things, rough as if they'd had chunks bitten out, as if elastic held the notes together and was fraying round the edges.

The notes were nostalgia, and they echoed. Ernest could hear them now with his eyes open, with the plain wall before him and the hard seat beneath. It was almost as if they were in the room with him, as if he could turn his head and they'd be there, their shadows on the wall, on bookshelves stuffed with back issues of *Physikalische Zeitschrift* and *Philosophical Transactions of the Royal Society*. And Ernest would have resisted the impulse, would have kept his posture straight and his eyes forward, if that clumsy thumping hadn't degraded, suddenly, into the terrible (and terribly deliberate) scale that Charles had always defaulted to when revolting at practise and piano, before he'd given up scales for sea water. He'd done it for attention, always, to underline where he'd rather be, that he'd had enough, and at the repeat of it, so many years later, Ernest couldn't help but look, couldn't help but hope.

There was nothing. No shadows, no piano. No reminders of a life long gone, for as soon as Ernest moved from rigidity the music stopped and the room was silent.

'Charles?' said Ernest. 'Lad, are you there?' His big farmer hands clenched in on each other, his fingertips whitening under pressure. 'Charlie?'

He'd changed his mind, then. He could have done with footprints after all, with salt water and the evidence of seas long gone, the under-scent of rot. Perhaps if puddles waited by him, if he could look down at the hard floor and see prints either side of him, feel presence rather than absence, there'd be something of comfort in it. Something to say that loss was not a complete thing, that it was something more than catalyst, a way of untangling the universe and drawing meaning from it.

But there was nothing. No salt or sand or colour, no notes and no disturbance. An absence instead of presence, and when Ernest heard the knock upon his door, he knew they had come to tell him that his daughter was dead.

✳

It is clear in this case that on the whole the energy derived from transmutation of the atom is small compared with the energy of the bombarding particles. There thus seems to be little prospect that we can hope to obtain a new source of power by these processes. It has sometimes been suggested, from analogy with ordinary explosives, that the transmutation of one atom might cause the transmutation of a neighbouring nucleus, so that the explosion would spread throughout all the material. If this were true, we should long ago have had a gigantic explosion in our laboratories with no one remaining to tell the tale. The absence of these accidents indicates, as we should expect, that the explosion is confined to the individual nucleus and does not spread to the neighbouring nuclei, which may be regarded as relatively far removed from the centre of the explosion. (Ernest Rutherford, 'The Transmutation of the Atom', 1933.)

HAVELOCK, 1867

'You have to remember to trust your gut, Ern,' said James. 'To go with your instincts.'

And Ern, watching his father, could only think *That hasn't worked out so well for you, has it?* His father's instincts had led him to walk the Sounds for month after hopeless month, for a year, because he believed that if he just walked enough, looked enough, then he'd find the bodies of the children that had been lost. Perhaps that was instinct – or perhaps it was just the desire to get out of the house, to put distance between himself and his grief and the grief of his wife. The way the latter came with silence, the way it came with the shutting up of instruments and the cessation of piano notes.

But no. Ern couldn't believe that. His father was not such a coward, and if he found comfort in solitude sometimes then it was no more than anyone else did – his mother and brothers and sisters, Ern himself. No. It was instinct that caused that endless, painful search ... the deep gut feeling that hard work and hard love would pay off.

Ern wasn't so very old himself. Not a man yet, not truly, but close – and even he could see that his father's instinct was a lie. He could see it but he couldn't say it. That would be cruelty, and there was only so much cruelty he could fit into his mouth, a hard, stony truth-telling that his father would not, could not appreciate. Instead, he bit his tongue until the blood came, until he tasted iron. Iron was kindness, perhaps – or the magnetised needle within a compass. He couldn't tell anymore. The emotional swamp of his parents' loss was too much for him, the waters turbulent and the currents over-murky. Ern had gone past wishing for music, but he would have done almost anything now for mathematics, for physics and science and certainty – or at least an uncertainty that he had a hope to solve.

'You don't believe me,' said James.

'I didn't say that,' Ern replied. 'I didn't say anything.'

James sighed. It was a sound his son had heard too often. 'I know it's not your way,' he said. 'I don't have your gifts, Ern. I don't see things the way that you do.'

'You don't see things at all!' Ern blurted, and had he been even a couple of years younger he would have clapped his hands over his mouth, looked as guilty as he felt. What was the point of biting your tongue when you were going to speak regardless? But he wasn't a couple of years younger. He was close to a man, fifteen years old and he'd been watching his father drag himself out of the house earlier and earlier, come back later and later. He'd watched him spend his free time tramping coastlines, watched his siblings and his mother as they came to understand, to accept, that any free time wasn't theirs anymore. Watched his neighbours talk behind their hands, the pity on their faces or in their voices when, every so often, one would leave his own work to walk with his father, and not for Herbert's sake, not for Charlie's.

Why can't you just accept it? he wanted to scream. *They're goddamn dead and they're not coming back!* Ern wanted to scream this more than he'd ever wanted anything in his life. Under any other circumstances it might even have earned him a belting for taking the Lord's name in vain but beneath the anger and the guilt and the desire for cruelty (the desire to avoid it? he wasn't even sure anymore) was the fear that his father would smile at him sadly and turn away. That he wouldn't even *care*.

'You need to trust yourself,' James said again. There must have been something in his son's face that spoke to him then, even when the son did not. 'Even if you turn out to be wrong. Especially if you turn out to be wrong. No one can go through their life not ever being wrong, Ern. Not even you. It's all right,' he said. 'It's all right, son.'

'You're never going to find them,' said Ernest. He straightened his back, looked his father dead in the eye. 'It's been a year now. You're not going to find them.' It was an effort to keep his voice calm, and though he clenched his fists he could feel that his hands were shaking. 'I'm sorry for it, Dad, I am. I'd do anything for it to be different. But it isn't. They're gone. Herbert and Charlie … they're gone. But we're still here.'

'I know,' said James. He knelt down briefly, the movement almost absent, his wiry body whippet-thin. When he stood again there were shells in his hand and as he spoke he tossed them into the sea, the movement jerky and thoughtless, as if he needed something to do with his hands while he talked. Early that morning, Ern had been woken by his father for the first time in a long while, been woken to go walking with him, go searching. 'I always said to myself, I'll give it a good year,' said James. It was almost conversational. 'A good year. They were good boys. They deserved that much.'

'What?' said Ern, off balance and suddenly dizzy in the sand. He could hear blood rushing in his ears, hear it over the ocean, and there was blood in his mouth.

'I'm going to stop now,' said James. 'I always meant to. I'm sorry I didn't tell you. I meant to do that too, but it all got away from me.' There were tears in his eyes, and Ern had never seen his father cry before. 'Then I looked round one day and saw you watching me, and I knew I hadn't told you. Knew it was too late for that. That you'd already built up in yourself what you wanted to say to me. But Ern … you needed to be able say it. You needed to know that you could.'

✖

It is of course true that some of the advances of science may occasionally be used for ignoble ends but this is not the fault of the scientific man, but rather of the community which fails to control this prostitution … It is sometimes suggested that scientific men should be more active in controlling the wrong use of their discoveries. I am doubtful however whether even the most imaginative scientific man, except in rare cases, is able to foresee the ultimate effect of any discovery. (Ernest Rutherford, Norman Lockyer Lecture, November 1936.)

ENGLAND, 1930s

Could he have been so wrong, all along? Could there be more in the atom than prizes, more than electrons and protons and the miniaturisation of power?

What a thing to be responsible for. Ernest had no illusions: he was not immutable in his point of success, not so very individual a pivot. Had he never been, had he stayed in New Zealand, a professor at a frontier university, a smaller man than he had become, then another physicist would eventually have done what he had done. Another physicist would have opened the same door, would have done it in confidence and ignorance both. And had Ernest met that man, met that woman, he would have shaken their hand and told them it wasn't their fault, what could arise, and that they should be congratulated for what they'd done – the expansion of knowledge, that tiny step towards the unravelling of the universe.

But it had been him. The knowledge of the atom, the dissection of its structure, had come to a man who had lived through one World War, who had contributed to the development of technology used in that war – when he had been able to, when the naval forces of his second country had allowed him, though that allowance was a thin one and short-sighted. But for all that, he'd never fought on the front line, never died there – as young Moseley had in Gallipoli, and what a waste of a mind that had been!

It had hurt, losing Harry, but there'd always been the comfort in the back of Ernest's mind that the lads who were lost had at least not been his. None of the children had been his – he'd been safe that way, with his young daughter. The only child, the one he'd never have to give up to uniforms and parades and the distance between the trenches and his laboratories, the possibility of poison gas. He'd sympathised with the other parents, of course. That was only decent, and Ernest had felt for them as he'd felt for his own parents, long ago. But the compassion he'd been able to give had been a starveling thing, something still with little colour in it. Then Eileen had died, and he had understood.

'I feel old,' he said to Mary, after it happened, and he could see in the faces around him the belief that he was growing older faster than he'd done before. It was true, too. When he emerged from the fog that was her funeral and the first months of his life without her (and that absence was so different from life before her, the life with her) his joints seemed to ache easier, his hands to sink and quiver more rapidly.

The worst of it was his mind. Never quick, but he had prided himself on the long slow workings, of the ability to seize and hold and worry. Once, on a long night when he had lain awake, still and silent and trying not to picture his daughter's face, he had overlaid her image with that of another woman – one distant to him, the connection made through pity and disgust and the horrified rising of guilt.

Fritz Haber had worked at a chemistry so different to Ernest's – the chemistry of war and chlorine gas. While Ernest had spent his war research on underwater sounds and signalling, Haber had learned to kill at distance, to use science as a method of slaughter. Ernest had looked down on him for that. Turned his back, refused to shake his hand. Had refused to help the other man find work – and his contempt had been all the sharper for what Haber's work had done to his wife. Clara Immerwahr had shot herself to death in her own garden – and that was too close to home, a wife who loved gardens – because she couldn't stand what her husband had made of war. A deliberate act, to follow another deliberate act.

The analogy was not a complete one, Ernest knew. It was not fitting. If a weapon could be made from atoms then he had given the impetus all unsuspecting. Eileen, too, had died in a manner other than suicide. She hadn't meant to die in the labour of her last child; there was nothing deliberate about her loss. And she was a daughter, not a wife. The analogy was flawed. But even so, once he had connected them the contamination was there, the comparison caught in his mind, rendered immobile: the father of chemical slaughter lost one woman to their mutual deliberation, and the man who had stumbled into fatherhood of another kind had lost another woman, quite by accident.

'You're a silly old fool,' he said, staring at himself in the mirror one morning. The basin was full of cold water, clean where he had hoped somehow for salt. Then Mary had knocked on the door to call him to breakfast and Ernest did his best to pinch colour into his cheeks, to make himself look normal, as though he didn't feel anything but. A fool, yes, but a fool with a wife who had her own grief and he would never have been so self-indulgent as to add to it with the spectres of his conscience, made over-sensitive with insomnia and sorrow.

There was no one he could tell.

Instead, he cornered Maurice Hankey at a committee meeting, spoke to him of the potential of atomic weapons, the ghosts of his nightmares. 'Keep an eye on the matter,' he said, as if he hadn't said for years that such a thing was impossible, that such a device could never be made. 'Keep an eye on the matter.'

'You'll likely know before I will,' said Hankey.

'Perhaps,' said Ernest.

He was an old man, with grandchildren.

About the Authors

AC BUCHANAN

AC Buchanan lives just north of Wellington and would welcome a visit from any passing sauropods. They're the author of the recent novella *Liquid City* and their short fiction has most recently been published in the *Accessing the Future* anthology from FutureFire.net and the Crossed Genres Publications anthology *Fierce Family*. Because there's no such thing as too many projects, they also co-chair LexiCon 2017—The 38th New Zealand National Science Fiction and Fantasy Convention and edit the recently launched speculative fiction magazine *Capricious*. You can find them on Twitter at @andicbuchanan or www.acbuchanan.org.

GRANT STONE

Grant Stone's stories have appeared in *Shimmer*, *Strange Horizons*, *Andromeda Spaceways Inflight Magazine*, *Semaphore Magazine*, and *Use Only As Directed*, and have twice won the Sir Julius Vogel Award. He's also one-third of the Cerberus Writing Band, along with Dan Rabarts and Matthew Sanborn Smith. You can find him on Twitter as @discorobot or his website at www.grant-stone.com.

IK PATERSON-HARKNESS

IK Paterson-Harkness lives on a grimy street on the fringe of Auckland's CBD, watching seagulls squabble on the roof of the Chinese supermarket across the road while she tries to write her stories. With university degrees in music, philosophy and creative writing she doesn't quite know what to do with herself. Mostly, when not writing, she's doodling on a pad or thinking about time travel. Her prose and poetry publications, as well as music and weird, lo-fi music videos, can be found at www.ikpatersonharkness.com, or @IKPatersonHark.

LEE MURRAY

Lee Murray writes fiction for adults and children, for which she has been lucky enough to win some literary prizes. Her novels include *A Dash of Reality*, *Battle of the Birds*, and *Misplaced*. Lee lives with her family in New Zealand.

OCTAVIA CADE

Octavia Cade has sold stories to *Strange Horizons, Apex Magazine*, and *Aurealis*, amongst others. She has a PhD in science communication, and enjoys mixing science history with her fiction. Octavia has recently published her first novel, *The August Birds* (also containing Ernest Rutherford), and has a sci-fi poetry collection about the periodic table currently in press. Her short fiction has been shortlisted for the BSFA and Sir Julius Vogel Award.

PIPER MEJIA

Piper Mejia is an advocate for New Zealand writers and literature. She was the co-editor of *Write Off Line* (2012/2013) and *Beyond This …* (2012/2013), collections of writing by New Zealand intermediate and secondary students, and continues to manage both national writing competitions. In 2014 her short story "Lockdown" (included in the horror flash fiction collection *Baby Teeth: Bite-Sized Tales of Terror*) was shortlisted for the Sir Julius Vogel Award for science fiction and fantasy writing. Her young adult novella, *The Fence*, appeared in *Conclave: A Collection of Science Fiction and Fantasy* and she won a national poetry competition for her poem "Sounds of Evolution". In her spare time she is a high school English teacher.

TIM JONES

Tim Jones is a poet and author. He was awarded the New Zealand Society of Authors Janet Frame Memorial Award for Literature in 2010, and his recent books include short story collection *Transported* (Vintage, 2008), poetry anthology *Voyagers: Science Fiction Poetry from New Zealand* (co-edited with Mark Pirie; Interactive Press, 2009), and poetry collection *Men Briefly Explained* (Interactive Press, 2011). Tim's short fiction has appeared in *Best New Zealand Fiction 4* (2007), *The Penguin Book of Contemporary New Zealand Short Stories* (2009), and *The Apex Book of World SF 2* (2012). Tim's latest book, a companion anthology to

Voyagers, is *The Stars Like Sand: Australian Speculative Poetry,* co-edited with PS Cottier and published by Interactive Press (IP) in 2014. For more information, see Tim's Amazon author page: www.amazon.com/Tim-Jones/e/B004MGX7Z8/ and Tim's blog: www.timjonesbooks.blogspot.com.

www.ingramcontent.com/pod-product-compliance
Lightning Source LLC
Chambersburg PA
CBHW051503030726
47592CB00006B/2075